She pulled out the letter that she had tucked inside the book of fairy tales.

The strange address was printed at the top: Pendragon Hall, Land's End, Cornwall. A crest, a shield of three black crosses on gold and a band of black in an upward arrow, lay below.

Dear Miss Wilmot,

Your acceptance of the situation as governess has been received. Train tickets are enclosed. I will expect you at Pendragon Hall at your earliest convenience.

Yours sincerely,

Dominic Jago

The handwriting was strong and large, the words in black ink across the paper, the message curt.

Jago. It was an unusual name. She had never heard it before.

All she had to hope now was that he had never heard her real name.

Author Note

Meet the new governess...

The role of the governess was not always an easy one in Victorian England. Like Maud Wilmot, the heroine of this tale, many governesses existed "between stairs," accepted neither by the servants nor by the family, and some were at the mercy of their more unscrupulous employers. Governesses were expected to provide both academic and moral education, and to be of high moral character themselves. Any slur on their character, whether true or not, could mean ruin.

But during the nineteenth century, governesses began to stand up for their profession. Some were "bluestockings," passionately committed to the education of women. Like Maud, many governesses used fables and fairy tales for the moral education of their young charges. Such stories were full of wonder, wisdom and, often, warning to women. A well-known governess, Madame Leprince de Beaumont, published educational guides for young ladies in the 1800s. Her *Moral Tales* became famous handbooks and included the fairy tale *Beauty and the Beast*.

I hope you enjoy this romance of a storytelling governess who learns never to give up on a happy ending.

ELIZA REDGOLD

The Master's New Governess

HARLEQUIN
HISTORICAL

Recycling programs
for this product may
not exist in your area.

ISBN-13: 978-1-335-50549-1

The Master's New Governess

Copyright © 2020 by Eliza Redgold

This edition published by arrangement with Harlequin Books S.A.

For questions and comments about the quality of this book,
please contact us at CustomerService@Harlequin.com.

Harlequin Enterprises ULC
22 Adelaide St. West, 40th Floor
Toronto, Ontario M5H 4E3, Canada
www.Harlequin.com

Printed in U.S.A.

Eliza Redgold is an author, academic and unashamed romantic. She was born in Scotland, is married to an Englishman and currently lives in Australia. She loves to share stories with readers! Get in touch with Eliza via Twitter, @elizaredgold; on Facebook, Facebook.com/elizaredgoldauthor; and Pinterest, Pinterest.com/elizaredgold. Or visit her at Goodreads.com and elizaredgold.com.

Books by Eliza Redgold

Harlequin Historical

Enticing Benedict Cole
Playing the Duke's Mistress
The Scandalous Suffragette
The Master's New Governess

Visit the Author Profile page
at Harlequin.com.

Chapter One

'*She is near, she is near;*'
                —*Alfred, Lord Tennyson:* Maud *(1855)*

Cornwall, 1855—

'**O**nce upon a time…'

The words blurred in front of Maud Wilmot's eyes. Before she could stop it, a tear trembled at the edge of her lashes, but she blinked it away.

With shaking fingers, she closed the book of fairy tales and laid the worn blue leather volume with its faded gilt lettering on her lap. She traced her gloved finger over the title: *Fairy Tales for Children*.

Even the familiar stories couldn't comfort her.

Another tear splashed on to the blue leather.

Leaning her bonnet against the back of the leather carriage seat, she pressed her eyes shut, her shaking fingers still clutched around the book.

'This will never do,' she told herself, in her firmest governess voice.

One deep breath.

Then another.

She wouldn't cry. She mustn't. She hadn't let herself so far, and if she started now, seated in the train carriage bearing her nearer and nearer an unknown situation—her last, desperate chance—she might never stop. She hauled a third breath from deep inside her corset as the tears threatened to overcome her.

No matter how anxious she felt, she wouldn't let it get the better of her.

Another breath. She let the motion of the locomotive lull her. She'd always loved travelling by train, not that she did it often, but it didn't ease her agitation. She hadn't managed to sleep the night before, tossing and turning, worrying about what lay ahead.

What else could she do? It went against every fibre of her being, but she had no choice.

Lord Melville's voice jeered inside her head.

No one will believe your story.

As the train rolled along the tracks, her thoughts went back to the last few dreadful weeks.

'Oh, Maud.' Her sister, Martha, had hugged her. 'How is it possible you have been dismissed? You're the best governess I know.'

'Thank you, Martha,' Maud choked out. 'But I have been dismissed without pay and without references, too.'

She had applied for funds from the Governesses' Benevolent Institution and was in lodgings; but the money wouldn't last long.

Martha hugged her again. 'Perhaps I can talk to Albert—you can come and live with us.'

'Absolutely not,' Maud had replied, even as her heart was sinking. She was running out of time. Soon she would be on the street. 'You're newlyweds, Martha. I have no intention of making myself a nuisance.'

'You'd never be a nuisance,' said Martha. 'That's why this is all so unfair!'

'Unfair or not, I must find a way out of it.' Maud knew she sounded braver than she felt, but she wasn't going to burden Martha, not when her sister had just found happiness with Albert. And she hadn't told Martha the full story.

She could not.

It was unspeakable.

'What will you do now?' Martha asked, her soft brown eyes wide and worried.

Maud bit her lip. 'I must find another position as a governess. It will be difficult, without references. Perhaps impossible. But I have no other means of supporting myself and I love teaching children. But after what happened—' she clenched her hands '—no one will employ Miss Maud Wilmot.'

It was then the idea had struck her. 'Martha. Didn't you tell me you had been offered a situation in Cornwall?'

Martha nodded. 'Yes, it was before Albert proposed. I applied and it took ever so long for them to get back to me. But then I got a letter, saying that they would be pleased to employ me at Pendragon Hall.'

'Have you written back to them?' Maud asked, hardly daring to voice the other question that came to mind. Of course, Martha would say no and that would be that. It was an absurd idea anyway.

Martha shook the blonde ringlets on either side of her head. 'Not yet.'

'So they are still expecting a Miss Wilmot,' Maud said slowly.

She and Martha were around the same age, Martha two years older than Maud's six and twenty. They had both spent quite a few years in service as governesses. They were both experienced.

It could be done. It was foolhardy. Why, it was positively scandalous. But she had nothing left to lose. It *must* be done.

'That's right,' Martha said, her eyes even wider. 'Oh, Maud, you've got that look on your face, the one you get when you are telling a story…'

Maud opened her eyes. Now here she was, in Cornwall, the wheels of the train turning on the track beneath her.

To lift her spirits, she forced herself to register the beauties passing by. From the moment she'd left London, there had been plenty to see.

Setting forth on the journey had been an intense relief. As the train moved further west, she'd even begun to experience a sense of freedom. The train moved so much faster than a horse and carriage, it was almost dizzying. There was so much to see, the landscape becoming wilder, more foreign, the deeper they moved into Cornwall. They had left the outskirts of London and the view of the backs of the houses, with their gardens and washing lines, then into the countryside of rolling hills and green fields dotted with sheep and cows. They had made a stop overnight in Exeter, where she had stayed at an inn near the train station, in surprisingly comfortable accommodation provided by her new employer, before continuing further south-west, where the clusters of villages and isolated country houses became sparser as they moved towards the remote, rugged coast.

A tiny thrill of excitement ran through her.

She pulled out the letter that she had tucked inside the book of fairy tales.

The strange address was printed at the top: Pendragon Hall, West Cornwall. A crest, a shield of three black crosses on gold and a band of black in an upward arrow lay below.

Dear Miss Wilmot

That was correct, at least.

She laid the paper down momentarily in her lap. Her hands were trembling. At least it didn't say *Dear Miss Martha Wilmot*. She could take some comfort in that. A Miss Wilmot they wanted, and a Miss Wilmot they would get.

Swallowing hard, she read on.

Your acceptance of the situation as the new governess has been received. Train tickets are enclosed.

I will expect you at Pendragon Hall at your earliest convenience.
Yours sincerely,
Sir Dominic Jago

She traced the name with her gloved finger. The handwriting was strong and large, the words in black ink across the paper. The message curt.

Jago. It was an unusual name. She had never encountered it before.

All she had to hope now was that he had never heard her real name.

No one will believe your story.

Her fingers were still shaking as she folded up the letter. From the other information that Martha had passed on to her, she knew that the terms for her new employment were handsome, much better than she had expected, especially for a post in the country. It was not uncommon for a governess to be offered a home and no salary at all, but the post at Pendragon Hall paid a good wage, enough for her to save a little. She'd never had that opportunity before. Her last post had left her with nothing.

She would only be teaching one child: a girl, Rosabel, aged seven, who was recovering from illness. The application made no mention of any other children and, Martha had also informed her, Sir Dominic Jago was a widower.

To her surprise, the letter from Sir Dominic had also been accompanied by a first-class ticket on the West Cornish Railway for the final leg of her journey. On the previous trains, for she had changed twice, she had travelled in a second-class carriage, as governesses, footmen, ladies' maids and other servants usually did. First-class travel was for gentry, not governesses.

She laid her head back against the leather seat. It was astonishing to be travelling first class. She must waste no more time on tears. The West Cornish Railway first-class carriage was so clean and new, she could smell the polish. The brass fittings and handles gleamed and a handsome brass lamp stayed lit so that she could read even as they went through woods and tunnels. There were three private compartments within the carriage, separated by a wooden screen, each with a pair of leather seats that faced each other.

It was so roomy. She stretched out her legs beneath her petticoats, resisting the urge to kick at them a little. How constricting they were! She still wore layers of them, in cambric, flannel, wool and cotton, rather than the new hooped skirt.

She stifled her sigh of yearning. Oh, how she longed for hoops. She could never afford to have her dresses made over in the new style. Hoops would probably be out of date before she could manage it.

To lift her spirits, she forced her attention back to the view. She would not miss a moment of the journey pining for things that could not be. In the large carriage window she could see her reflection, ghostly against the scenery of hedgerows, meadows and cottages. Underneath her green eyes were dark shadows and lines around her mouth that hadn't been there mere weeks before. Wisps of brown hair escaped from her dove-grey bonnet, resting on the white collar of her grey dress.

Opposite her own reflection, Maud could see the only other occupant of the carriage, a sweet old lady, who had slept for most of the journey, Maud was pleased to note.

Earlier, Maud had helped her to settle into the window seat and find her smelling salts.

'Thank you, my dear,' the lady had whispered. 'How kind you are. I find travel by locomotive very trying. It makes me quite ill.'

The train slowed and the whistle shrieked as they drew into a station.

Now the old lady awoke with a start. 'Have we arrived already?'

'Not yet. We still have a way to go to Penponds Station,' Maud reassured her with a smile. They had discovered they shared the same destination. 'We're just making a stop.'

She peered through the glass.

A puff of steam obscured the platform, then swirled away, to reveal a man staring straight at her.

He was the kind of man it was impossible to miss. Tall, dark-haired, long-legged, he wore a long dark grey coat, with a scarlet cravat tied carelessly around his neck. His hands were gloveless and she saw the flash of a gold signet ring on his right hand. Yet it was the energy that emanated from him that she noticed most of all. Even standing still, he seemed to convey a restlessness, a sense of contained speed, as though, like the train in front of him, he wanted to move fast in a determined direction.

His dark gaze was intent as he stared through the train window into her eyes, before another puff of steam obscured him once again from view.

Maud drew back. The man's gaze had been magnetic, powerful, as though there was not a glass window between them, but nothing at all.

The cloud of steam cleared once again, but the dark-haired man had vanished.

'I say!'

Maud spun around on her seat.

Another passenger had entered the carriage, a portly young man in a checked overcoat, red-faced beneath his top hat.

'Excuse me, madam,' he said to the old lady in braying tones. 'You are in my seat.'

'Oh, dear, oh, dear,' the old lady quavered. 'What did you say?'

The young man scowled. 'I tell you, that's my seat! I especially wanted a window.'

The old lady's mouth trembled.

Maud looked around for the train conductor. He was nowhere to be seen.

She leaned forward. 'Excuse me, sir. Might I see your ticket?'

The young man turned. 'What?' he demanded, in an imperious tone, looking down on her, his blue eyes bulbous.

Maud lifted her chin. She hadn't been a governess for five years to be intimidated by this overgrown boy.

'Might I see your ticket?' she repeated, in a tone that no child had ever refused.

The young man puffed out his breath and looked about to argue. Muttering under his breath, he handed it over.

'Thank you.' Maud scrutinised it, then glanced at the seat number. She bit her lip, vexed. When she had helped the old lady settle into her seat, she hadn't thought to check her ticket.

'I'm so sorry,' she said to the old lady. 'It seems there has been some mistake. You do appear to be in the wrong seat.'

The old lady clutched her lace handkerchief. 'Oh, how dreadful!'

'I told you so!' said the young man, triumphantly.

Maud returned the ticket to him.

'I'm sure this lady would like to remain in her seat,' she said quietly. 'She is suffering from travel sickness. Will you do her the kindness?'

Maud caught a whiff of claret as the young man puffed out his cheeks. 'Certainly not! That's my seat and I want it.'

'That is the height of discourtesy!' Maud couldn't hold back the reprimand. 'This lady is old enough to be your grandmother!'

The man turned even redder. 'Who are you to try to teach me manners?'

'It's a pity no one else has taught you,' Maud retorted. 'Please, let this lady stay where she is.'

The old lady began to struggle up. 'I don't want to cause any inconvenience.'

Maud jumped to her feet, the book of fairy tales tumbling from her lap. 'Please take my seat, if it is a window seat you're after.'

'I don't want your seat,' the young man said stubbornly. 'I want the seat I paid for!'

Another, taller man had entered the carriage.

It was the man from the platform, Maud realised in a flash. The sense of suppressed purpose, of energy around him, was even more palpable in close proximity. Yet his demeanour was impassive as he surveyed the scene.

'What seems to be the matter?' he asked coolly.

'This young gentleman…' Maud allowed some scorn to enter her voice '…insists that this lady vacate her seat.'

'I tell you. She is in the wrong seat!' The young man brandished his ticket.

'Wrong seat or no, surely you can allow her to remain. As I told you, she's not well.'

'That's not my concern,' the young man snarled.

The dark-haired man stepped forward. His voice was low, but the authority in it was unmistakable. 'The train's about to depart. I happen to know there is a window seat available in the other first-class carriage. If you would care to take it, these ladies can remain here.'

The young man began to bluster, but after a look

into the eyes of the man in front of him, he appeared to change his mind.

'Very well,' he said with a sulky expression.

'Excellent.' The dark-haired man turned to the conductor, who had finally appeared. 'Could you show this gentleman to his new seat?'

The conductor bowed. 'Very good, sir.'

With another puff of claret-fumed annoyance, the young man followed the conductor out of the carriage.

Maud let out a sigh of relief.

The dark-haired man leaned down and picked up the book of fairy tales. He frowned as he glanced at the title. 'Is this yours?'

She nodded. His fingers grazed hers as he returned it to her.

He bowed and left the carriage.

Maud took her seat. She clutched the book, the sensation of his warm fingers still imprinted on hers.

'Thank you, my dear,' the old lady said, with a grateful smile, as the train began to move away from the station.

A few minutes later the conductor returned. He tipped his cap. 'I hope you two ladies are settled now.'

'Very well, thank you.' Maud was unable to restrain her curiosity. 'The gentleman who came to our assistance. How did he know there was a seat available in the other carriage? Did he offer his own seat?'

The conductor chuckled. 'They're all his seats.'

Maud drew back her head. 'What on earth do you mean?'

'He's the owner of the West Cornish Railway Line. That's Sir Dominic Jago.'

Chapter Two

To the turrets and the walls;
—*Alfred, Lord Tennyson:* Maud *(1855)*

'Welcome to Pendragon Hall.'

Maud jumped. She had been watching a small copper butterfly dancing among the daisies on the chamomile lawn, when a deep voice spoke behind her.

One hand to her bodice, she spun around. 'Oh!'

On the gravel drive stood Sir Dominic Jago.

He was silhouetted against Pendragon Hall, half in light, half in shadow, against the setting sun. In the golden light, the house behind him looked like an illustration from a fairy tale.

Maud drew in her breath. Never had she expected her place of employment to be so enchanting. Her previous post had been in a far bigger house, but it did not match this for pure charm. She had imagined a version of a thatched farmhouse—a long house—but for once, her imagination had failed her. Pendragon Hall was a large hall, built of golden-grey stone with a steep slate roof, chimneys as tall as turrets and arched stone windows. It seemed to glow in the sunset.

The house was situated some miles inland, away from the coast, but the fresh breeze ruffling the daisies—and her hair—was rich with the scent of the sea.

Now the wind blew her new employer's dark hair away from his forehead, which creased as he studied her with his penetrating eyes.

Beneath her bodice, Maud could feel the rising and falling of her corset. Ever since what had happened in her previous post, she had been more easily startled. She jumped if someone entered the room unexpectedly, or even at a loud noise. Her nerves were strained. Yet it wasn't only that which unnerved her now. It was Sir Dominic Jago, her new employer, with that aura of energy around him.

He inclined his head slightly. 'My apologies. I had no wish to startle you.'

'Not at all, Sir Dominic.' To her relief, her voice sounded steadier than she felt. She wasn't quite sure how to address him. She knew that knights used their first name with their title, rather than their surname, yet it seemed strangely intimate to address him so.

The corner of his mouth lifted. 'So, you know my name.'

She nodded.

His gaze was as intent as it had been during their first encounter, through the glass of the train window. 'And I know yours.'

Maud's stomach turned over.

'Perhaps I ought to have introduced myself on the train,' he said. 'I guessed who you were. The new governess.'

He had a very faint Cornish accent, Maud noted, yet there was no doubting he was a gentleman. He had received his title of knight, Martha had told her in awe, from Queen Victoria herself, for services rendered to the Crown. He was young to have received such an honour. The West Cornish Railway Company would never have been developed without his drive and determination, Martha had said, and Queen Victoria was known to be most enthusiastic about travelling by train.

He appeared younger than Maud had expected from Martha's description. She had still anticipated a much older, perhaps portly, grey-haired gentleman to have accomplished all that Sir Dominic Jago had done before he was thirty-five years old, for she guessed that was about his age.

'I appreciated your help on the train,' Maud said to him. 'The situation had become most uncomfortable. I hope you did not give up your own seat.'

'It's not the first time I've travelled in the engine.' He brushed at his hair. 'Coal dust doesn't bother me. I want all passengers to be comfortable on the West Cornish Railway Line.'

'It's a marvellous train,' said Maud, frankly. 'I enjoyed the journey, in spite of the altercation. The conductor told me you're the owner of the railway.'

'Not entirely. I am one of a group of local investors who are committed to taking control of our railway lines and trains. Properly managed, they will bring prosperity to Cornwall. Prosperity, and something even more important.'

'What's that?'

'Hope, Miss Wilmot,' he said. 'Hope is the engine of prosperity. Our aim is to have the West Cornish Railway Line enable travel by train all the way from London to Land's End.'

'Here be dragons,' Maud said, before she could stop herself.

'I'm sorry?'

Maud bit her tongue. Their conversation so far had been surprisingly easy, as if they were not new acquaintances at all, let alone governess and employer, and the phrase had slipped out. 'It's what they used to put on old maps. When the end of the land was marked and what lay beyond it was unknown. "Here be dragons."'

The corner of his mouth lifted. 'There are no dragons here, Miss Wilmot, in spite of the name of the estate. At least, I hope not. Have you had a chance to familiarise yourself with Pendragon Hall?'

'Not the house,' Maud admitted. 'I was shown to my room, of course, and I hoped to see Rosabel, but she was having her afternoon rest and I needed some air after the train journey. I'm afraid I have been outdoors for some time. These gardens are so beautiful.'

She turned towards the rolling green lawn, where the butterfly still danced. The grass was well manicured, edged with flower beds, but it had a wildness to it. Climbing roses tangled together, thick with thorns, as if to protect a sleeping princess. There were woods on the estate, too, as well as leafy orchards that she had seen on her way from the small village station of Penponds. She'd half expected Sir Dominic to travel to the house in the carriage sent for her, but he had not appeared.

She'd questioned the coach driver, who had chuckled. 'Sir Dominic's got no time for travelling in carriages. Rides his horse to the train station and back, he does. A stallion. Goes like the blazes.'

'So you like to be out of doors?' Sir Dominic asked her now, unexpectedly.

'Very much,' she replied. 'I am no botanist, but I enjoy studying the natural world. And I am particularly fond of butterflies.'

'Butterflies. Do you collect them?'

Maud shuddered. 'If you mean sticking them with a pin, certainly not. But I like being able to identify them and know their names. Did you know that butterflies return to the same place? You can always rely on finding them again.'

'I wasn't aware of that fact, no,' he drawled.

Maud flushed. Once again, to her amazement, she had been far more at ease with him than she had expected and spoken more freely than she ought. 'I'm sorry. I often provide too many facts.'

The corner of his mouth quirked again. 'As a good governess should.'

'I also enjoy walking,' Maud added. She wanted to make that clear, at the outset. 'Both in the daytime and in the evening, too. Sometimes at night.'

He raised an eyebrow. 'Can butterflies be seen at night?'

She smiled. 'Not butterflies. Moths. And…' She swallowed hard, keeping down the anxiety that instantly threatened her equilibrium. 'Sometimes, I find it difficult to sleep.'

His dark eyes seemed to become even more perceptive. 'A woman being out alone at night is unusual.'

'I hope that won't be a difficulty,' Maud said. The night air was the only antidote, sometimes, to counteract the terrible nightmares she had been experiencing recently and that had not been getting any better. Increasingly, her sleep was disturbed. The fear of the nightmares often kept her awake.

'To the contrary.' Sir Dominic bowed. 'I appreciate your interest in the outdoors. But if you would care to come indoors for a while, Miss Wilmot, we can begin our interview for your position as governess.' He indicated towards the house, now sunk into evening shadow. 'If you will accompany me?'

Her agitation built as she kept up with his long-legged stride across the lawn and gravel drive, indoors to a room on the ground floor of Pendragon Hall. It was a large room lined with leather-bound books, which normally would have sent a warm tingle of delight through her. Even at first glance, she could see the works of Shakespeare and Gibbon. On the burgundy walls above the wooden wainscot panelling hung fine prints and paintings, too, but she could hardly take it all in.

Maud lifted her chin. 'There appears to have been some mistake, Sir Dominic.'

He frowned as he moved behind a green-topped leather desk. He removed his coat to reveal a dark wine-coloured waistcoat and a pristine white shirt that showed no trace of coal dust. 'What kind of mistake?'

'I thought I had been accepted into your employ already.' Her voice quavered a little. 'Have I come all this way just for an interview?'

'Ah.' He drummed his fingers on the desk. 'Please sit down, Miss Wilmot. There are a few matters I need to discuss with you that are...sensitive. I wanted to do so in person. It is not my intention to ask you to return to London before you have even taken up your post. But it's possible that after hearing what I have to say that you will consider this position...unsuitable.'

'This is very unusual,' Maud replied indignantly, trying to mask her anxiety.

'If you will allow me to explain...'

Maud smoothed out her skirts with hands that only trembled a little and took a seat on the carved wooden chair. He could not make her change her mind about taking the post.

It was her only hope.

Opposite her, Sir Dominic moved to sit in the high-backed wooden chair located behind the desk. He pushed it back and crossed one long leg, but his relaxed posture belied the intensity of his eyes that still seemed to blaze into her.

'First, your character references are excellent. It is the main reason I employed you.'

'Oh,' Maud said faintly. They were Martha's references, of course. It pained her to have to use them, but her only comfort was that her references for teaching the Melville boys, of whom she had become very fond, would also have been excellent, if their uncle had not been quite so cruel.

She forced her attention back to Sir Dominic.

'You will find Rosabel an easy charge, I expect,' he told her. 'She has experienced some ill health over the years and, of late, she has become timid. I can barely encourage her out of doors.'

'Is Rosabel in poor health now?'

He shook his head. 'She is not robust, a result of her history of illness, but she is well enough now. I've had the local doctor to see her. He says there is nothing physically wrong.'

Maud frowned, perplexed. 'Fresh air is good for children. I will certainly see if I can encourage her out of doors.'

'Thank you. You will understand, then, why I am pleased to learn you enjoy fresh air yourself,' he said. 'The grounds here are extensive and I hope you will be able to make good use of them with Rosabel. There are a number of gardens and orchards, and there are woods, too. She is not to spend all her time at lessons.'

'I entirely agree,' said Maud. She hesitated for a moment. She had planned what to say all the way on the train. 'About Rosabel's lessons…'

'They are to be the usual lessons for a girl her age. Music, languages and drawing.'

'That is not enough,' Maud said firmly. 'Young ladies need to learn much more than music and drawing, Sir Dominic.'

The corner of his mouth lifted. 'Do they indeed? Are you a bluestocking, Miss Wilmot?'

'I am a passionate supporter of female education,' she retorted. 'If that makes me a bluestocking, so be it.'

'Do not mistake me,' he said. 'I would not be educating Rosabel if I, too, did not believe in women's education.'

Maud clasped her hands together. 'If she is in my charge, I would like to ensure that Rosabel is educated not only in the refinements befitting a lady, but that her mind, too, is broadened. Geography, mathematics, Latin and botany would also benefit her.'

He drew back his head. 'Latin? Botany? Are you qualified to teach them, Miss Wilmot? Did you study such subjects?'

'Certainly. My mama and papa were somewhat unusual in that they were committed to female education.

My father was a schoolmaster. That's why my sister and I had such a good education. We followed the same curriculum as the boys at the school, even though we studied at home. My sister…' She hesitated, unable to call Martha by her own name. 'My sister and I both studied hard and became governesses.'

He steepled his fingers as he regarded her from across the desk. 'Rosabel is but seven years old.'

'It's never too early to learn,' Maud assured him. 'Do not think I would make it too challenging or unpleasant for her. On the contrary, Sir Dominic. My goal would be for Rosabel to love her lessons, or, even better, to not realise she is having lessons at all.'

'How so?'

'I have my methods,' said Maud. 'A child's imagination must be awoken in order to learn.' She leaned forward. 'Please. Let me try my teaching methods with Rosabel. If she does not take to them, I will not pursue the curriculum. But surely she deserves the chance?'

'You are most convincing.' He deliberated for a moment. 'Very well. You may have free rein.'

'Thank you, Sir Dominic.' She breathed out with relief. It meant so much to her, to be able to try her new ideas in the schoolroom. 'You won't regret it.'

'I hope not, Miss Wilmot,' he murmured.

'I encourage you to observe my methods,' she said. It was valuable for parents and guardians to be involved in their children's education, yet so few parents ever did so, in her experience. Some of her charges had rarely seen their parents. 'You will be welcome in the schoolroom at any time.'

'You can be assured I will take up that offer, Miss Wilmot.'

He fell silent for a moment. 'Now we have settled the academic pursuits, there are some other matters. Rosabel's mother, Sarah, died not long after she was born.'

He spoke without expression, yet she sensed the grief that still lingered in him. There was a bleakness behind his eyes.

'I'm very sorry,' Maud said with sympathy.

He nodded his thanks, but that was all. 'It is particularly because of her lack of maternal care that Rosabel requires a governess. She has a nursemaid who is devoted to her and will remain here at Pendragon Hall. But Rosabel also needs a woman of good character, such as yourself, not only to guide her in academic instruction, but also in manners and etiquette, in her moral education.'

'Of course.' Maud bit her lip. 'That is a usual part of a governess's duties.'

'For Rosabel, it will be a most important part. As her father, I can guide her in some parts of her moral development, but not in all, and, of course, a governess is someone who can provide her the guidance she needs in the absence of a mother.'

'You have not considered remarriage?' Maud asked, innocently.

The change in Dominic Jago's face was startling. On the platform, when she first saw him, it had been as if no glass was between them. Now there was a stone wall. 'Is my marital status of interest to you, Miss Wilmot? Is it a reason you took the post?'

Maud shook her head, bewildered. 'I knew that you were a widower, Sir Dominic. But it is certainly not the reason I took this post. Why would it be?'

'What were your reasons, if I may ask?' His voice had hardened.

'My reasons…' She faltered.

'Indeed. Why did you leave your last post?'

Maud took a deep, shaky breath. 'I wanted a new start,' she said, uncertainly. 'A position in the country.'

'I see.' He didn't sound convinced.

He stood and went to the window. When he swung around his jaw was set. 'This is a delicate matter, Miss Wilmot, but I fear it must be addressed at the outset.'

Maud began to tremble. Somehow, he'd found out that she wasn't Martha. Somehow, he had heard what had happened in her employment by Lord Melville.

No one will believe your story.

Sir Dominic moved back behind the desk, but remained standing. His expression was more severe than when he had appeared out of doors, in the garden.

'I am forced to speak bluntly,' he said. 'You realise that there was a delay before I contacted you and offered you this post.'

'Yes,' Maud whispered, trying to still her trembling body.

'There have been other governesses.' He exhaled. 'Two, in fact.'

The trembling in her body turned to shaking she could barely disguise.

'As a widower, I have discovered myself to be the subject of some…romantic notions.' He laid his hand flat on the desk. His signet ring glinted. 'It seems to be a fantasy of certain governesses that they might marry the master of the house.'

'Oh!' Maud felt as if he had thrown cold water over her.

'Surely you have heard of such things?' he asked curtly.

'Indeed I have.' As his meaning sank in, the shaking in her body disappeared as anger made its way through her limbs. 'But in my experience, it is less to do with the expectations of the governess and more to do with those of the master of the house.'

He lifted his eyebrow. 'Is that so?'

'Women are all too often blamed for the behaviour of men.' She was unable to keep the bitterness from her voice. She knew, all too well.

'I can assure you that the previous governesses left of their own accord when they realised the position was not what they hoped it might be,' he said evenly. 'I merely wish to be honest and straightforward with you about this matter, Miss Wilmot, from the start.'

She jerked up her chin. 'As do I. And you can be assured, Sir Dominic, that I have no romantic notions. None whatsoever.'

'On the train I saw that you were reading a book of fairy tales,' he said. 'I thought you may be a woman who gives way to fanciful ideas.'

Maud tried to keep her voice steady. 'I have an imagination. That is all.'

He looked at her keenly. 'I do not seek to offend you.'

'You have judged me without knowing me.' Maud could barely contain her anger. 'Simply because I am a governess.'

He drew back. 'I meant no judgement. Please accept my apology if that is how you have taken it. My goal was to be clear about the nature of your employment.'

'You have been very clear, Sir Dominic.' Maud raised her head high. 'You can be sure I will not pursue any… *romantic notions* about you.'

He inclined his head. 'I regret if I have caused you offence.'

'Perhaps it is better that the matter has been discussed.' That was true, at least.

'Are you willing to take the post under these conditions?' he asked, after a moment.

'Certainly, Sir Dominic.' Maud stood to face him. He was a foot taller than she was, but she met his gaze, eye to eye. 'Believe me, I would take the post under no other.'

Dominic drummed his fingers on the desk. His interview with the new governess—if it could be called an interview—had not gone entirely as planned.

Miss Martha Wilmot.

She had left the room without banging the door behind her, but he got the distinct impression she had been strongly tempted.

He picked up the letters from the table and tucked them into the drawer of his oak desk. The drawer still open, he stared down at them, perplexed. Her letters of recommendation had been excellent. By all accounts, she was an outstanding governess. Exemplary, in fact, to the point of being almost bland. There had been nothing out of the ordinary. Yet the impression he had formed of her upon reading the letters of reference was quite different from his perception of her on first sight.

When he had first spotted her from the platform, she had been looking out of the train window unguarded, with such interest and curiosity. So eager, so alive. His attention had been immediately drawn to her. She had reminded him of a bright-eyed wren, an image emphasised by the colours of her clothing, in shades of brown and grey. Drab colours, no doubt suited to a governess. Her hair, too, was light brown, her eyes green. They were not remarkable, yet at the moment their eyes met, Dominic had experienced a moment of unmistakable response to that eagerness, to those bright eyes that revealed, beneath the drab colours, a lively and enquiring mind.

In the conversation that had just taken place—for as she had pointed out, it could not be called an interview—he'd been forced to be blunt about his previous experiences with governesses. He'd already decided that upon her arrival it would be essential to warn the new governess against any fancies she might have, and when he'd seen Miss Wilmot's book of fairy tales, it had only seemed more pressing.

But he'd affronted her. It was a risk he'd known he would have to take, to quell any possible misunderstanding right from the start, in light of what had happened before, but he had sounded more pompous, and more arrogant than he'd meant. It was damned unfortunate. And her response...

Dominic frowned.

She had been more than affronted. She had ably defended the position of a governess and she was right: all too often male employers took advantage of the women in their employment. It was a matter of which he was aware and it was one of the reasons he'd decided to be straightforward about what had previously occurred. He wanted absolutely no confusion on that score. But he'd mishandled it. And he'd sensed there was more to it, for her.

He'd witnessed pain, and a kind of terror, in her eyes when the subject had been raised. It had been quickly disguised, but it wasn't an expression he cared to see in those bright eyes.

He closed the desk drawer.

Miss Wilmot was a puzzle. She had modern ideas about women's education, too. He was willing to see the results from her methods before he made any judgement upon them.

He wanted the best for Rosabel. If Miss Wilmot could bring the roses back into his daughter's cheeks, he would have no quarrel with the new governess. And she had made it perfectly clear that her interest lay only in teaching children.

It was a relief.

Dominic drummed his fingers again absently on the green leather top of his desk. He wondered how soon he would forget the enchanting expression he'd first seen, unguarded, in those bright eyes.

Maud washed her face and hands with rather more vigour than necessary in the white basin and pitcher provided in her new bedroom. She doused her cheeks again and again, tendrils of hair about her forehead dampened and curled, but her anger didn't abate.

Romantic notions!

How dared Sir Dominic Jago suggest that she had taken on the post as the new governess simply because he was a widower! Did he think himself so handsome? Did he expect all governesses to drop at his feet? Or that *she* would find him so hard to resist? Did he really believe she had come all the way to Cornwall, not for employment, but to catch a husband?

If only he knew.

Hot tears joined the chill water on Maud's cheeks.

Governesses sometimes married their employers, it was true. It happened. But it would never happen to her.

Marriage—to anyone, let alone the master of the house—was not in her future. Not now, not ever. Any promise of it had been torn away. No man could accept her and she could never explain. A future with a husband and a family would never be. Any dreams of such happy-ever-afters had been stolen from her.

She'd vowed, instead, to educate the children in her care with all the love and encouragement she had to give. She would dedicate herself to her vocation.

It was the only way she could go on.

Not all governesses considered themselves professional women, but Maud did. Some thought being a governess a last resort of penniless gentlewomen. But it was so much more to her. The work of private teaching was changing. Members of the Governesses' Benevolent Institution not only received support in dire straits, but their membership was also beginning to share their experiences and expertise among themselves. Recommendation of teaching ideas and textbooks was becoming more common. Yet governesses still had the reputation of mere husband-hunters in disguise.

Or worse.

Maud shuddered.

Sir Dominic's warning had cut her to the quick. She was already sensitive about such matters. Worse, much worse—she forced herself into the severest honesty—she had instantly liked him. That energy, she had to admit, was attractive and there was no arguing with his handsome dark looks. Had she looked at him with the eyes of a husband-hunter, even for an instant? No, it had been the ease with which they had conversed in the sunlit garden that had made her begin to believe that her new position as governess might prove to be a post she could truly enjoy.

Now she wished she could take the very next train away from Pendragon Hall, especially when what he suggested about governesses was, in her case, so far from the truth.

But perhaps—her brain began to tick—perhaps this post was ideal for her. Why, it was practically providential. A master of the house who had no interest in romance or marriage might not suit every governess, but it certainly suited Maud.

She threw more water on her face, washing away the tears. She would stay at Pendragon Hall. And she would, for the sake of her new charge, make the best of it.

Carefully she dried her face. The towel was of a fine snowy-white linen, clearly of good quality. In fact, all the appointments of her bedroom were the same. The room was large and airy, with tall arched windows that looked out over the gardens. There was an oak bureau and wardrobe that was far too big for the number of dresses she possessed. She only owned three: her grey cotton and her brown wool, for workday attire, and her dark green cotton, for special occasions. There had not been many of those, so it was still in good repair.

To one side of the room was a particularly beautiful four-poster oak bed. All in all, the room was far grander than the room she had occupied beneath the attics at her previous post.

Her bedroom had a connecting door to the adjacent schoolroom. She had glanced in when she had first arrived, but retreated, vaguely disappointed. It was well-furnished and decorated, but somewhat lacking, in her view. She had noted plenty of toys, a dolls' house and a rocking chair, tables and chairs, but less of the equipment she considered essential to teaching than she had expected. The previous governesses had left no imprint on their surroundings, it seemed.

Perhaps they had been too busy having romantic notions about Sir Dominic Jago.

Maud smiled ruefully. At least her sense of humour was returning. Of all the governesses in the world, she was the last to have harboured such ideas.

The master of Pendragon Hall was safe from Maud.

Folding the towel and hanging it carefully back on the rail, she glanced in the mirror and smoothed back her hair. Wisps were escaping from the severe bun she wore, softening her profile. Most unfortunate. She'd not been wearing her bonnet outside and her complexion appeared to have caught another freckle. Perhaps not wearing her bonnet on the way to Pendragon Hall—for she had sat next to the coach driver in the open air, rather than inside the Jago carriage—had not been the best idea. But she did love to be out of doors.

If she could, she would help Rosabel learn to love it, too.

She crossed to the schoolroom door. Rosabel's bedroom was on the other side.

It was time to make the acquaintance of a little girl who needed her care and to forget about her infuriating father, Sir Dominic Jago.

Maud pushed open the schoolroom door.

Chapter Three

On the little flower that clings;
—Alfred, Lord Tennyson: Maud *(1855)*

'Hello,' said Maud gently.

A little girl was seated at a table, eating a supper of bread and milk. She had dark hair, the same raven black as her father's, smoothed back under a black velvet snood. She wore a white ruffled pinafore over a yellow dress that didn't suit her colouring—her skin had a slight olive tint that looked almost sallow, as if she spent too much time indoors.

She did need to spend more time in the garden, thought Maud, to make her cheeks as rosy as her name.

Seated beside the little girl was a nursemaid in a black-and-white uniform, a plump, blonde-haired girl of little more than twenty, with a broad face and a friendly expression.

'Hello, miss,' the nursemaid said, in an accent like the coach driver's, with the same lilting burr that Maud had noticed tingeing Sir Dominic Jago's voice. 'You must be the new governess. I'm Netta.'

'How do you do.' Maud smiled at her. 'Sir Dominic told me you looked after Rosabel, and that you will be continuing to do so.'

'That's right, miss. I give Rosabel her baths and meals and so on. She's almost ready for bed now.'

Maud bent her knees slightly, to make herself closer to the girl's level. She disliked leaning over her charges. It made her unapproachable. 'I've been looking forward to meeting you.'

The little girl didn't respond.

Maud moved closer and saw the girl draw back. On her lap was a golden-haired porcelain doll. Her gaze was fixed upon the toy and she clutched it tightly in her hands.

'I see you've got a doll,' Maud said. 'Does she have a name?'

Rosabel hesitated, her eyes still cast down, then shook her head fiercely.

'Oh, dear,' said Maud. 'A doll with no name. How does she come when you call?'

A splutter of surprised laughter escaped from the little girl's lips, though she still did not look up. 'She's a doll! She can't come when I call!'

'How do you know if you've never called her?'

Rosabel lifted her head and stared at Maud. She didn't respond, merely continued to look suspicious with her dark eyes. They were the same deep brown as her father's.

'The right names are very important.' Maud ignored the tremor of unease that ran through her as she spoke. It bothered her more than she had expected, not to be using her own name. At least Wilmot was the same.

Maud sank down on her knees beside Rosabel's chair.

'You must have a name that a doll likes, otherwise she won't play properly with you.'

For the first time Maud saw a dimple in Rosabel's cheeks.

'I wonder what her name might be...' Maud mused. 'Could it be... Mergetrude?'

'Mergetrude isn't a name!' the girl burst out, with a giggle.

'Isn't it?' Maud pursed her lips and stared at the ceiling, as if in deep thought. 'Perhaps her name is Dorothea-Millicent-Margaret-Anne.'

Rosabel giggled. It was a sound that seemed awkward, as if it didn't happen very often. The doll in front of her, she held it towards Maud. 'She does have a name! It's Polly.'

'Of course!' Maud touched her hand to her forehead, as if in mock foolishness. 'How could I have thought otherwise? I'm very pleased to make your acquaintance, Miss Polly.'

She gave a curtsy.

With another shy giggle, Rosabel inclined the doll into a bow in return.

'You made up those names,' she said.

'Of course,' said Maud. 'Don't you ever make things up?'

Rosabel once again looked suspicious.

'Why, I do all the time,' said Maud.

'Is that so, Miss Wilmot?'

Maud swung around. The schoolroom door that opened on to the upstairs hall must have been ajar and she hadn't heard Dominic Jago enter. Her attention had been fully focused on the child in front of her.

He leaned against the doorframe, his dark eyes surveying the scene.

'Papa!' Rosabel exclaimed.

He moved around the table and dropped a kiss on the girl's raven head. The little girl beamed. Clearly, she adored her father, and it was mutual, judging by the way Sir Dominic regarded at his daughter. The angles of his face softened as he gazed down at the small girl.

'I see you have been making Rosabel's acquaintance,' he said, as he ruffled her hair.

Rosabel giggled. 'She thought Polly's name was Merget... Merg...'

'Mergetrude,' put in Maud.

'She made it up!'

Sir Dominic raised an eyebrow.

'I encourage imagination,' said Maud, quickly.

'I see.' He glanced around the schoolroom. 'I hope you have found everything here is satisfactory to your methods.'

Maud bit her lip. She didn't want to appear critical, but from their previous conversation, it was clear that Sir Dominic Jago prized being straightforward, to say the least.

In for a penny, in for a pound, she thought to herself.

'Not quite,' she replied.

She heard Netta the nursemaid's stunned intake of breath.

'What is it you require?' Sir Dominic asked. She thought there was the slightest upturn of his mouth, but she couldn't be sure.

'Some more books,' she said. She had brought her book of fairy tales and some other volumes, but they would need a great deal more. 'And other educational materials. A globe of the world, for a start. I saw one or two in the library.'

'A globe of the world,' he repeated.

'For geography.'

After a moment he nodded. 'The library is at your disposal. You must help yourself to whatever you need.'

'Thank you.' She hesitated. 'Might I fetch one of the globes now?'

His eyebrow rose. 'This evening?'

Maud nodded. 'It would be most useful.' She turned her attention back to Rosabel. 'Do you like stories, Rosabel?'

'Yes,' she replied doubtfully.

'I can tell you and Polly a bedtime story tonight. Would you like that?'

'Will you make it up?' the little girl asked.

'Certainly,' said Maud.

'Then I think I might like it,' she said. 'And so would Polly,' she added as an afterthought.

Maud smiled. 'Then while Netta puts you to bed, I will go and fetch the globe from the library.'

Sir Dominic stepped forward. His eyes glinted.

'Allow me,' he drawled. 'I will fetch the globe for you, Miss Wilmot, if you will allow me to stay for the bedtime story.'

Maud halted the twisting of her hands. She would not reveal her nervousness to Sir Dominic.

She sat by Rosabel's bed in her pretty bedroom. It was all done in pink silk, with roses on the wallpaper. It must have been decorated recently, for wallpapers were the height of fashion and this was one of the most delightful Maud had seen. The room was light and airy, looking over the same aspect of the garden as Maud's.

Tucked up under the pink silk eiderdown was Rosabel, in her white nightgown. Polly had been dressed in a white nightdress, too.

'That will be all for me, miss,' Netta said now. 'I'll be going to have my tea in the servants' hall. I suppose you will be having your supper on a tray in the schoolroom? All the other governesses did.'

Maud hid her sigh. The governess always hovered between stairs, neither upstairs nor down, not welcome to dine with the family, nor particularly welcome among the servants. Often, Maud felt lonely when she dined alone in the schoolroom, night after night. But she had learnt to manage being alone. She read books, or wrote letters, or prepared lessons. She would often mend and sew, too, and of course, when she could, she would slip out for a walk.

'Thank you, Netta.' Maud smiled at her. It wasn't Netta's fault that the governess wasn't to be included below stairs. It was the way things were done. 'A supper tray would be most welcome. I can fetch it myself, if that would be of help.'

'Oh, no, miss. I'll bring it. And your morning tray, too.'

Netta gave Maud one last curious look. The story of how the new governess had found fault with the schoolroom and spoken in such a forthright manner to the master of the house would be all over the servants' hall in minutes, Maud guessed.

A few moments later he reappeared, carrying the globe. Again, she was aware of how he moved. He strode into the room with a casual ease that would have been attractive, had he not been so infuriating. She supposed she could see why previous governesses had been drawn to him—not that she would, of course, fall under his spell.

He bowed slightly as he passed the globe to Maud.

She made sure her fingers did not touch his as she took it. 'Thank you.'

He gave a glimmer of a smile before pulling up a chair on the other side of Rosabel's bed.

So, he did intend to stay and listen to the bedtime story.

'Tonight's story is about Little Swallowtail.' Maud fought down her unexpected anxiety. She was never nervous when storytelling, but Sir Dominic Jago's presence had an unsettling effect. He had said nothing at all since he came back with the globe, yet she could not help being aware of him.

'Little Swallowtail is a fairy—a butterfly fairy, in fact. She is tiny and delicate, so tiny that from a distance you might mistake her for a butterfly herself.' Maud leaned forward and whispered to Rosabel, 'I think some of them might live in your garden.'

Rosabel's eyes became saucers.

A fleeting smile passed across Sir Dominic's face.

Maud settled back in the chair. Her nerves were abating now. 'Once upon a time, there was a young butterfly fairy called Little Swallowtail. Though she wasn't quite a butterfly fairy, not yet. You see, she didn't want to grow her wings.'

Rosabel's eyes were wide. 'Don't all fairies have wings?'

'Not when they're little fairies,' said Maud. 'At the beginning, they don't have wings when they are born.

They have lovely black-and-white-striped caterpillar bodies with yellow spots, and they stay on the ground.'

'Ugh.' Rosabel shuddered and hugged Polly tighter. 'I don't like caterpillars.'

'Perhaps you haven't met the right ones,' said Maud. 'Little Swallowtail is friendly, though the Red Admiral can be a rather unpleasant caterpillar, at times, and Speckled Wood can be a crosspatch in bad weather. But I've never met a Small Tortoiseshell I didn't like.'

A muffled cough came from Sir Dominic.

Maud glanced up. His face, however, was expressionless.

She went on with the story. 'Now, let me tell you about Little Swallowtail. She was born into a beautiful garden. Her family had settled in Cornwall long ago, though long ago, they came from tropical climes.'

Maud held up the globe so that Rosabel could see it.

'Swallowtail's family came from North Africa...' she put her finger on the map '...and Asia.' She showed Rosabel the landmass before spinning the globe. 'And this is where we are, in Cornwall.'

She turned the globe again to show Rosabel the long distance between the two countries and held it steady so that Rosabel could spin it around.

Sir Dominic smiled. He leaned in. 'Is that a little girl I see in Cornwall?' He pointed to the location on the globe.

Rosabel giggled.

Maud almost dropped the globe on to the eiderdown. She hadn't expected him to join in the fun of storytelling.

He reached out and steadied the globe with his long fingers.

His lips curved. 'Shall I hold the world for you, Miss Wilmot?'

Maud quickly removed her own hand. 'We have almost finished with it.'

His half-smile remained as he laid the globe on the bedside table next to him.

'The Swallowtails liked the weather here in Cornwall,' Maud went on. She had to focus. She refused to be perturbed by his presence as she continued the story, all about how Little Swallowtail didn't want to fly like the other butterflies and how she found her courage, and her wings.

Rosabel listened with her doll gripped tight. Sir Dominic Jago, too, appeared to take in every word, as Maud described Little Swallowtail's adventures as a caterpillar: how she got lost in the jungle of long grass by the meadow near the river and found her way home.

'Finally…' Maud got to the end of the story '… Little Swallowtail saw the vegetable patch and knew she was home. Her mother wrapped Little Swallowtail in her wings. "We thought we had lost you for ever!"

'"I want to grow my wings," said Little Swallowtail, "so I don't ever get lost again." So, she was wrapped up in her soft white cocoon, that is like the most comfortable of featherbeds, and when she came out of the cocoon, she had become Princess Swallowtail, with wings of pale yellow veined with black, a pretty blue frill and two scarlet spots.'

Rosabel had been listening eagerly. 'Have you ever seen Princess Swallowtail?'

Maud smiled. 'The butterflies are all asleep now and you must go to sleep, too. But one day, if you can show me the vegetable patch, we can try to find Princess Swallowtail, or perhaps one of her cousins.'

Rosabel drew back. 'I don't like to go out of doors.'

Maud clasped her hands together. 'Why, that is just how some of the butterflies feel, about coming *indoors*.'

'They do?' Rosabel asked.

Maud sensed Sir Dominic's hidden chuckle.

'Indeed,' Maud said. 'I wonder if you can help. It would be most useful if you could allow some of the butterflies to visit you, indoors. They are used to the outdoors, you see, and if you would allow them to make a morning call on you, they might become more used to the environment.'

Rosabel thought for a moment. 'How will they come indoors?'

'I will bring them,' said Maud, 'in a large jar, with plenty of holes for air. Some might be bold enough to go free in the schoolroom, but we will have to see.'

'Might I also be present for this morning visit?' Sir Dominic asked.

'Of course.' Maud inclined her head without enthusiasm.

She stood and smoothed out her skirt. 'I will say goodnight now, Rosabel.'

'Goodnight.'

'Goodnight, Sir Dominic.'

Idly, he spun the globe with his finger. 'Goodnight, Miss Wilmot. Until tomorrow.'

Maud hurried through the schoolroom and into her own bedroom. She shut the door and leaned against it. She had no intention of lingering.

Sir Dominic's presence during the storytelling had been more enjoyable than she had anticipated. She had to admit, as her heart gave another thud, he was the most disturbing man she had ever met. Most disturbing, indeed.

Chapter Four

It leads me forth at evening;
—*Alfred, Lord Tennyson:* Maud *(1855)*

'Good morning, Miss Wilmot.'

Maud entered the schoolroom to find Sir Dominic standing by the window. The sunlight streamed in, putting his face half in profile. It emphasised the set of his jaw.

She stepped back, then raised her own chin as she crossed the room and placed on the table the large jars she had borrowed from the kitchen earlier that morning. The glass glistened in the sunlight, making the foliage she had gathered inside them appear even more vivid green.

'Good morning,' she replied, unsmiling, with the slightest nod of her head. Overnight, for she had struggled to sleep as usual, her indignation at the master of the house had not abated. She had resolved to display the utmost propriety towards him at all times.

'I thought I would come and see that you have what

you need here in the schoolroom for today's lesson. But I see you have already been busy,' he said.

'Since just after dawn,' she admitted. 'I was fortunate to find what I needed around the vegetable patch.'

He frowned slightly as he studied the contents of the jars. 'Are these of sufficient size for your purposes?'

She ran her finger over the lid of one of the jars, where she had made the holes for air. She'd not only caught caterpillars, but a butterfly, too. 'These jars are large enough for insect homes.' She couldn't suppress a sigh. 'Ideally, of course, I'd have a vivarium.'

His raised eyebrow met the other in a slight frown. 'You are already teaching me something, Miss Wilmot. I'm not familiar with the word. What is a vivarium?'

'It's a Latin term,' she told him eagerly, unable to hold back her enthusiasm. She picked up one of the glass jars. 'It's a most innovative idea. Imagine this insect home being four or five times the size. That is the size of a vivarium. They are big glass cases or domes, with ventilation, where caterpillars and butterflies can be observed alive, without harm. Mr Ward of London has made some marvellous ones that are being used on long sea voyages to collect specimens, I believe. But we can make do.'

'Thank you for enlightening me.'

Maud stiffened as she put the jar back with the others on the table. She wondered, for a moment, if he was mocking her enthusiasm, but she could discern no trace of mockery on his face. Instead, he was studying the insect homes with increased interest.

The door from the nursery opened.

Maud smiled. 'Good morning, Rosabel.'

Rosabel edged towards the table, her doll Polly clutched against her ruffled pinafore.

Sir Dominic reached out and put his arm around her, drawing the little girl close to him. He pointed to the insect homes. 'Come and see what Miss Wilmot has found.'

Rosabel peered cautiously at the jars. 'Is that Princess Swallowtail?'

Maud shook her head. 'I couldn't find her this morning. She must be off on one of her adventures. Some of her friends have come to call instead. Would you like to meet them?'

Rosabel leaned further into her papa's side, but she nodded.

Maud pointed at the brown-and-yellow butterfly fluttering against the glass. 'This is Mr Speckled Wood come to say how do you do. I'm sure he is very pleased to make your and Polly's acquaintance.'

'How do you do,' Sir Dominic murmured.

Rosabel giggled. 'How do you do.'

'I trust Mr Wood has found adequate refreshment,' said Sir Dominic.

'Indeed he has,' Maud replied, repressing another smile. She hadn't expected the master of the house to play along. 'Long grass is his preference, so I have put plenty in the jar.'

'We aim to please at Pendragon Hall.' Sir Dominic leaned in. 'I see there are leaves, also. Are they to Mr Wood's taste?'

Maud couldn't repress a chuckle. 'I hope not.'

'Can you see what is on one of the leaves in the other jar, Rosabel?' Sir Dominic asked.

Rosabel cringed. 'Is that a caterpillar?'

'Indeed it is.' Maud turned the glass around so that the little green creature was more visible.

'Will it come out of the jar?' Rosabel's voice was high with fear.

Maud was quick to reassure her. 'Oh, no, not unless you invite it to do so specifically. Caterpillars are extremely shy. They like to stay on their leaves. It is not a good idea to move them too quickly. They also get very, very hungry. We shall have to feed it lots of grass, in its new home.'

Maud moved the jar aside and took up the other. 'And here is someone who likes to stay in bed.'

Sir Dominic leaned in. After a moment, Rosabel followed her father's example.

'This is a cocoon,' Maud explained. 'A more proper name for it is chrysalis.' It was a little early in the year, but she'd found it on a loose piece of bark, near the scullery door. She never liked to disturb a cocoon unnecessarily and often they were attached to walls or fences. This one had transferred easily.

Rosabel's shoulders were hunched, but Maud was pleased to see she couldn't restrain a closer look at the hard white case that was stuck to the bark. It was only a couple of inches long. 'Is there a caterpillar inside?'

'It was a caterpillar,' Maud went on. 'Now it is sleeping on its pillow. But while it is sleeping, safe and sound, it is changing into a beautiful butterfly. A white-and-pale-green one, I think. When it is ready, it will come out.'

Sir Dominic glanced at her over the top of Rosabel's head. 'How long do you think it will take?'

'A week,' Maud told him. 'Maybe two.'

His face was still, but he drew his daughter closer to him. 'I hope I am there to see it.'

'I can assure you, Sir Dominic,' Maud said softly. 'It will happen. The butterfly will emerge.'

Dominic slid the engraved card out of the envelope and sighed. Another dinner invitation.

He dropped the white card on the mantelpiece. He was not an unfriendly man, far from it, but at the end of a day's work running the railway, let alone Pendragon Hall and the surrounding estate, he never particularly looked forward to idle banter around a dinner table.

Strange, how a mere piece of card could bring back so many memories.

The arguments. The misunderstandings. The complaints. The tears.

He returned to his desk, gritted his teeth and opened the book of railway accounts.

As he did so, the clock on the mantelpiece chimed.

He didn't need to look at a timetable to know that a West Cornish Railway train would be arriving at a Cornish station at that very moment. Over the past few years, he'd memorised the train timetable almost without realising it. Every time a train arrived or pulled out, he knew it.

His challenge in the future would be to keep them running.

At least he'd been able to focus more easily on his work for the last few days, since the new governess had arrived. It was hard to put his finger on exactly what had altered, but one of the burdens he'd been carrying alone had been eased, at least.

Not that he had too much contact with the new governess. When he did, she was most stern in her manner. Even so, something had shifted in the house; some tension had disappeared. The change was almost imperceptible, but it was there.

Yet his other burdens remained. He squared his shoulders, took up his fountain pen and went over the figures again.

They didn't add up any differently.

He exhaled as he dropped the pen on to the desk. For a moment he rested his elbows on the leather, put his head in his hands and pressed his fingers into his scalp, as if different numbers would emerge if he pressed hard enough.

Mentally, he calculated again. He'd trimmed back costs by taking on even more of the financial responsibility. It was a risk, but he had to take it, at least until he could find an alternative. He was not only a major investor, he also managed much of the line himself. No detail escaped him. He wanted the line to be the best in Britain, if not in Europe. Cornwall had lagged behind for so long. His county deserved to thrive in the new railway age. He must do everything possible to ensure it did.

The study door flung open.

'Papa!'

Dominic leapt to his feet. 'What is it, Rosabel?'

His daughter's black ringlets flew around her head as she rushed into the room. 'The butterfly has come out!'

Behind her came Miss Wilmot, carrying one of the insect homes. 'Forgive the interruption, Sir Dominic.'

'Not at all, Miss Wilmot.'

'Butterflies often come out in the morning,' she explained. 'Rosabel and I were fortunate enough to see it in time, just after breakfast. It has occurred much earlier than I expected. The new butterfly had just begun to break free.'

Rosabel clapped her hands together. 'We watched it come out, Papa! And now we're going to let it out of the jar. Come out and watch it with us!'

Dominic turned away and cleared his suddenly choked throat. He'd barely realised how much Rosabel's nervousness had been preying on his mind and heart.

He'd tried to convince himself that it was merely his young daughter's temperament, that she took after him more than her mama. Sarah had been pretty, friendly and gregarious. She'd been sociable, loving to attend dinners and parties, to go and stay with acquaintances, to host a stream of guests at Pendragon Hall. Rosabel was more reserved. But he'd known, deep down, it was something else than temperament that had kept her indoors for so long.

He'd been more worried about his daughter than he'd ever been able to acknowledge.

Dominic turned and met the gaze of Miss Wilmot. Her face was grave, but in her eyes, he saw her relief.

His throat choked again. Until the new governess had come along, he had struggled alone with his fears for his daughter. Now he saw that she had shared his concern. An understanding, more profound than sympathy, emanated from every aspect of her being.

'Papa! Didn't you hear me?' Rosabel came around the desk and tugged at his sleeve. 'We're going to let the butterfly into the garden.'

Under the guise of adjusting his cravat, Dominic cleared his throat.

'Is it ready to fly?' he asked Miss Wilmot, his voice rasping. He was unable to say more. 'It is not too soon?'

That deep understanding flared in her eyes.

'Not at all,' she assured him quietly. 'It is time to test its wings.'

Rosabel tugged his sleeve again. 'Come with us, Papa!'

He tousled his daughter's curls. 'Of course.'

She half ran out of the study.

Dominic came out from behind his desk. As he did so, he caught Miss Wilmot's fresh, clean scent—pure and natural, like the outdoors.

She held out the jar. The empty chrysalis lay on the bottom of the glass and a white butterfly was fluttering within. 'Perhaps you would care to do the honours, Sir Dominic.'

She wore no gloves. As he took it, their fingers touched. Hers were warm before she quickly withdrew them.

'Miss Wilmot! Papa!' Rosabel called from the hall.

'We're coming, Rosabel,' she replied.

Her grey skirt swished over the smooth wooden boards as he followed her into the hall.

He blinked as the new governess stepped forward and opened the front door. The morning sun streamed in. It turned the hall to gold, sending coppery glints into her hair.

Dominic gripped the jar.

As they watched, Rosabel ran out into the sunlight.

A twig snapped.

Maud shrieked.

'Miss Wilmot!'

An owl screeched as she spun around, her boots slipping in the soft grass. Her breath came in jagged, painful gasps.

Her shawl fell back from her head. 'Sir Dominic!'

He bowed slightly. 'I didn't mean to startle you. I seem to be making a habit of it.'

She drew her shawl tight. Her whole body shook. 'I didn't hear you come up behind me.'

'I can see that.' He cast an eye over her as she stood before him.

She became aware of the rise and fall of her bodice as she clutched the shawl. Her heart was still pounding, her breath coming fast.

He stepped back. 'I meant no cause for alarm. I noticed a light here in the bushes and recalled what you told me about moth-hunting.'

Maud glanced around. She hadn't gone right into the woods, just stayed at the edge, among some of the oaks and blackthorn bushes. 'Is there any difficulty in my being here?'

He shook his head. 'Not in the least. I merely thought I would take the opportunity to thank you for what you did for Rosabel today.'

'There's no need to thank me,' Maud replied as she counted her breaths, trying to slow them.

'We both know that there is.' He studied her. 'Are you all right now?'

'Yes. I mean, no. I mean, you surprised me.' Her breath still came in those painful, jagged gasps. Tremors tore at her body like fingers. Ever since what had happened, as she now thought of it as a way of both trying to deal with it and keep the memories at bay, she had become easily startled. She jumped if someone entered the room unexpectedly, or even at a loud noise. Her nerves were strained, she knew, fluttering like a butterfly in a net.

He stood silently as she tried to regain her composure, his face half in darkness, half in lamplight.

Maud lifted her head to let the cool night air fan her face. 'I didn't mean to shriek.'

He pushed back his hair from his brow. His signet ring gleamed. 'You gave the night owls a run for their money.'

He continued to study her, as if trying to assess her reaction. 'If I may say, you don't seem the type to startle easily.'

'What type do I seem?'

His mouth quirked. 'I am still making you out.'

Her stomach fluttered. His scrutiny was unnerving.

'Miss Wilmot,' he said, after a moment, 'I believe we got off to a bad start and I am sorry for that. I am in your debt for what you have achieved with Rosabel in such a short amount of time.'

Maud drew back, stunned. She had never expected him to say such a thing.

'Rosabel's achievements are her own,' she protested.

'That is very modest of you, Miss Wilmot, but it is not entirely the case. You have more than proved your competence as a governess.'

'Thank you,' she said simply. It was what she taught her charges. To accept a compliment with grace. But it was more difficult, coming, as it did, with an apology from Sir Dominic Jago.

'Changes make things difficult for Rosabel,' he said. 'After having lost her mother, new governesses, one after another…'

She nodded.

'I understand,' she said gently. More than he realised, perhaps.

He exhaled. 'I believe you shared my pleasure at witnessing the butterfly emerge.'

'I believe I did.' She couldn't deny it.

He glanced over to where she had placed the lamp carefully on the ground. 'I have never seen moth-hunting before.'

Maud pointed to the lamp. Even burning low, a variety of moths were drawn to it, some of them large, some small, in shades of brown, white and grey. They fluttered around it now. It silvered their wings. 'Moths are attracted to light, of course, and I can only catch them at night. They are interesting to compare to butterflies.'

'I needed some air myself tonight,' he admitted. 'The railway is keeping me busy.'

'Surely the railway doesn't run at night,' Maud said lightly. He'd said something similar to her about butterflies.

His smile was fleeting in the lamplight. 'Trains need more than coal to keep them running. They need money. The West Cornish Railway Company needs other investors and needs them urgently. I am committed to connecting Cornwall to the rest of the world. The line has to expand, in both terms of track miles and more carriages and customers, or it will fail, taking away opportunities for all the workers and travellers, along with trade. The West Cornish Railway lacks funds and it is my job to find it. Failure is not an option, Miss Wilmot.'

'It's a big responsibility.' It explained why his light was so often burning in the library, late at night.

'Many people depend on me. It's important for me to increase work and prosperity in Cornwall. My father was not a man of business and Pendragon Hall needs more than rents to keep going. I have been working hard to not only improve my father's estate but the lives of all those nearby. There have been Jagos in this area for centuries. Once, they were tenant farmers, not landowners. I do not forget that. I have a horror of taking advantage of those who work for a living.'

He exhaled. 'The railway needs my full attention at this crucial stage. Investment is essential if it is to reach its full potential, and investors must be found and cultivated. I must admit, it is the part of the business I like least, but unless money is found to ensure the prosperity of the line, my hopes and dreams for the railway may never come true. We need investors urgently.'

'The West Cornish Railway is a fine train line,' she protested. 'Surely investors will be keen to support it.'

'That is very kind of you to say, but there is little money here in my county and Cornwall has always struggled to gain English investment.'

'You speak as if Cornwall and England are two different lands.'

'To a Cornishman they are,' he said. 'We are accepted by English, but also not accepted. Not quite.'

'Like governesses,' Maud said. 'We, too, are outsiders. Between stairs.'

'I had not thought of it that way. Then we are alike, it seems.'

Silence fell over them again, like a net. She felt no wish to break it, as the moths fluttered by.

Nor, it appeared, did he. It was some moments later that he bowed. 'I have imposed upon your leisure time. I will wish you goodnight, Miss Wilmot. Happy hunting.'

He vanished into the darkness.

Maud stared after him. What he'd told her about the railway line explained a great deal. He was a hard-work-

ing man, a driven one, committed to the people who relied upon him.

But it was a heavy burden to carry alone.

Picking up her lamp and net, she slowly made her
way back to the house.

Chapter Five

'Tis a morning pure and sweet;
—*Alfred, Lord Tennyson:* Maud *(1855)*

Dominic leaned back on his horse. 'Whoa, Taran.'

On the gravel drive he paused and looked across the lawn to where Miss Wilmot and Rosabel were busy with their botany activities, as they had been every morning, without fail, for the past few weeks. Her unusual methods had continued to work. He had now become accustomed to stopping and watching them before he rode off to spend most of the day at the railway office, just as he had become accustomed to spending the early part of his evening in the nursery listening to Miss Wilmot tell one of her butterfly fables.

He had to admit it had become a most pleasant pastime.

This morning, he had been observing them more closely than usual. Usually, they carried butterfly nets with long wooden handles. Rosabel's was some inches shorter than the governess's net. Miss Wilmot's also appeared to be adjustable. She was able to lengthen or shorten it with a sharp flick of her fingers, as if she were fly-fishing. At first, she had spent a great deal of time demonstrating to Rosabel how to leap and jump to make the best use of a net, much to Dominic's hidden amusement. He had almost laughed out loud at one particularly adventurous swipe through the air, but he'd restrained himself. She hadn't looked much older than Rosabel, with her enthusiasm and energy as, with her net aloft, she almost flew through the air.

It was in sharp contrast to the reserved, almost reproving manner with which she treated him, even after their nighttime encounter. He could not fault her behaviour in that regard. There was a distance between them that, to his amazement, he almost regretted. His initial warning had been entirely unnecessary, he realised, with some chagrin. She did not seek him out. She kept any conversation with him to a minimum. Each night she told her tale, bid Rosabel goodnight and vanished into the cocoon of her bedroom.

But his daughter was thriving under her care. Miss Wilmot had proved to be a gift and he had been able to relax in that regard, at least. Rosabel's increased appetite, pink cheeks and general air of happiness showed that the new governess's routine was continuing to make a difference. Miss Wilmot was much more than a good storyteller. She possessed that rare gift of being able to enchant children into learning. The stories she told each night were full of charm, but they also carried information, and usually held an intriguing lesson that would lead Rosabel out of doors the next day.

He had become intrigued himself.

As well as butterfly-catching, the pair of them seemed to spend a great deal of time hunting for caterpillars, or at least that was what he presumed they were doing. It was something he had never thought he would see Rosabel do. But there she was, digging among the bushes and plants and emerging with her white pinafore covered with dirt, her normally neat ringlets a mass of wild curls. Miss Wilmot was often not much better. She, too, was not averse to diving into the undergrowth, and, as it had this morning, her bonnet generally fell back completely, revealing curls that rivalled Rosabel's ringlets in a shade that he now saw had warm reddish lights in the sunlight.

This morning there had been even more activity than usual. Netta, the nursemaid, and other kitchen staff had been going to and from the Hall, carrying more glass pickling bottles and jars, with Miss Wilmot directing their placement in certain areas of the garden. From the smiling response and interest of the servants, he gauged that the new governess was far more popular than any previous governess had been. She also seemed entirely unaware that there was foliage in her hair.

Dominic slid off the stallion's back.

'Watch me, Miss Wilmot!' Rosabel ran across the lawn, her butterfly net aloft. The sun beamed down on grass that still held the faintest touches of morning dew.

Maud laughed. 'That's right, Rosabel. Keep chasing them!'

On the gravel drive that led to the large iron gates, she had seen Sir Dominic astride a black stallion, a huge animal with a glossy coat. He often stopped and watched them, she'd noted, before he rode away. But this morning he'd turned the horse, dismounted and led it across the grass.

When he reached her, he pulled up the horse beside him with a casual turn of his wrist.

'Good morning.' He bowed. His riding coat was as black as the horse's mane, but his head was bare. 'It's good to see Rosabel so often out of doors. I must congratulate you on your methods.'

Maud nodded stiffly. Even though she had been at Pendragon Hall for a few weeks now, she made sure she never sought out Sir Dominic. He came and listened to her telling of The Butterfly Fables each night, but she carefully avoided being in his presence at all other times. It was imperative, in the circumstances. She must be certain not to lower her guard.

'Butterflies are more often out in the morning,' she said now.

'As is Rosabel, of late.' He moved the reins from one leather-gloved hand to the other as the horse shifted. 'I am continuing to enjoy listening to her bedtime stories.' His mouth curved in that half-smile again. 'You are something of a Scheherazade, entertaining us with her tales of one thousand and one Arabian Nights.'

'I do not seek to be an enchantress, Sir Dominic,' she replied with severity. What, did he think her a modern Scheherazade, luring her king into love by means of bedroom tales? He might think she had designs upon him, or, heaven forfend, romantic notions. She had no intention of implying any such intentions on her behalf. 'Nor, I believe, did Scheherazade. She was simply a woman who had the power of storytelling.'

'Forgive me.' Amusement gleamed in his dark eyes. 'I merely meant to praise you for your teaching methods.'

Maud lifted her chin. 'I am fully confident in their merit.'

He sketched her a small bow. 'You have already proved their worth, Miss Wilmot. Please do not think I have any complaints.'

'Papa! Miss Wilmot!' Rosabel raced over to them, the butterfly net now cupped in her hands. 'I've caught a butterfly!'

Maud clasped her hands together. 'Oh, well done, Rosabel!'

Rosabel danced with excitement. 'Is it Princess Swallowtail?'

'Let's look. Gently now.' Carefully, Maud took the net and covered the hooped steel top with a white cotton handkerchief she pulled from her pocket. She loosened the net, giving the butterfly room to move.

'It is a small blue butterfly,' she said. 'A male. His Latin name is *cupido*, named for Cupid, the little god of love. He is a good friend of Princess Swallowtail's. Look at the colour on his wings. He is one of the tiniest butterflies in England.'

'He's so small,' breathed Rosabel.

'Yes, but he's a good flier. Shall we keep him or set him free?'

'Surely Cupid should fly free,' murmured Sir Dominic.

Rosabel nodded.

'Very well.' Throwing off the handkerchief, Maud gave the butterfly net a shake. The dark blue butterfly fluttered momentarily in the net, then caught the opening and flew across the lawn towards the woods.

Rosabel clapped her hands in delight.

'Bravo, Miss Wilmot,' Sir Dominic Jago said. 'Another success.'

'It was Rosabel who caught the butterfly,' Maud responded.

'I wasn't referring to the butterfly,' he replied.

Maud glanced up at him.

His eyes were on Rosabel, pink-cheeked and laughing, before his gaze met hers.

Understanding flashed between them.

Instantly Maud broke the connection.

'Shall we go and see if we can find some other butterflies in the woods?' she asked Rosabel quickly. 'We don't need to go far.'

'You can go as far as you wish, Miss Wilmot,' Sir Dominic said. 'Pendragon Woods are part of the estate.'

'Thank you.'

'We're going to have a picnic in the woods, Papa,' Rosabel said. 'Miss Wilmot says that everything tastes better out of doors. Can you come, too?'

He smiled at his daughter. 'Another time, I hope, if Miss Wilmot will allow it.'

'Of course,' Maud replied.

He bowed again.

Maud took Rosabel by the hand, the butterfly net in the other. She was aware of him still standing with his horse as they walked away.

When they returned from the woods a little later, there was no sign of Sir Dominic Jago. Not that she had been looking for him, she reproved herself.

A carriage had drawn up at in front of the house, and, with the help of a footman, a woman was descending, her hooped taffeta skirt swaying in the breeze. The fabric shimmered as if it were the ocean itself.

Maud sighed. The dress was so beautiful. With Rosabel's hand still in hers, she moved closer, across the lawn.

The woman turned. She was probably the most fashionable woman Maud had ever seen, even in London, she thought, half-dazzled. Her hair was dark and her long-lashed eyes were an unusual blue-green, a light turquoise that matched the velvet of the ribbons that held her black cape.

With an imperious, gloved hand, she beckoned.

Maud stiffened. She disliked being summoned in such a way, but it would be rude not to respond. She had to be careful, always, to be polite to visitors to the house. It was part of the role of a governess.

The woman looked Maud up and down as they drew near, as if Maud were a specimen on a pin. 'You must be the new governess. Dominic has mentioned you.'

Maud inclined her head. Governesses did not curtsy or bob, in general, but she always aimed to be courteous. 'Yes. I am Miss Wilmot. How do you do?'

'I am Averill Trevose.' The other woman's voice was crisp and high. 'Soon to be mistress of Pendragon Hall.'

Chapter Six

When all my spirit reels;
                —Alfred, Lord Tennyson: Maud *(1855)*

Maud almost dropped the butterfly net.

So, Sir Dominic Jago was engaged to be married. No wonder he had been at such pains to tell her that he did not want governesses chasing after him. But it still came as a shock that he had not informed her of his impending wedding.

Yet why should he? she chided herself. He was not required to disclose his personal affairs to her.

'My apologies,' Maud said. 'I wasn't aware that Sir Dominic was engaged.'

Two red spots appeared on Miss Averill Trevose's cheeks.

'Our engagement has not been formally announced, not that it is any concern of yours. I am mistress here in all but name, and soon I will have that, too.' She spoke with all the assurance of a woman who always got what she wanted. Maud knew that haughty tone. She'd come across it in her previous employment—it emanated from women who wanted their desires met instantly, who expected Maud to fetch and carry for them, even though her role as governess was not that of a general servant.

Averill tossed her glossy ringlets. 'I told Dominic that I could take charge of employing his servants. He has had such trouble with governesses. How they chase him! But I understand you are something of a bluestocking.'

Maud's corset tightened, seemed to clamp her chest. 'I support women's education, yes,' she managed to reply.

'I suppose some women need an education,' said Averill, in a dismissive, almost pitying tone. 'Especially if they have nothing else in life.'

Maud bit back her retort.

Miss Trevose's black ringlets fell over her shoulder as she bent towards Rosabel, who had been listening to the conversation, wide-eyed, all the while pressed against Maud's grey skirt.

Maud reached to put an arm around her and draw the little girl closer in. It was entirely inappropriate for Miss Averill Trevose to have mentioned the possibility of marrying Rosabel's father in front of the child, she thought indignantly. Miss Trevose obviously had no consideration for how it could affect a child to hear such news, especially a child such as Rosabel. Still, it was none of her concern who Sir Dominic Jago chose to marry.

Averill gave Rosabel a smile that didn't warm her blue eyes.

'I've come to take Rosabel home to Trevose Hall with me for the day,' she cooed. 'I thought we ought to spend some time getting to know each other better. Would you like that, Rosabel?'

Rosabel shrank back.

Averill rolled her eyes. 'It is absurd that a knight's

daughter should be so shy. She must learn to take her place in society. Her disposition is much too nervous.'

Maud bit her tongue. She loathed hearing children criticised in their presence. Rosabel was shy and sensitive, it was true, but there was nothing wrong with that. She would become more confident, even in new situations, if she was allowed time and care. She had already made such excellent progress. Maud did not want it undone.

Averill held out her hand. 'Come along now, Rosabel.'

Rosabel shrank even further behind Maud's skirt.

Averill exhaled in exasperation. 'Come along, I said.'

One look into Rosabel's white face and pleading eyes was enough for Maud.

She thought quickly. 'My apologies, Miss Trevose. Sir Dominic left no instructions for Rosabel to visit you today, or any other day, for that matter.'

Averill drew back, her elbows bent. Her cooing demeanour had vanished. 'Don't be impertinent! He didn't need to leave instructions. Dominic will entirely approve of Rosabel coming with me.'

Maud felt Rosabel's small hand grasp tighter in hers. 'I cannot allow Rosabel to leave without Sir Dominic's permission.'

'I'm quite certain that *Dominic*,' Averill emphasised the use of his first name, as if underlining their intimacy, 'would have no objection to my taking Rosabel out for the day. He can collect the child later.'

'Nevertheless,' Maud said with a calmness that belied her inner anger at Rosabel being described as if she were no more than a parcel to be picked up, 'I have been given no explicit instructions. Until I receive Sir Dominic's permission for you to take Rosabel, I cannot do so.'

She would not. Not with Rosabel quivering beside her.

'That's ridiculous,' Miss Averill hissed.

'In any case,' said Maud, 'there are Rosabel's lessons to think of.'

Miss Averill tossed her head. 'Surely her lessons can wait.'

'I'm afraid not.' Maud squeezed Rosabel's trembling hand. 'Come with me, Rosabel. We must finish our botany lesson.'

Rosabel peeped out from behind Maud's skirt. Relief was obvious on her pinched face.

Fury at being thwarted flashed in Averill's stunning blue eyes. 'Dominic shall hear about your impertinence. I'll have you dismissed.'

Her skirt whirled as she turned her back on them both and stalked back to the carriage.

Still holding Rosabel's hand, Maud raised the butterfly net and walked across the lawn towards the woods. Rosabel's hand was not the only one shaking. Rarely had Maud met another woman to whom she had taken such an instinctive dislike.

There was no doubt that Miss Averill Trevose was a beautiful woman, but there was a coldness to her that chilled Maud's heart. Was this the kind of woman that Sir Dominic wanted to marry? Was she soon to become Rosabel's mother?

Maud's heart sank.

She had thought that her position as her governess was secure.

Far from it.

'Miss Wilmot?'

Maud smiled down at Rosabel, who lay tucked beneath the bedclothes, her teddy bear beside her. She had just finished listening, wide-eyed, to the latest adventures of Princess Swallowtail.

The bedtime story had started later than usual. Almost a week had passed since the unfortunate interlude with Miss Trevose, and Maud had allowed herself to hope that it had been forgotten. Each night, when Sir Dominic Jago appeared in the nursery, and, with no words spoken, took a seat on the other side of Rosabel's bed to listen to Maud's tale, she had expected him to raise the matter, but he had not.

Tonight, however, the nursery clock had chimed seven and he had not appeared. Perhaps he had lost interest in her storytelling. Maud suppressed an odd pang at the thought. She had begun to listen for his approach in the corridor outside, had come to recognise his tread. It had become part of the evening ritual, his being there, listening intently. He rarely spoke. But tonight, she had been forced to start the new instalment of the story without him. She and Rosabel had both become engrossed in the adventure.

'What is it, Rosabel?' she asked the little girl now, with a stroke of her hair. It was dark, almost black against the white pillow. The same shade as her papa's.

'What colour are your stockings, Miss Wilmot?'

Maud drew back with a chuckle. 'Why, Rosabel! That's a funny question.'

'When she came to visit Pendragon Hall, Miss Trevose said you had blue stockings.'

'Oh, I see! So she did. How clever of you to remember. That's what some people call governesses and women who like books and learning.'

Rosabel clutched her teddy bear. She cocked her head in its pillow nest. 'Do you have blue stockings?'

Maud laughed. Rising to her feet, she lifted her skirt a few inches. With a flourish, she raised one leg for Rosabel's inspection.

'Why, they're black,' said Rosabel, disappointed.

And well darned, Maud noted ruefully, as she cast her eyes down at her ankles. They had been mended more than once, and the wool, once thick, was now threadbare, providing little more than a shadowy outline of her legs.

'Good evening.'

Maud turned sharply, one foot still aloft. Off balance, she tottered and nearly fell. As it was, her skirts flounced most indecorously. 'Sir Dominic!'

He stood by the nursery door, lounged against its frame in his now-familiar relaxed, yet taut, posture, his eyes fixed upon her.

'Look, Papa,' said Rosabel. 'Miss Wilmot doesn't wear blue stockings!'

'So I see,' he murmured.

Maud dropped as if shot into the chair by Rosabel's bed. Her legs, just a moment ago wafted aloft, now refused to hold her up. There was no way he had not fully taken in her darned stockings and well-polished but worn button boots. Her cheeks burned.

His lips lifted, stretched. White teeth appeared, followed by a dimple.

Heavens above, Sir Dominic Jago possesses dimples.

She couldn't help it. She found herself smiling in return. A giggle rose. *No!* She clapped a hand across her offending mouth.

'Miss Wilmot says she is a blue stocking, even though she hasn't any,' Rosabel confided.

'Who knows, maybe she keeps her blue stockings for Sunday best.'

The dimple lingered. One more trait he had passed on to his daughter. She wished he would put it away. It was most distracting.

Maud lifted her chin. 'I own no blue stockings, Sir Dominic. I have no need to. It is what I am. I know some people use the term in a derogatory way, but it is one I am proud of.'

His lips curved. 'I must confess I also admire blue-stockings, Miss Wilmot.'

'Can we buy Miss Wilmot some blue stockings, Papa?' Rosabel asked.

His lips curved further. 'If she would like some.'

'I don't need new stockings,' Maud managed to say. If only he hadn't seen hers, so old and darned!

Fortunately, he did not pursue the subject.

'I've come to say goodnight to Rosabel, if I may,' he said smoothly. 'Have you finished your story? And your...um, demonstration?'

Maud nodded, mute with embarrassment.

Leaving his place by the door, he entered the nursery. Tonight, he was dressed in a dark, long-tailed dinner jacket and a shirt of pristine white, a black bow tie expertly tied around his throat. There was no denying he was a most attractive man. It stunned her that she found him—or indeed, any man—physically attractive. It rippled over her skin, like a warm breeze. She had dismissed any such idea from her mind—and her heart. That part of her life was gone, or so she'd believed. Yet her eye was drawn to the way the formal garments only seemed to emphasise his masculinity.

'You missed hearing about Princess Swallowtail to-night, Papa,' Rosabel reproached him.

'So I have. I was delayed at the railway.'

'Princess Swallowtail only just managed to escape from the Red Emperor,' Rosabel said.

'Is that so?' Sir Dominic glanced at Maud. 'I regret to have missed such an exciting instalment.'

It was merely an expression of politeness. What seemed like a flicker of interest in his eyes was a mere trick of the lamplight. He, truly sorry to have missed her story? Certainly not. Railway magnates were not interested in fairy tales.

'You must hear the rest of the story tomorrow night,' Rosabel said.

'I hope I am there to do so.' He smiled at her. 'But to-night, I am going to dine at Trevose Hall.'

Oh. He was going to dine with Miss Averill Trevose. Her time at Pendragon Hall was over, before it had really begun.

Maud moved to the nature table and began to tidy the leaves and twigs that had been left over. The insect homes were supposed to have stayed in the schoolroom, but Rosabel had begged to be able to keep them in her bedroom, and the entire nature table had been brought in.

A fern shredded beneath Maud's fingers. There was no chance she would still be employed as Rosabel's governess when Sir Dominic heard about what had transpired. Maud was in no doubt that Miss Averill would cast her in the worst possible light. She would be instantly dismissed.

Her fingers tightened around a sharp-edged twig. For a moment she wondered if she ought to say something, to tell her side of the story. No, she decided. She would not stoop to that.

After all she had gone through to get the post, the risk of losing it was devastating. The butterflies, the woods and gardens, the beautiful rambling old house. And Rosabel. Sweet, shy Rosabel, who had ventured out of her cocoon under Maud's gentle tutelage. All she had gained over patient weeks would be lost in an evening's spiteful tale-telling. And Sir Dominic. No, she would not think of him.

She glanced over towards where he stood beside Rosabel's bed. To her consternation, he met her gaze.

Immediately she turned away and gathered up more fern fronds.

He would have no choice but to take Miss Trevose's side. After all, she was about to be his bride. He would not take the side of a governess. No employer ever did. No employer ever would.

Her eyesight blurred as she stared at the insect homes. She wouldn't see the caterpillars grow, or any more butterflies emerge. No, she would be told to pack her bags. Tomorrow, perhaps. In the morning, before Sir Dominic departed for the railway, he would call her before him. She would have to fold her grey and brown dresses and her green gown into her old carpetbag and make her way back to London.

She didn't even have enough money for a return train fare. Her ticket to Cornwall had been one way and she would be unlikely to receive any wages, in the circumstances. Somehow, she would have to find a way to travel back to London and hope that Martha could take her in.

To her horror, a tear slipped down her cheek, like a caterpillar trail, followed by another, then another.

'Are you quite well, Miss Wilmot?'

Maud started. Sir Dominic had moved to stand beside her at the table.

'Oh!' Keeping her head down, she quickly wiped her eyes. The fern brushed her cheek. 'Yes. I was just checking on the caterpillars.'

Yet he remained beside her. She could feel the heat of his body and the breadth and height of him. Normally, under such close quarters with him, she would step aside. Yet she didn't want to move away. Sir Dominic seemed to emanate a strange comfort.

'Up close, butterflies are very fragile,' he commented, after a moment. 'Are you sure they have enough room to breathe?'

She glanced up at him. He was no longer looking at the insect homes, in their pickling jars. He looked straight at her.

'Butterflies are surprising creatures,' Maud replied at last. 'They are stronger than they look.'

'I hope so, Miss Wilmot.'

Again, that connection flared between them as he continued to study her, his eyebrows angled.

She took a deep breath, willing her tears to subside. She laid down the fern frond. 'I will leave you to say goodnight to Rosabel.'

She stepped away from him.

He nodded, as he picked up the fern frond she had left on the table and ran it through his fingers, his gaze remaining upon her. 'Goodnight, Miss Wilmot.'

'Goodnight, Sir Dominic.' She went to the bed and dropped a kiss on the glossy hair. 'Goodnight, Rosabel. Sweet dreams.'

Her throat constricted. She hurried through the connecting door, barely seeing what she was about. She always made sure that when he came to say goodnight to Rosabel she discreetly exited the room and retired to her own quarters immediately. She had no wish to imply any untoward interest in the master of the house.

Not that it mattered any more.

Safe in her bedroom, she stared out of the window. The moon was rising, a crescent in a clear sky, casting a faint silvery light over the garden and the dark woods beyond where she had already spent so many happy hours with Rosabel, chasing butterflies.

Tears smarted again. There would be no more butterfly chasing for her.

She lifted her hairbrush from the dressing table. It trembled in her hand.

Perhaps Miss Trevose's threat to report her to Sir Dominic had been an empty one. There was still a chance. Not that she regretted refusing to allow Rosabel to leave her care. Every instinct as a governess had told her not to do so. It wasn't that Rosabel would be in danger. It was more that even in the short time that Rosabel had been in her care, Maud had become attuned to the sensitive child, with an instinctive urge to protect her. Rosabel was afraid of Miss Averill Trevose.

And there was something else. Miss Trevose had told Maud she was about to become mistress of Pendragon Hall. Yet she had overheard no such talk among the servants, who always knew such things, nor so much as a hint from Sir Dominic himself, although she supposed he saw no need to inform a governess of his marriage intentions.

Maud released her hair from its customary bun and applied an unsteady hairbrush to it. The long strands had become painfully tangled. She tugged at the knots ineffectually, painfully.

No master of the house would ever believe a governess.

Chapter Seven

But the rose was awake all night for your sake;
—*Alfred, Lord Tennyson:* Maud *(1855)*

Dominic ran a finger along his black tie.

Dinner had not yet been served and already he was wishing he could remove the thin piece of fabric that encircled his neck. It felt more stifling than usual.

He tugged again at his bow tie. He'd been sorry to miss the nightly entertainment in the nursery. If he was honest with himself, and he always tried to be so, he would have preferred to have spent the evening listening to Miss Wilmot tell fairy tales, rather than being where he was, in an elegant candlelit dining room, surrounded by members of the local gentry, their conversation buzzing around him.

'It's so difficult to entice you to come to dinner, Dominic, and then you hardly speak.'

Averill leaned across the polished table. Diamonds nestled amid the low décolletage of her turquoise evening gown.

Dominic lifted his wine glass to his hostess. 'My apologies, Averill.'

Averill leaned in further as she continued to scold him. 'I'm expecting a party of guests later this month, from London. I've chosen them especially for their interest in railways. You may find an investor among them. You must host them with me. You're too reclusive for your own good.'

'Hardly reclusive,' he replied with a smile. He ran a railway, after all, dealt with employees each day.

'But distracted.' Averill pouted. 'Whatever can you be thinking about?'

'The new governess.' He chuckled to himself. He hadn't expected to come across Miss Wilmot with her petticoats lifted high, revealing her long legs in their black stockings. It hadn't really been unseemly. He'd have left immediately if it had been so. The frills of her petticoats had covered her knees. At first, she had appeared alarmed, but he was relieved to see that she shared the humour of the situation, even if her cheeks had been pinker than Rosabel's.

'Oh! Your new governess!' Averill produced a fan and proceeded to flutter it, setting her carefully arranged curls dancing. 'Dear Dominic, I fear you have been duped.'

Dominic took a draught of claret. 'How so?'

With heat colouring her cheeks, Averill recounted the interaction she'd had with Miss Wilmot.

'She was quite impertinent!' Averill exclaimed.

'I'm sorry to hear that.' He was surprised, too. It didn't sound like Miss Wilmot, with her air of decorum. What he had learnt of her character did not chime with what Averill described.

He frowned. Rosabel had been outdoors every day recently. Miss Wilmot had achieved more than he had ever hoped. Nevertheless, he would need to speak to her. He could not have her display impertinence to his neighbours in front of Rosabel.

'I've told you that you ought to allow me to engage your nursery staff in future,' Averill chided with a pretty smile that didn't disguise the annoyance in her eyes.

Averill had become almost proprietary, Dominic realised. She'd offered help when Sarah had died and he was grateful, but he was able to hire his own staff.

He took a sip of claret. 'Thank you, Averill. I will let you know if I need assistance.'

'The new governess is quite unsuitable,' Averill insisted. 'She ought to be dismissed!'

'Miss Wilmot has only recently arrived,' Dominic found himself replying. 'So far she has been more than satisfactory. She has a great interest in the sciences. She collects insects, day and night. I came across her one evening down near the woods, hunting moths, of all things.'

'But what on earth was she doing out alone at night?' Averill eyed him from behind the fluttering fan. 'Oh, how positively scandalous! I thought she was a blue-stocking, not a creature of light morals!'

Dominic laughed outright. 'Miss Wilmot, a creature of light morals? I don't think so, Averill.'

Averill raised a delicately arched eyebrow. 'You are too generous, Dominic. Let me tell you, I am certain that she is not all she seems. You know how these women try to take advantage of your good nature.'

Dominic tensed. He took another draught of claret as he recalled Miss Wilmot's impassioned defence of her profession.

'We ask a great deal of governesses,' he said at last. 'There were some misunderstandings in the past, nothing more. I don't think Miss Wilmot is trying to take advantage.'

Averill's chest heaved. It set her diamonds sparkling.

'So, you're defending governesses now.' She spoke lightly, yet her words held a sharp edge.

He shrugged.

'I see I will have to be careful how I speak in future about your new governess.' With another of her pretty smiles Averill changed the subject.

The awkwardness between them had passed, Dominic reflected later as he returned to Pendragon Hall, but he knew he would not forget the conversation.

He had allowed Averill to become more invested in their lives than he had intended. He would not, of course, have had her employ a governess for Rosabel. It was beyond the bounds of neighbourly. And he had not cared for the way she had spoken about the new governess. He had to admit, he had not cared for it at all.

As always, the sight of his home lifted his spirits. It looked particularly well at night, with its turrets and towers, lit from within by gas and candles. It emanated a warmth and brightness from the mullioned windows.

Unexpectedly, it reminded him of the new governess. Her exterior was plain, like the grey stone of the Hall, but it possessed the same fine lines and elegance. It was made of stuff that would last, that had strength. Eyes were known as the windows of the soul, and her eyes, those green eyes that held those unexpected lights, were as warm and golden as the candlelit windows of his home.

He laughed drily to himself. It was not like him to be

fanciful, but there was much more to Miss Wilmot than the moth-grey garments she wore.

She wore such sombre clothing. It suited her vocation, he supposed. He frowned. Did she do it on purpose? Why did she go to such lengths to hide her beauty? Many women wouldn't, of course. Miss Wilmot kept herself hidden, always in a cocoon of her grey clothes.

Perhaps she merely thought it more suitable to a governess.

He glanced across the dark lawn, but he could see no lamplight. Miss Wilmot was not out moth-hunting tonight.

When he had come across her that night in the woods, her eyes had not been dancing. Instead, in her white face framed by that russet hair, her eyes had been dark and huge in fright. She had been quite terrified when he startled her.

Her level of panic had seemed out of place. Certainly, he'd come across her unawares, but she had been trembling from head to foot. It wasn't that some alarm wouldn't be expected in the circumstances. It was more that she appeared to be the opposite of the cool-headed confident young woman he generally observed.

He frowned. What Averill had told him at dinner didn't sound like Miss Wilmot. He was a man who trusted his own instincts. What he had observed of her character did not chime with what Averill described. Yet he had seen her, when they first met, giving what could only be described as a dressing-down to the young man who had tried to make an elderly passenger give up her seat on the train. There was a passionate woman beneath her carefully guarded manner. In any case, he would have to get to the bottom of it.

Loosening his tie at last, Dominic crossed the threshold. Taking up the lamp that had been left in the hall, he made his way up the stairs.

Then he heard it. A cry, sharp with terror.

He gripped the lamp and finished the stairs two at a time.

Outside Rosabel's nursery door, he stopped and listened.

Had he imagined it? Some night bird, perhaps? Gulls often sounded eerily like children.

It came again, lifting the very hairs on his neck. High, pained and full of panic. Very nearly a scream. He threw back the door of the nursery and would have run to Rosabel's bedside, save it only took him two strides.

He stared down at his daughter in puzzlement. The lamp glow played over a sweetly slumbering face. She was sleeping soundly.

Her hair lay smooth on the pillow, her hand tucked under her cheek, and her breathing was even.

He was withdrawing, shielding the lamplight from her eyes, when the cry jolted through him again.

Now he realised. It came from the room beyond the schoolroom next door, from the governess's room. A terrified cry, as if in mortal danger.

Miss Wilmot.

Without a second thought, Dominic threw open the connecting door.

Chapter Eight

Half in dreams I sorrow after;
—*Alfred, Lord Tennyson:* Maud *(1855)*

'Miss Wilmot. *Miss Wilmot!* Martha!'

Through the horror of the nightmare Maud heard a deep male voice.

She moaned.

'Martha. Wake up!' the voice commanded her.

Strong arms pulled her up, out of the nightmarish depths. She did not resist. She did not want to. With a sob, she instead leaned into them, her whole body knowing instinctively that she was safe in those arms. So sure, so powerful, she knew they could hold her and protect her from the nightmare that had pulled her back into the dreadful memory she fought so hard to keep from her mind by day: the sensation of being slowly suffocated beneath an immovable weight that she could not fight or escape. In her waking hours her brain seemed to protect her and shield her memory from the full horror. But at night, oh, at night, as she slept, the remembrance would return without mercy, without buffer. She lived the experience again, night after night.

Yet now, as she came out of it, still shuddering, she realised that she was not defenceless against it for the first time. Someone had come to her aid and pulled her out of the morass.

Sir Dominic Jago.

'It's all right.' His low voice was full of a strange tenderness. 'You're awake now. You're safe.'

The firmness of his hold, the strength of those arms. Instinctively she laid her head against his chest while his arms wrapped around her, so close she could hear his heartbeat. For a moment she let herself relax, her breath still coming in painful jags, then slowing, easing.

'It's all right, Martha.' He soothed her again, as his arms briefly cradled her against him. 'It's all right.'

She pulled back with a gasp. 'You're calling me Martha.'

Instantly he released her from his grip and moved away to the edge of the bed. 'My apologies, Miss Wilmot. You were having a nightmare. At least, that is what it seemed to be. I needed to try to reach you.'

He *had* reached her, but it hadn't been through his voice alone. His touch had reached her through sleep in a way she had never expected.

There had been a strange, physical honesty between them as he cradled her in his arms, but now, hearing him call her by Martha's name and not her own, that honesty vanished.

She was in his home under false pretences.

Her panic must have shown on her face.

Instantly he rose from the bed and took a step back. He must have assumed that she withdrew from him in alarm at his familiarity, for his breach of the master–governess gulf between them, when he called her by her first name. He didn't know that she wasn't who she claimed to be.

She shuddered again.

'I tried to wake you for some time,' he said, low. 'I did not know how else to do so. You didn't seem to respond when I called you, Miss Wilmot. I'm sorry for the breach of propriety in my taking hold of you, but you were in great distress. I feared for your well-being. There was no other way.'

'It's not that,' she whispered. 'I mean, I'm glad you woke me. Thank you.'

His face was shadowed as he studied her by the light from the nightstand. He must have brought the lamp with him. Beneath his regard her body was a swirl of sensations: her unsteady heart, the tingle where his arms had cradled her and the warmth where her cheek had leaned against his shirt.

'I heard a scream,' he explained. 'I thought it was Rosabel.'

Maud struggled to sit up, but her whole body trembled as she reached for the bedcovers to hold them up against her nightgown. 'Is she all right?'

'Rosabel is sound asleep,' he reassured her.

Taking up the lamp, he backed towards the door.

He was still dressed, unlike Maud, but his bow tie was loose and his shirt was unbuttoned, revealing his neck and a glimpse of his chest. The chest she had leaned against, only moments before. Where she had rested her head and found unexpected solace.

He scanned her intently once more. 'You are still

clearly distressed. May I be of any further assistance to you? Do you think you can get back to sleep?'

'I'm not sure.' If she slept now, there was every chance the dream would reclaim her. She could feel it there, lingering in the back of her mind. Respite had come only when Sir Dominic had held her so close. Of course she could not ask him to stay, nor to hold her again. That would be unthinkable.

'It may be better if you get up for a while,' he said after a moment. 'I suppose I should suggest cocoa, or a cup of tea, but I'm tempted to prescribe brandy.' His half-smile played around his lips. 'For both of us.'

'Brandy would be very welcome,' Maud admitted. She rarely drank spirits, but she needed something to still her frantic heartbeat. 'Thank you.'

Dominic moved the lamp closer towards her. 'Follow the light, Miss Wilmot.'

Maud pushed back the covers. Her body was damp with perspiration.

She'd thrown herself into Sir Dominic's arms. The comfort of that moment, of being held by him, so securely. The fear had been beaten back.

But that nightmare had been one of the worst. One of the terrible ones, where she feared she would suffocate entirely, when she was stifled, trapped—

No! She wouldn't think about it.

She seized her grey woollen dressing gown and buttoned it up tightly. It took longer than usual, for her fingers were trembling so. Thank goodness Sir Dominic had already departed the room. Doubtless he realised it was indecorous in the highest degree for him to linger in a governess's bedchamber. She would follow his light as soon as her fingers managed to secure her some modesty.

She hardly knew now what made her tremble: the remnants of the nightmare, or the embrace she had shared with Sir Dominic.

He'd taken her in his arms, he'd said, in order to get through to her. He must have realised that she had not responded to her name, or rather, to her sister's name. Hopefully he had thought it part of the terrible dream.

She stared at her white face in the looking glass, ghostly in the lamplight, as she plaited her hair. She draped it, one long fox tail, over her shoulder and hurried through the connecting door to check on Rosabel. To her relief, the little girl lay asleep, clutching her teddy bear, her breath slow and steady.

Lamp in hand, she made her way downstairs into the study.

The door was ajar. Firelight glowed in the grate.

Sir Dominic stood beside it. In one cupped hand he held a rounded brandy glass, its colours catching the brown-and-gold firelight.

'Come in, Miss Wilmot.' He indicated one of the leather chairs by the fireplace. 'Take a seat. I'll pour you a brandy.'

'Thank you.' She settled by the fire, feeling as if she were still in a dream. She supposed she ought to have felt uncomfortable drinking brandy in the middle of the night with the master of the house, but she didn't. She felt strangely at peace, as if Dominic's presence cradled her as securely as his arms.

It was odd, especially in the circumstances. She might have expected that in any situation where she was alone with a man, particularly the master of the house, she would be frightened.

Sir Dominic was strong, masculine, but he did not

frighten her. He held his strength in check in the same easy way he had held the reins of his stallion.

The crystal clinked on the silver tray as he poured her a drink.

Returning to the fire, he held out the brandy glass. His fingers brushed hers as he passed it to her.

'Thank you.'

The brandy flared down her throat, like the fire in the grate.

Maud choked.

He leaned over her. 'Are you all right?'

Maud reached to smooth her skirt, but her fingers encountered her dressing gown, instead.

'I'm not used to spirits,' she explained, coughing.

'Perhaps you'd prefer a cup of tea after all.'

'No!' Maud said quickly. She threw back the remaining brandy in a single gulp.

'That's one way to get used to it,' he said with a grin.

The brandy burned to settle in her stomach. Sir Dominic ensconced himself in the seat opposite her.

Between them the fire flared.

'Now, Miss Wilmot,' Sir Dominic said. 'Are you going to tell me the truth?'

'The truth?' Maud gasped.

Sir Dominic took a draught of brandy. 'You're like a filly who has been spooked. You're nervous, frightened. You jump at the slightest noise—I've seen you—yet I do not believe you have a naturally nervous disposition.'

'I haven't always been nervous,' Maud admitted. 'Why, when I was a small child, my mother was nearly driven to distraction by my foolhardiness. M—' She stopped. She had so nearly said *Martha*. 'My...my sister was by far the more cautious and sensible of us two.'

'I see. Then there are the night terrors that I witnessed tonight. Have such nightmares happened before?'

She nodded.

'Regularly?'

Again, she nodded.

'But you didn't grow up having nightmares.'

Maud curled her fingers around the brandy glass and shook her head. They had begun when…

No. She refused to let the memory come into her mind. She had some control over that, when she was awake, at least.

He leaned forward. 'There is something mysterious about you, Miss Wilmot. Something you are hiding. You can trust me. I will not betray your confidence.'

Maud hesitated. How she longed to be able to lay down the burden she had carried alone for so long. She hadn't even told Martha the full story.

Telling Sir Dominic the truth about her identity would mean telling him everything.

She couldn't take the risk.

'It isn't as simple as that,' she said at last.

He raised an eyebrow. 'Isn't it?'

She evaded his gaze. 'I prefer not to think about my troubles.'

'Perhaps not thinking about them is why you are experiencing nightmares,' he said, far too shrewdly. 'It may be better to share your burdens.'

'I can't,' she whispered.

How could she disclose to him what had happened, when she had never been able to speak of it and been forced to come to Pendragon Hall under a false identity? It would take too much to explain and he might send her away. Oh, he was almost certain to send her away anyway, as soon as Averill Trevose had her way. But just in case she didn't…no, no, it must remain a secret. As long as her nightmares didn't bring him running into her bedchamber again and then he might demand she reveal all.

She shook her head, as if she could shake the confusion of thoughts into some order.

'Very well. I don't want to distress you any further,' he said abruptly. 'You do not have to confide in me.'

Maud bit her lip. Less than an hour before, she had leaned against his chest, felt his heartbeat slow and steady her own.

'There's something else I need to discuss with you, Sir Dominic.' She took a deep breath. 'Miss Trevose came to the Hall earlier this week.'

'Ah. Yes.' He reached for his bow tie, tossed it aside. 'Your name did come up over dinner, Miss Wilmot. I won't deny it. I planned to speak to you about it tomorrow.'

'Please.' Maud reached out her hand in appeal. She couldn't bear to toss and turn in her bed again, waiting for the axe to fall. 'I would rather hear about it now.'

He exhaled as he took up his brandy glass again. 'I have no wish to upset you further. You have been through enough tonight. This doesn't seem the appropriate time or place.'

'Is there any appropriate time or place to be dismissed?' Maud was unable to keep a painful edge of bitterness from her voice.

The brandy splashed in his glass as he jerked back. 'Is that what you think is going to happen to you?'

'I don't expect you to listen to my side of the story.' She knew how matters played out in that regard. Whoever listened to a governess?

'That's where you are wrong, Miss Wilmot,' he replied. 'Since your arrival at Pendragon Hall, I find I have become quite interested in your stories. Tell me what happened with Miss Trevose.'

Faltering, Maud described what had occurred in as balanced a manner as possible.

When she finished, he exhaled sharply. 'She wanted to take Rosabel for the day?'

Maud nodded. 'I must be honest. I did not disallow Rosabel to go with Miss Trevose solely because you had not given your explicit permission. It was because Rosabel did not seem to want to go.'

'I see.' He was silent for a moment as he swirled his brandy. 'Did Rosabel tell you so?'

'No.' She had to admit it. 'It is more my sense of her feelings, based on how she behaved. She appeared anxious in Miss Trevose's company.' Now she was unable to keep the indignation from her voice. 'Miss Trevose was critical of Rosabel. It has never helped a sensitive child to be spoken of in such a manner in her presence.'

'What manner do you mean, precisely?'

Maud hesitated. But she might as well speak her mind. 'Miss Trevose showed no understanding of how Rosabel might be feeling and Rosabel is a child who feels things deeply. She may be shy, but that is not an affliction. The true affliction is surely that displayed by Miss Trevose.'

He breathed out in a whistle.

'I have spoken out of turn.' But Maud didn't regret it. Once she was dismissed, she might not be there to defend Rosabel, so she must take her opportunity to speak out. She had grown so fond of her young charge.

'I prefer your honesty,' Sir Dominic replied, to her surprise. 'And you may be correct about Miss Trevose's imagination. Certainly, I can't picture her telling…fairy tales.'

A smile hinted again at the corners of his mouth. Then his jaw hardened. 'However, she said you were impertinent. I did not care to hear that such behaviour was witnessed by my neighbour and by Rosabel.'

Maud bit her lip. 'Any outspokenness in a servant would be considered impertinence by Miss Trevose.'

She thought for a moment that she saw the dent in his cheek, before he took a quick gulp of brandy.

'I'm sorry,' Maud said quickly. 'I don't seek to cause offence, speaking in such a manner about your fiancée.'

'My what?' Dominic demanded.

Chapter Nine

All night have the roses heard
The flute, violin, bassoon;
All night has the casement jessamine stirr'd
To the dancers dancing in tune;
> —*Alfred, Lord Tennyson:* Maud *(1855)*

Maud drew back. In the firelight she could see the astonishment on Sir Dominic's face.

'Your fiancée…' she faltered.

'So I heard you correctly.' He drew his eyebrows together. 'I am not engaged to Miss Trevose, or any other woman,' he said at last. 'I thought I made it perfectly clear upon your arrival. All of my acquaintance know I have no plans to remarry.'

'Oh!' Why, she had not meant to bring up the matter. Now he would think her a purveyor of cheap gossip. Gossip, she always told her charges in the nursery, put the person who told the tale in a poor light, not the person discussed.

'Perhaps I misunderstood,' she said rapidly. Somehow, she had to retract what she had said and quickly. 'Yes, I'm sure that was it.'

He raised an eyebrow. 'Perhaps?'

'It is my mistake,' she hastened to add. 'Please, take no notice of it. I would not like my mistake repeated to anyone and perhaps cause any further misunderstanding.'

Even disliking Averill Trevose as she did, she would never have purposely disclosed the other woman's presumptive comment. It would be unkind and she had not meant to be.

'Very well,' he replied, after a moment. 'I will not specifically raise the matter of your misunderstanding further with—anyone.'

Maud sighed with relief. 'Thank you.'

He swirled the brandy in his glass. 'But let me clear up your other misunderstanding, Miss Wilmot. We have established that I am not to be married. Neither am I planning to dismiss you as Rosabel's governess.'

Maud laid down her brandy glass and put her hand to her bodice, surprised to find it was still trembling. 'You're not?'

He shook his head. 'I trust my own judgement, Miss Wilmot. I always have and I always will. I do not rely on the opinions of others.'

Maud breathed out.

'You have exceeded my expectations,' he said, to her further amazement. 'Rosabel is happier and healthier than she has been under anyone else's care. And I should not like to deprive Rosabel of any further tales of Princess Swallowtail. Nor myself, for that matter.' His half-smile glimmered. 'You are quite the Scheherazade, Miss Wilmot.'

'I told you before, Sir Dominic, that is not so,' she protested. Then she smiled, too. 'But I expect I do have enough stories for a thousand and one nights.'

He chuckled, before taking another draught of brandy. 'Perhaps we ought to make that the terms of your employment.'

Was he teasing her? He must be, Maud decided.

'Thank you,' she said. 'For giving me another chance.'

He frowned. 'From what you have told me, it is the same chance. You assured me you were not rude to Miss Trevose. Merely outspoken, on Rosabel's behalf.'

And she would do the same again, she knew, to ensure Rosabel's happiness.

'Such protectiveness is what I want in a governess,' he said next. 'But perhaps in future, however, you can ensure that you keep your outspokenness to a minimum when guests appear at Pendragon Hall.'

Maud blinked. He might have dismissed her. Many employers would have, given the same circumstances, as Maud knew very well. A governess was rarely given the benefit of the doubt. 'Thank you, Sir Dominic. You won't regret it. I wouldn't want to leave Pendragon Hall.'

He swirled his glass again, his long fingers cupped around it. 'You said you were happy here in Cornwall.'

'Of course,' she replied. 'How could anyone not be happy at Pendragon Hall?'

His mouth twisted. 'You would be surprised. There are those for whom the wilds of Cornwall seem dull and countrified.'

Maud fell silent.

A shadow passed across his face. 'My late wife, Sarah—Rosabel's mother—did not care for my home.'

Quietly, Maud laid down her glass. He needed to talk. She could sense it.

Dominic exhaled. 'My late wife and I met in London, during the Season. It was her debut. I suppose Cornwall seemed distant and romantic to her at the time. As did I, a railway man. What she didn't know is that a man who must build a life and business of his own does not have much leisure.'

He breathed heavily. 'We married young. Too young. Sarah never settled in Cornwall, nor did she find the railway as captivating as I do. At first, she showed great interest in it, but she anticipated we would live in London. She had friends there, in fashionable circles, in society. She resented any time she was forced to spend here at Pendragon Hall. Neither of us was prepared for her to become quite so bored and discontented. Even the arrival of Rosabel did not alter her feelings.'

For a moment he stared into the flames. 'It is my great regret that I did not make her happy. I know myself better now. I am simply not the marrying kind.'

Maud stayed still. The only sound was the fire, flickering in the grate.

'I was here in Cornwall on railway business when she died,' he said at last. 'It was tuberculosis of the lung. She was in London at the time. She worsened suddenly and I did not get to her in time.'

'How could you possibly have predicted that?' Maud exclaimed.

'I find it hard to forgive myself.'

He stood and threw another log on the fire. It sparked and blazed.

'Sarah often accused me of working too hard, of being distant and not available to her when she needed me,' he said at last, staring into the flames. 'Of lacking feeling. In the end, it seemed she was right.'

Impulsively Maud got to her feet. 'That is not what I have observed, Sir Dominic. In my experience as a governess, you do not lack feeling at all. You are exceptionally kind to your daughter.' She breathed out. 'As you have been tonight. To me.'

He turned to look at her. Bleak lines etched his mouth. 'I ought to have been there. There was a great deal of guilt for me when she died. Guilt as well as grief. I did not give her the attention she craved. I thought we would have more time.'

Maud shook her head. 'When my parents died after an outbreak of influenza, I experienced some of what you are feeling. A sense of guilt that I could have done more. Perhaps it is normal, in the circumstances.'

His gaze was acute. 'How old were you when you lost your parents, if you do not mind my asking?'

'I was seventeen.' Maud reached for her brandy glass. There was still some of the liquor left, gleaming in the crystal cup. It warmed her, inside. 'As I told you, my father was a schoolmaster. The influenza outbreak began at the school. Both my sister and I caught it, too, but we survived it. We had to. We had not only lost our parents. We lost our home.'

He raised an eyebrow. 'Why so?'

'Our house near Winchester was provided by the school trustees. When we lost our parents, we had to make way for the new incumbent. That's why I had to seek work as a governess as soon as possible.'

He studied her over the edge of his own glass. 'It seems it is a night for confidences, Miss Wilmot. I'm sorry to hear of such a loss. It does not sound as if life has been easy for you.'

Her fingers tightened. 'No, it was not easy. But I had stories. They kept me going, always.'

'Being a governess must have been difficult for you in the circumstances.'

'A little,' she admitted, unable to disguise a shudder.

But he'd noted it. 'Tell me. In your previous employment, did they treat you well?'

Maud hesitated. He had confided in her. She longed to do the same, but she could not. 'I have no wish to complain of past situations. I do not want you to think I am the kind of governess who is constantly griping about her circumstances.'

'You do not strike me in that way, Miss Wilmot.'

How tempting it was to tell him. But though he might have given her another chance after the complaint from Miss Trevose, he would not give her another if he knew she was there under false pretences.

'It's different here,' she added. 'You treat your staff well.'

He was a fair man, to all his employees. In the servants' hall, he was spoken of with an affection Maud had never encountered before, certainly not in her previous employer's household.

Dominic grinned wryly. 'I've never found that treating someone badly brought out the best in them.'

'Not all employers agree with you.'

He played idly with the stem of his glass as he studied her silently.

Again, the desire to lay down the burden of her memories almost overcame her. But she must not be misled by the warm room and his unexpected kindness to her.

She stood up. She was tired and vulnerable. She couldn't risk staying here in such an unexpectedly intimate *tête-à-tête* any longer. 'Thank you, Sir Dominic, for the brandy. And for your understanding.'

He drained his own glass and inclined his head. To her relief, he did not pursue the subject. 'Goodnight.'

'Goodnight.'

As she reached the door, his voice stopped her. 'Pleasant dreams, Miss Wilmot.'

Dominic poured himself more brandy. By God, he needed it, after the night of revelations with his new governess.

He had never anticipated confiding in her in such a manner. Nor had he expected having to enter her bedroom to wake her from such a nightmare.

He ran his hand through his hair.

Something troubled Miss Wilmot and troubled her deeply. The look in her eyes, the flash of sheer terror when she'd awoken from sleep, had appalled him. He was sure it was terror, but then she had quickly disguised it with a resolve that was admirable. Yet that panic, that wide-eyed fright which had induced him to wrap his arms about her, he knew, would stay with him. She held it in check, but it was there.

She'd looked younger in her white nightgown, with her hair tumbling over her shoulders. Tonight, he'd noticed that her lashes were dark, fringing those unusually coloured eyes. But he'd seen the shadows now, too, the faint smudges under her eyes that told of other restless nights, of shadows also, in her mind.

He wondered if he'd be able to forget the scent of her hair as he held her. Fresh, clean, like a green day.

He regretted that he'd been required to go into her bedroom at night, but he could not ignore such terrified screams, any more than he could have ignored someone trapped in a burning building.

He took another sip of brandy. When Miss Wilmot had awoken, it was almost as if she had expected to see someone else. As if her fright was because she had experienced something similar before.

Dominic frowned. She'd recovered well enough as she had sat in the study. The brandy, he'd been pleased to note, had brought the colour stealing back into her cheeks.

Then she had told him what had transpired with Averill.

He shook his head. At dinner earlier that evening, he'd been surprised when Averill had expressed her willingness to hire his staff, but he'd been shocked to learn that she had sought to take his child without his permission. That was not acceptable to him. Averill had gone too far. Miss Wilmot had handled the situation with tact.

He had made it perfectly clear, not just to the previous governesses who had expressed interest in his marital status, but also to Averill and other women in the neighbouring area, that he had no intention of marrying again. He hadn't felt the need to explain himself. It had probably been assumed that it was because of his grief over the loss of Sarah. Perhaps it had also been assumed that his grief would pass. But there was more to it than that.

Miss Wilmot was the first person with whom he'd been able to share the guilt that haunted him about not being there when Sarah died.

Dominic cleared his throat. Perhaps some guilt was

a normal part of grief. Miss Wilmot certainly seemed to think so.

He moved to the window and stared out into the night. He'd loved Sarah. He'd been attracted by her high spirits and enjoyment of life. He'd never expected it to go wrong. But he'd realised, as time went on, that he'd only seen what he'd wanted to see in her. He'd come to suspect that during their courtship she had feigned more interest in the railway than she really possessed. Certainly, he'd never expected her to resent his spending time and energy in Cornwall. It was his life. He'd wanted her to share it and, at first, he'd believed that she wanted to.

He drummed his fingers together. Sarah had been friends with Averill Trevose. They were similar women, with a liking for fashion and the *ton*. Averill had shown Dominic a great deal of neighbourliness since Sarah's death and he'd appreciated it. She had a kind nature beneath her society manners. Clearly, however, his appreciation had been taken as more, as a particular kind of attention.

He shook his head. He hadn't led Averill to think he sought marriage. His conscience was entirely clear on that score. He had not encouraged her in any way. Their friendship had not strayed beyond the bounds of propriety. He hadn't hidden from anyone, including the new governess, his firm intention to remain a widower, but it seemed that Averill planned to change his mind.

Now, Miss Wilmot had unwittingly made this fact known to him. He'd promised her that he would not reveal what she had told him. He would keep her counsel, but he would have to ensure that Averill laboured under no false expectations. Somehow, without exposing Miss Wilmot, he would have to communicate that he did not seek his neighbourliness with Averill to be any more than that. It was damned awkward.

Dominic exhaled. He was not a man to put off an unpleasant duty, but he would deal with the matter of Averill's expectations of him and promptly. He must ensure that he made it very clear that his views about marriage had not changed.

As he'd told the new governess, he was not the marrying kind.

He hadn't expected that he would be such an object of interest as a widower. The only woman who did not seem to crave his attention was Miss Wilmot. She had made no attempt to intrigue him, as the previous governesses had done. From her there was no posing prettily in his line of sight, no seeking time alone to purportedly discuss Rosabel's progress, no extra demands on his time or attention.

Miss Wilmot was as elusive as a butterfly. Yet as Dominic finally made his way to his bedroom, he was still thinking about her.

Chapter Ten

Till a silence fell with the waking bird,
And a hush with the setting moon.
　　　　—Alfred, Lord Tennyson: Maud *(1855)*

'What did you say to Dominic?'

Maud jumped as sharp fingers pressed into her sleeve. She spun around to find Averill Trevose had come up behind her on the gravel drive. She was dressed in an exquisite sprigged morning gown, shirred in layers of lace and silk over her swaying skirt that Maud regarded with a brief flash of envy, and a bonnet lined in azure silk that captured the colour of her glorious eyes, now narrowed with hostility.

'Good morning, Miss Trevose.' Maud managed to keep any incivility from her voice. She had no wish for another encounter with Pendragon Hall's closest neighbour, but nor did it do to be impolite. At least Rosabel was inside the house having her nap and could not be upset by her again.

'It certainly is not a good morning.' Miss Trevose dug her gloved fingers even harder into Maud's arm.

Maud stepped back, gently brushing off the painful grip, and held herself upright. She would not allow herself to be bullied. 'Is something the matter?'

Averill stamped her foot, sending small particles of gravel flying towards Maud.

Maud nearly smiled at the woman's nursery antics.

'Don't stand there looking as if butter wouldn't melt in your mouth!' Averill exclaimed. 'I know exactly what's going on! You've somehow managed to turn Dominic against me.'

'Indeed I have not,' Maud replied indignantly, her good intentions not to answer back falling away. Why, there were no grounds for any such accusation. It was not her fault that Miss Trevose had embellished her relationship with the master of Pendragon Hall.

'Dominic came to call at Trevose Hall and practically warned me off! I knew immediately you must have had a hand in it. I insist on knowing exactly what you said to him!'

Maud lifted her chin. 'I told him the truth. From you, I understood that you were affianced. I regret that I spoke out of turn, but I did so in all innocence. It was not I who created the situation.' She would not have said anything about it, but nothing would have held her back from speaking out on Rosabel's behalf. She didn't regret that for a moment.

'How dare you speak about matters that don't concern you!' Averill's voice became shrill. 'I knew from the moment you arrived that you would be trouble. You are evidently harbouring ideas above your station.'

'My ideas are precisely suited to my station,' Maud retorted, unable to hold back.

'You must have designs upon Dominic,' Averill Trevose hissed. 'That is why you have cast aspersions on me. It's the oldest trick in the book. But I can see through you and so will Dominic—in time. You governesses are all alike, fawning on the master of Pendragon Hall.'

Maud pursed her lips. It was on the tip of her tongue to remark that it was Miss Trevose who was pursuing Sir Dominic Jago, rather than the governess.

'I do not have designs upon Sir Dominic.'

'Don't lie to me.' Averill's blue eyes flashed. She stepped closer. 'You've interfered in my relationship with Dominic, somehow. I'll have you removed from your post as governess if it's the last thing I do. Keep your bags packed.'

'Averill. This is a surprise.'

A deep voice came from the doorway of the Hall. Maud looked up to see Sir Dominic leaned against the doorframe. He wore his riding clothes, one long leg casually draped in front of the other, his boots as polished as black mirrors.

She had avoided him in the few days since he had saved her from her nightmare. She'd had to.

'Why, Dominic!' Averill put her bonnet to one side. 'I didn't know you were at home.'

He strolled out and stood between them. The morning sun glinted on his dark head. How much of their conversation he had overheard, Maud could not be sure, but it was impossible to imagine he had heard none of it.

Maud pressed her lips together. Sir Dominic had specifically asked her not to be impertinent to Averill Trevose, yet once again, she had been unable to hold her tongue. Impertinence or self-defence? No doubt she was about to find out.

But Sir Dominic did not look her way. Instead, he

smiled at Averill. 'What brings you to Pendragon Hall, Averill? Not that it isn't pleasant to see you, of course.'

'Aren't I always welcome to call?' Averill cooed; her angry demeanour quite vanished.

'Of course,' he said easily. 'Neighbours are always welcome.'

'And we are such close neighbours.' She smiled as sweetly as sunshine on spring flowers. 'I came to remind you of the party of guests I'm expecting next week. I hope you haven't forgotten you agreed to help entertain them.'

He raised an eyebrow. 'I did?'

'Dear Dominic.' She gave a light, musical laugh. 'How you like to tease me. Of course you did. They are very important guests. They won't be used to a backwater like Cornwall.'

Dominic's mouth hardened. 'If they think Cornwall is a backwater, then they are not important to me.'

Averill laughed again. 'You and Cornwall.'

Finally, Dominic glanced at Maud. His expression was inscrutable. 'Did you need me, Miss Wilmot?'

Maud shook her head. 'I was just collecting some ferns for Rosabel's botany lesson.'

'Don't let us keep you.' Averill's voice was a model in politeness.

'I will see you this evening,' Dominic said to Maud.

'This evening?' Averill asked sharply, looking from one of them to the other.

'Miss Wilmot is telling Rosabel a fairy story,' he explained. 'There are nightly instalments at bedtime.'

'How sweet!' Averill's lips curved. Maud wasn't certain they formed a smile. 'I didn't know you liked stories, Dominic.'

He shrugged. 'Miss Wilmot has a talent for it.'

'Somehow I'm not surprised to hear that.' From under her bonnet, Averill gave Maud a look as sharp as her fingertips had been.

'How kind you are to encourage your servants, Dominic.' She did not need to emphasise the word 'servants.' It blared like a brass horn in Maud's ears. 'If I knew you were fond of fairy tales, I would have begun telling them myself.'

He chuckled. 'I didn't know that storytelling was one of your talents, Averill.'

'I have many talents you don't know of yet,' she replied, with an arched eyebrow.

Maud couldn't watch. 'If you will excuse me, Sir Dominic, it is almost time for Rosabel's lessons. I must hurry if I am to collect the ferns.'

He nodded. 'Of course.'

Before Maud turned away, Averill tucked her hand into Dominic's elbow and flashed her a sweetly pointed smile.

Maud fled into the house.

Averill Trevose was not a woman to be crossed.

Unfortunately, she had managed to do so, yet again.

Dominic stared down the long driveway, with its lines of oak trees on either side. Averill had gone, leaving a waft of exquisite perfume after her. There was no doubt she was a fashionable woman.

He had called on her and reiterated his view on marriage, without giving away Miss Wilmot's role in the affair. Averill had brushed it aside with a smile, in her society manner, but he'd seen comprehension quicken in her eyes. From the heated exchange he'd witnessed between the two women through the window of the library, Averill must have realised that his words had some connection to her imprudent comment to Miss Wilmot about becoming the future mistress of Pendragon Hall.

Since the conversation with Miss Wilmot by the fire, his first marriage had been on his mind even more than usual.

He glanced at the clouds hovering in the sky. The day was cast over. He turned and headed to the stables. He'd intended to go for a long ride, but he stopped, hesitated, then veered off instead on to the path that led to the corner of the grounds.

A few raindrops fell. He lifted the collar of his riding coat and shrugged them off as he strode along the path until he reached the old family chapel. The building itself was disused, lacking a roof, little more than a heap of stones that was a home for pigeons, but the ground was still consecrated. Members of the Jago family had been buried there for many years. His parents lay there, in graves next to each other. His mother had not long survived his father, when he had gone.

He opened the wooden gate and made his way to the newest grave, with its carved granite memorial. Beneath it lay Sarah. He had spent many hours sitting there, after she had died.

For some time, Dominic stood in silence, the memories flashing through his mind.

Taking a wild rose from the bramble bush that grew over the gate, he laid it on her grave.

The burden of his guilt and grief would not disappear

overnight, if it ever would. Yet some long-held tension had gone from his body.

The rain broke overhead.

He lifted his face to it and let it fall.

Maud stared out into the driving rain. It was as grey as the night. Dusk had fallen and a long evening stretched ahead.

There would be no moth-hunting tonight.

She paced up and down the schoolroom, restless. She relied upon going out of doors in the evenings, but of course, it wasn't always possible, especially in such weather.

She picked up her old book of fairy tales. The memory of Sir Dominic picking up the book on the train came back as a physical sensation. His fingers had grazed hers as he returned the volume to her.

How angry she had been with him when she'd first arrived. But she'd begun to see a different side of him. He was a good man, a kind man. One who had so much love and care for his daughter.

And a lot of books in his library.

Maud cast aside the book of fairy tales and tiptoed down the stairs.

The house was quiet. Outside his study door, she stopped and listened. There was no sound.

She knocked, but there was no reply.

Gingerly she turned the brass door handle. 'Sir Dominic?'

The library was empty, the fire low. She stepped inside and inhaled. There was a scent of woodsmoke and leather, and—books.

Maud tiptoed across the patterned carpet.

The books ran from floor to ceiling, in old, wooden shelves. Most were leather-bound, in rich red, green, blue, brown and wine. In one corner of the room was a ladder, attached to the shelves, so that it was possible to reach the books on the top.

But they weren't what Maud wanted.

She bypassed the old atlases, tempting as they were. Past the books of natural history, many titles she recognised, that she hadn't known were there. Past the tomes of history and a shelf of books about railways. She chuckled to herself. She knew to whom they belonged.

There they were, in their blue leather binding. The gilt lettering of the titles glittered.

She reached out her hand. Her fingers caressed the leather as she pulled the one she wanted from the shelf. She flicked the book open, sat down on the armchair by the fireplace and began to read.

'Good evening.'

Sir Dominic had entered the library, as silent as a cat. He stood by the door.

The book dropped into Maud's lap.

'Please, don't get up.' He crossed the room. 'I said you could make use of the books to prepare lessons.'

Maud's cheeks flamed. 'I am not reading for the purposes of Rosabel's education.'

He crooked an eyebrow.

She held up the blue leather-bound volume. 'I must confess I am reading a fairy tale.'

He stepped closer and read the title aloud. *'A Midsummer Night's Dream.'*

'Shakespeare's fairy tale,' she said. 'Titania, Oberon, Puck and Peaseblossom…'

He chuckled. 'I'm familiar with the play. And you're quite right, Miss Wilmot. It *is* a fairy tale.'

'Perhaps you can revise your prejudices against them,' Maud could not help saying, then bit her lip.

To her relief, his chuckle became a laugh, denting in his cheek. Instantly, he looked younger.

'I'm glad you found it.' He glanced at the fireplace. 'But the fire has almost gone out. You ought not to sit in the cold.'

He crouched to reignite the flames. The shape of his shoulders beneath his jacket was emphasised in the lamplight. He wore a dark jacket, a loose white shirt with the neck open and a paisley waistcoat carelessly buttoned down to dark brown woollen trousers, his feet clad in well-polished boots.

He stood and dusted off his hands.

'I should go to my room,' Maud said, tensing her own fingers around the volume of Shakespeare.

'Please stay, if you wish.' He drew a breath and regarded her with unsmiling directness. 'I am glad to have an opportunity to thank you. I was able to confide in you what I have not been able to confide to anyone else. It is a gift you have, Miss Wilmot. It is a rare woman who can both tell a story and listen to one.'

You are easy to listen to, she wanted to say, but she did not. Instead, she stayed silent. She sensed he had more to share.

He took a poker and prodded the fire. 'After our conversation, I realised that my feelings must be faced.'

'You must forgive yourself,' she said softly. 'For Rosabel's sake.'

He clenched his jaw as he laid down the poker. It clattered on the granite hearth.

He turned to her. 'You're welcome to remain where you are. I do believe I would be glad of the company tonight.'

His tone, clipped tight as if holding back some emotion, halted her from rising from her chair. She knew that measure. She'd practised it herself, often enough.

'Very well,' she said softly.

In silence, he went to his desk. Opening a large folio, he took up a fountain pen, making notations as he ran the pen over the pages.

How hard he worked. Maud peeped over her book. More than once he impatiently pushed back a lock of hair that fell over his forehead, down towards two lines that creased between his eyebrows as he frowned in concentration.

The clock ticked, then chimed.

Maud continued her reading.

An hour passed, then another.

At the sound of a muttered expletive, she looked up.

'Forgive me.' Sir Dominic shook his head. 'I always think I can improve upon the train schedules. It is something of a puzzle.'

'You do the train timetables?' she asked, amazed.

'It's not my role specifically,' he admitted. 'But the smoother they run, they more cost-effective they are. Currently, every penny counts.'

He glanced at the clock. 'It's been a change to have company in the evening.'

'Not an intrusion, I hope.'

'Not at all. I invited you.' He exhaled. 'I'm a man accustomed to solitude. I was an only child. I suppose it seems unusual that there was not a whole row of brothers and sisters lined up beside me, but my parents were older than most.'

'Were you lonely?'

'My childhood was an isolated one,' he admitted. 'Perhaps that is why I learnt to enjoy my own company. My parents were content with each other. They often sat in this library in the evenings. They were exceptionally close friends as well as husband and wife. Neither of them lived to see me build the railway. They lived quietly at Pendragon Hall, with hardly a quarrel, or none that I ever witnessed. It was what I anticipated in a marriage.'

All Maud's senses as a governess came alert. 'Still, it can be hard for a child to be alone.'

He shrugged. 'I suppose it isn't something I wanted for Rosabel. But we cannot always have what we want.'

Silent, Maud waited for him to continue. It was a trick she employed with the children she cared for. They would often tell her their troubles, if she gave them the space to do so.

'When I married Sarah, it was her liveliness that attracted me.' He laid down the pen. 'It was the opposite of my own, more retiring nature. But my parents used to sit here, in this library, much as we are doing now. Peaceful evenings spent in companionship. Without even having to speak. That was my expectation of marriage, when it came to it.' He gave a bleak smile. 'As I've said, you seem to encourage confidences, Miss Wilmot.'

'It's a skill of a governess.'

'Ah. It seems I am in capable hands.' He leaned back in his chair. 'What of your own childhood? Was it a happy one?'

'Most happy. Bookish. And quiet, like yours.' She raised the book she held. 'I was the more talkative one, until I learnt to read. Then I, too, learnt the joys of quiet evenings.'

He took up his pen and rolled it in his hand. 'Have you ever given thought to writing your own stories?'

'They're not good enough,' Maud protested.

'You underestimate yourself,' he replied. 'In my opinion they are fit to be published.'

Maud gaped. 'They're simply tales I have imagined, to entertain myself and my charges.'

He shifted to meet her gaze. 'There's a lot more to your stories than that.'

The clock chimed again. Maud closed her book.

'You've finished reading Shakespeare's fairy tale?' he asked with a curve of his lips.

'I have. It's an old friend,' she answered as she returned the book to its companions, aware of his gaze upon her.

'Your father would have owned many books, I imagine, as a schoolmaster.'

'Yes.' She brushed the volumes with her finger. 'But not as fine a collection as this and most of them belonged to the school in Winchester.'

'I hope you will not hold back from availing yourself of them again,' Sir Dominic said lightly. 'Or of the study in the evenings, if you wish.'

He meant it. She could tell.

Maud couldn't hide her smile. 'Thank you. I believe I will.'

Chapter Eleven

For a breeze of morning moves,
And the planet of Love is on high.
      —Alfred, Lord Tennyson: Maud *(1855)*

Maud stretched.

Sleep. Pure, uninterrupted sleep.

The sheer bliss of it. She had gone without unbroken nights for so long, she had never imagined what relief it could bring, to have rest without horrifying dreams.

For weeks now, she had slept through the night. From the moment she laid her head on the pillow, she slept peacefully. When she awoke, she felt different, more light-hearted then she had in months.

Alert.

Alive.

The days at Pendragon Hall now formed a pleasant pattern. Lessons and nature walks with Rosabel. The bedside story, which Sir Dominic never missed. Her night walks and some moth-hunting, if the weather was good. And if the weather was inclement, as it had been on a number of occasions, a quiet evening in the study by the fireside, in the company of Sir Dominic. Mostly, she read by the fire while he worked at the desk, running his fingers through his hair in an unconscious gesture that she had observed was habitual to him. Sometimes they would exchange conversation before the clock chimed ten, about Rosabel's progress, or what she was reading, or his work. Once, she had even tried to help him with the train timetable.

She watched the morning light play at the edges of the brocade curtains.

Sir Dominic's figure by the side of the bed came back to her. That was how it had all started, when he had awoken her from the nightmare. The stern man she had first met had vanished for ever, transformed into the man who had held her so close, who had sat by the fire with her and shown concerned interest in her previous life. The unexpected connection, the sense of understanding and warmth between them had calmed her, body and mind.

She hadn't been able to tell him much, of course. That had not changed. Nor could she talk for too long about her supposed previous employment, for that could lead to dangerous questions. She had quizzed Martha on her sister's previous position—demanded detailed descriptions of the children just in case she was called upon to substantiate her identity. But descriptions were not the same as *knowing* the children, or the household. She could not be sure she would not slip up if put on the spot.

She had never foreseen such difficulties. The lie shadowed each interaction she had with Sir Dominic and it went against her nature. She had always prided herself on being straightforward and honest.

She winced. It caused her physical pain, to go against her usual truthfulness. If only she did not need to tell such a story to stay at Pendragon Hall, where she no longer felt so desperately alone. Oh, she had tried to hide it, with her chin up and her stern governess air. But she had been forced to cope with so much, on her own.

She threw back the covers and rose from the bed as lightly as if she had grown wings. She smiled at the thought. At the window she pulled back the curtains. The moon had gone and in its place sunlight dappled the lawn. It was a perfect morning. She would take Rosabel out to the woods as soon as they had eaten breakfast and they would search for butterflies, for once feeling as light and free as those delicately winged creatures.

With a spring in her step, she collected her breakfast tray with its tea and toast from outside her bedroom door and dressed quickly, for when she glanced at the small clock by her bed, she realised she had overslept. That, too, was new. As she put on her familiar grey dress, she had an unexpected urge to choose a garment with more colour.

She looked at the green evening gown in her wardrobe. It was the only dress she owned that wasn't in a drab shade. But of course, she could not wear an evening gown during the day, she thought with a chuckle, even if it did accord so well with her new mood. Instead, she took out a piece of green velvet ribbon and wound it around her index finger.

She'd not cared to draw any attention to herself for so long. Focusing her attention on others had helped keep the dreadful sensations in her mind and body at bay.

But after a quick nod at herself in the looking glass, she rapidly bundled her long tresses into a slightly different style than usual. She still wore it up, of course, but it was not in such a strictly confined bun. Tendrils curled about her face rather than being scraped back, and she tied the green velvet ribbon around her bun in a bow, its ends floating free. She glanced at the clock. She needed to hurry. It had taken longer than usual to style her hair.

'Good morning, Miss Wilmot.' A now-familiar deep voice greeted her as she hastened down the stairs.

Sir Dominic stood in the hall, next to the silver tray that held the morning mail, flicking through the envelopes with his long fingers.

He looked up.

Her foot slipped. She grabbed hold of the banister.

'Good morning, Sir Dominic.'

They never strayed beyond their formal roles as master and governess, in spite of the increasing amount of time they spent together, she realised, as she took another step down the stairs. She lowered her gaze, keeping her hand on the smooth wooden rail. Yes, better not to fall.

When she ventured another glance at her employer, it was to find him smiling at her. It was as well she had almost finished her descent, for the effect was positively dizzying. It was a smile of reassurance, almost of conspiracy, that sent a warmth through her body, but contributed absolutely nothing to her steadiness.

She felt her own lips widen in reply.

'I've been meaning to ask. How are you sleeping now?' he enquired in an undertone.

'Much better,' she replied. 'Thank you. I have not had a nightmare for some time.'

'That's good news.' He exhaled. 'That night was an unusual occurrence. An aberration. I hope you know that I would not have entered your bedroom under any other circumstances, except the thought that you were in danger.'

His words reverberated within her, soothing and healing her in the same way his arms had soothed and healed her that night, as if he touched her again.

'The brandy you had that night did the trick, then,' he said.

It wasn't the brandy. It was you.

It was on the tip of her tongue to say those words. She stopped herself just in time. It was the truth; she knew that. But if she said such a thing it would have sounded as if she were attracted to him, like all those other governesses.

And it wasn't his smile that made her sway and grasp at the banister this time. It was the realisation forming in her brain.

Shocking.

Unthinkable.

'Yes, it must have been the brandy,' she managed to reply.

Suddenly, she wasn't sure if she could stand upright, let alone go any further down the stairs. 'I must have some more. Brandy, I mean. But not with you. I mean, I won't make a habit of it.'

He lifted an eyebrow. 'It's all right. You don't seem to me to be one of those kinds of governesses.'

'Those kinds of governesses?' Her voice came out in a squeak. Had he read her mind?

'The kind who drink brandy every night.'

'Oh!' Maud gave a breathless, nervous laugh. 'No, of course not. I'm not one of those kinds of governesses. Not at all. Please, excuse me, Sir Dominic. I have left something in my room.'

She spun on her heel and disappeared up the stairs with as much speed as decorum would allow.

Dominic stared after Miss Wilmot. The ends of a green ribbon in her hair wafted after her like butterfly wings.

What had he said to send her flying away like that? After all the time they had spent together recently, he was surprised by her reaction. There had been nervousness in her again. He'd hoped that she felt more at ease with him now. Perhaps she regretted the familiarity that had developed between them in the past weeks and wanted to re-establish some propriety.

Not that there was any real impropriety between them, of course. No master and governess could be seemlier as they sat together in the evenings. They were often alone in his study, it was true, but their relationship was purely a professional one. No, he corrected himself. It was more companionable than that, but no decorum had been breached, not since he had been forced to enter her bedroom, that night he had heard her terrible cries.

It still bothered him, that anguished nightmare of hers. The agony in her expression. He'd never pressed her to confide in him. That would have been inappropriate, even though, to his wry amazement, he had begun to confide in her. She had such a way of waiting for him to speak that seemed to bring out in him a need to talk that he'd never been aware of before. But he respected her privacy.

He was pleased to hear that she was sleeping well. The dark smudges under her eyes had almost disappeared. They'd been steadily diminishing and the roses were coming into her cheeks, just as they were to Rosabel's.

She'd looked brighter, happier—at least, she had before she'd raced off like that.

He looked down at the letters in his hand. One was half out of its envelope. It was not addressed to him, but to Miss Wilmot. He would have to tell her that the flap had not been sealed correctly, for he did not want her to think that her letters were opened at Pendragon Hall.

As he slid the letter back into the envelope, he noticed the name at the bottom of the writing paper, in a fine, feminine hand.

With love, Martha

Martha. That was Miss Wilmot's name. He knew it from the exceedingly good references that had been provided to him. Perhaps she had a friend with the same name, or perhaps he'd misinterpreted what he read. Miss Wilmot's letters were her own.

He thrust it back into the envelope and laid it on the silver tray, face down. The return address was an outer area of London, written in the same feminine hand. He frowned slightly, perplexed. The address was oddly familiar.

It was none of his business, yet for some reason, it bothered him.

Dominic drummed his fingers on the tray and frowned.

Maud slammed the bedroom door behind her and leaned upon it for good measure. At least it held her up.

She tore the ribbon from her hair.

She had developed romantic notions about Sir Dominic Jago.

Rushing to the dressing table, she faced herself in the looking glass.

Her cheeks were flushed, her eyes bright.

It couldn't be!

Her reflection told her otherwise.

Casting the green ribbon aside, Maud seized her hairbrush and began to smooth back the loose tendrils of hair.

With every stroke of the hairbrush she reasoned with herself. It wasn't possible! No. She would not allow it. The very idea of being just like all the other previous governesses who had come to Pendragon Hall, of chasing the master of the house! She'd never anticipated that she would view Sir Dominic as anything more than her employer. When she'd told him that she had no interest in men, she had spoken the truth. She'd never expected her body to betray her, to react in such a way merely to his smile of greeting, as it had only minutes before.

Her hair back in its usual severe bun, she laid down the hairbrush and took an unsteady sip of water, then patted some of it on to her cheeks for good measure.

In the looking glass, her skin stayed resolutely pink.

No. No! She refused to be just like all the other governesses, infatuated with the master of the house. And he had made views about such infatuations perfectly clear. He had told her, in no uncertain terms.

She threw another splash of water on to her heated skin. After what had happened to her, she had thought she would never feel any emotions for a man. She had thought that the sensitive, precious part of her had been numbed, frozen, half-dead, unable to come alive.

Sir Dominic Jago had broken through that barrier.

The ribbon cut into her fingers as she took it up, rolled it and shut it away in the drawer with a determined snap.

She stood and smoothed her dress. She must not, she would not, under any circumstances, reveal the attraction she felt for him. Her romantic notions must be quashed, immediately. From this moment on, she would keep their interactions to the most professional and *minimal* level. She would not risk any further intimacy developing between them.

She would ensure an appropriate distance was kept between them now, so that her mind and body did not betray her. She would show nothing on her face. Her expression, from now on, would be severe, as befitting a governess. Not only because her professionalism demanded it, but because…

She wanted to stay at Pendragon Hall.

She would not give way to the romantic notions she had promised she would never entertain. Sir Dominic Jago must never know.

No, she would not stoop to chase the master of the house. It was essential that she revealed nothing of her newly discovered feelings.

Her hair restored to normal, she descended the stairs once more. She forced herself to move with dignity and utter steadiness, her head down as she concentrated on putting one foot in front of the other. Her resolve almost evaporated as she lifted her gaze to find Sir Dominic still in the hall. Looking at her.

'Miss Wilmot. I've been waiting for you to come down again. I have something for you.'

'What is it, Sir Dominic?' She focused again on navigating the stairs. One, two, swish, swish. Dignified steps.

Even breath. Hand on the banister. It was only when she achieved the hall that she trusted herself to look up again.

'This letter came for you.' He held out a white envelope. 'My apologies, but it was already open. I do not know why. I did not open it myself.'

It must be from Martha, she realised in a flash. Oh, how she hoped her sister had remembered not to put her full name on the envelope!

She almost snatched it from him. Thank goodness, Martha had only addressed it to 'Miss M. Wilmot' in her neat governess copperplate.

He had obviously noted her alarm. 'I have not intruded upon your privacy. Though the letter was open, I did no more than slide it back into the envelope. You have my word; your mail was not opened by me.'

She flushed. 'I'm sorry. I never suspected you of prying. I was eager to have my letter. That is all.'

He made no reply, yet his eyes narrowed. There was curiosity, a puzzlement in them. He glanced at her hair, as if noting the change.

She smoothed her hair even more firmly behind her ears.

'I am master of the house,' he said. 'But I would never take advantage of my position. I hope you know that.'

She raised her head and looked him full in the face.

'I have never doubted it,' she said honestly.

She knew that of him. It was more than an instinct. It was a truth that she felt deep in her soul.

A muscle in his jaw worked. 'Thank you. I have formed a good opinion of your moral standards, Miss Wilmot. I am pleased to have met them in myself.'

Maud stared down at the wooden floorboards, her

cheeks now burning. She couldn't meet his eyes. 'I am far from perfect.'

'As am I. Perfection would be tiresome, do you not think?'

When she looked up, he was smiling at her again, the half-smile that played around his lips, a smile that demanded she return it, despite her earlier determination upstairs to encourage no further intimacy or friendliness between them. Instead, she found herself responding instantly. All her new-found resolutions to ensure her manner remained strict and professional evaporated at the sight of his smile.

'I thought I would accompany you on your nature walk, if I may,' he said, after a moment.

She clutched the butterfly net more firmly in her grip. 'Oh?'

'I have an urge,' he said, 'to discover more about butterflies.'

Chapter Twelve

When I was wont to meet her
In the silent woody places
    —*Alfred, Lord Tennyson:* Maud *(1855)*

Rosabel raced across the daisy-studded grass, her ringlets bobbing.

Sir Dominic walked beside Maud as they followed close behind. He'd shrugged on a coat instead of riding away or disappearing into his study, but he wore no hat. The wind ruffled his hair in the breeze.

It was a relief to walk with him instead of standing face to face. The intensity of his presence could not be denied, but it was easier to withstand if he was beside her, rather than in her direct line of sight.

What was it about him? She peeped from under her bonnet, as they crossed the lawn. He was handsome, tall and strong, but that wasn't what made his presence so remarkable. It was the forcefulness of his character, a drive that emanated from him, like the steam around his trains.

'Miss Wilmot!' Rosabel called. 'I have one.'

'Copper, I believe,' said Dominic, as Rosabel showed them excitedly what she had caught in her net.

'You remembered,' Maud said, attempting to keep the amazement from her voice.

'You must set it free, Rosabel,' he said, after they had studied it for a moment.

'By the daisies, Rosabel,' Maud said. 'Copper butterflies love daisies.'

They had gone a little way through the woods, with its primroses and bluebells ablaze, when he asked: 'Have you followed the path all the way through the woods?'

Maud shook her head. She never walked too far alone, if she could help doing so.

'Not yet,' she admitted. 'I've wanted to explore the woods, but I wasn't sure how long it would take and if it was too far for Rosabel.'

'She is a different child since your arrival, but you are correct. It would be tiring for her to do so.' He gave her an acute look. 'So, you don't know what varieties of butterflies can be found deep in the forest?'

She shook her head again. It loosened the ribbons of her bonnet that were tied under her chin.

'Perhaps you will allow me to show you,' he murmured. 'Netta can look after Rosabel, if you are up to a longer walk than usual.'

'Oh!' she exclaimed. 'Yes, please. I mean, thank you. I would like that very much.' She studied her butterfly net, as if it would supply her with some coherence.

'I'll take Rosabel back to the Hall. She'll be happy with Netta.'

Rosabel tugged at her father's sleeve.

He ducked down and listened as she whispered in his ear.

With a laugh he straightened up. In one strong, smooth movement, he hoisted Rosabel on to his shoulders and carried her away, laughing with glee, ducking under the tree branches.

Maud watched them go, a smile tickling her lips. This was a Sir Dominic she sensed most people never encountered.

Her nails dug into her palms. She barely felt them, barely noticed her surroundings.

No! she told herself sternly, again. *This is nothing but a passing fancy. Ignore it, ignore him!*

Walking a little way further, she found a large stone. It was covered with moss and made a cushioned—if slightly damp—seat. She lifted her face to the sunshine that dappled through the leaves. She could still hear Rosabel laughing as Dominic carried her along the path. Then her voice died away and all was silent, except the rustle of the trees.

Maud felt a stillness come over her. Something magical and sacred. Something pure. The sense of healing she had experienced these past few days seemed even more intense here, in Pendragon Woods.

Sanctuary.

She tilted back her bonnet and closed her eyes. Her face was warmed by the sun's rays. She didn't know how long she sat there, soaking up the peace and silence. All she knew was that her woodland sanctuary was like a soothing balm to her soul, as Sir Dominic's arms had been.

When she finally opened her eyes, she took from her pocket the letter from Martha. It was full of enquiries about Maud's employment, descriptions of her own life as a newlywed and then one sentence that made her exclaim aloud in delight.

Dominic appeared on the path. She hadn't jumped, Maud realised. Previously, if she was approached, even if not unawares, she leapt as if burned by a fire. But with him, now, there was an easiness in her body.

He glanced at the letter in her hand. 'You have had news?'

Maud beamed. 'I have indeed. From my sister. She is newly married and she writes to tell me she is expecting a baby.'

He smiled. 'You love children.'

'Yes. Yes, of course. Teaching children is my vocation, after all. It is more than a mere occupation, to me.'

'You have never sought to have a family of your own? To have your own children?'

Maud stiffened. 'I am an unmarried woman.' She clipped out the words. She didn't know what else to say. His query had brought it all back, for a moment.

The nightmares.

The fears.

She did not dare to dream about marriage and a family. She might have once upon a time, but not any more. Her dreams were over. Ruined. That was the truth of it. She never let herself think about it. The pain was too great; it would overwhelm her. What had been taken away from her included her hope for the future, for the ordinary dreams of marriage, of having a husband and a family. Such dreams would never come true for her.

No one would ever want her, as she was. Not any more. Not now.

She bit her lip. Hiding her face, she busied herself folding the letter from Martha back into the envelope.

When she looked up again, he was studying her with a slight frown.

'I realise that you are unmarried,' he said, quietly. 'I am sorry if my question caused you any distress. I certainly meant to cause you no offence.'

She took a deep breath. 'I have taken none.'

'You must go and visit your sister, when the time comes,' he said.

'You would let me take time off?' she exclaimed. 'Ma—'

Once again, she had been about to say her sister's name, but of course she could not.

'I mean, my sister would like that,' she amended hastily.

'I give free or reduced fare tickets to all my staff,' he said. 'That extends to their families. When the baby is older, you can invite them down here, to Cornwall. For a holiday.'

'Really?'

The half-smile played at his lips before he inclined his head. 'If you wish it.'

'You're not what I expected,' she said on impulse.

He raised an eyebrow.

'You are so much kinder than you seem,' she explained. 'When I first met you, I found you...'

He raised his eyebrow further.

'Intimidating.'

'You had quite a severe air yourself, Miss Wilmot,' he drawled. 'I have sometimes been quite in awe of my new governess.'

She smoothed her skirt.

'You're teasing me,' she said.

'Not at all.'

He held out his hand to help her up.

She hesitated. She couldn't risk the touch of his hand, even gloved. She'd vowed that she would not reveal her new-found romantic notions for him and she could not let her body betray her.

Instantly, in response to her movement, he drew his hand away.

'Shall we go and look for the butterflies?' he asked, lightly.

'Yes, of course,' she replied, rising from the stone and fumbling for her butterfly net.

She sensed him observing her, making deductions.

Maud gripped the handle of her net as if it were a weapon. But the only person she must defend against was herself.

Her romantic notions about the master of the house had to pass.

Dreaming was too dangerous, especially for a governess.

As they went deeper into the wood, they fell in step together, side by side. She felt, for a moment, as if they always walked together.

Such thoughts were romantic notions, she reprimanded herself. They must stop. Immediately.

'It's said these woods were used for wild pagan rites, long ago,' Sir Dominic told her.

Maud shivered.

He chuckled. 'Does that scare you?'

'A little,' she conceded.

'You do not strike me as someone who lacks courage.'

'More than once I climbed a tree in an attempt to catch a butterfly,' she told him. 'I wanted to travel the world, looking for rare specimens. My favourite tales were about explorers of far lands. But now my daring goes into my stories, instead.'

'That seems a shame. Surely life is an adventure.'

'Princess Swallowtail's adventures are enough for me,' she said lightly.

She moved ahead on the path.

In a single stride he was beside her. They made their way deeper among the trees, to the sound of birdsong underscored by the occasional 'cuckoo...'

'I don't believe I have ever chased butterflies,' he admitted, after they had strolled for a while. 'I must admit, I'm intrigued.'

'They are intriguing creatures.'

'Indeed.'

They continued in silence. Maud felt herself unfurling, like a fern frond.

As they ventured further into the woods, it seemed to become more magical. The gnarled oak trees were like living giants and the hazel coppices were dappled with light. The morning was so bright, it was as light as if it was midday and already the sun was streaming through the leaf canopies.

For a moment she experienced again that strange sense that Sir Dominic's company was an everyday occurrence, just as she had that morning, when he had smiled at her on the stairs.

Beside her, he strode with the assured air of a man who knew his place in the world and took it.

Of course he did. They were his own woods, she supposed. She tried to imagine how it must feel to be the owner of such a vast amount of land. She could barely fathom it. Yet if she were to own anything—if nature could be owned—it would be a wood, an oak wood, just like this one.

Again, she felt a pang of pleasure that was almost painful in its intensity. Never had she felt so at home as she did at Pendragon Hall. It hadn't only been the sight of him at the foot of the stairs, leafing through the morning post and greeting her with a smile that gave her the strange sense of belonging, as if it had all happened before, or was meant to be. Here in the woods she felt the same sensation, the rightness of being beside him, as he strode, a full head taller than her, his black, polished boots keeping pace with hers.

The beauty of the woods only added to the intensity. The bluebells, wild garlic and primroses were out, and she noticed that he took them in, too, breathing in their fragrant scents.

'Watch out.' He lifted an overhanging tree bough, so that she could go underneath it, unharmed.

'Thank you,' she said.

He inclined his head in reply, but they spoke no more as they continued on the path.

Two wings flashed by her.

'Oh!' she cried out softly. 'Quickly!'

Lifting her petticoats, she ran across the forest floor, darting between tree trunks and dodging bushes in pursuit of the butterfly. It flitted across the path and led her deeper into the woods.

She slid to a halt.

Slowly, slowly, she lifted the butterfly net.

Dominic had followed her. 'Where is it?'

'Over there. Try not to move,' Maud instructed in a whisper. 'If you do, it will flee. Can you see it? Up there.'

Maud tilted her head towards where the butterfly

hovered about the lower limbs of an oak tree. 'See? It's mostly black with a white bar on each wing, but underneath it's all russet and white.'

Dominic shifted behind her.

She fought back an urge to lean into his arms. She instinctively sought the comfort of them now, after he had held her that night.

She bit her lip. What was happening to her? She had to control herself. Such sensations were entirely unseemly.

'What is it?' he murmured, his breath on her neck as he leaned in to minimise sound.

'It's a White Admiral,' she whispered in reply. 'It isn't the rarest of butterflies, but its pupation was in May, which means it has only just come out. Rosabel hasn't seen one yet.'

'I see it.' Dominic moved even nearer to her as he followed her line of sight. When her hands tightened around the wooden handle of the net, it had nothing to do with the butterfly.

She'd always been able to focus on an insect when she saw it and to stay still and stalk it patiently, but now it was impossible to concentrate. Every part of her body normally attuned to the flutter of wings, or for flash of colour, now seemed attuned to him.

The connection they'd made the night before was almost tangible here in the woods, as soundless as the movement of a butterfly wing, yet pulsating as effortlessly between them.

Did he feel it? If so, he made no indication. He stood motionless, like the experienced hunter he was.

A bead of perspiration trickled down the back of her corset as behind her he shifted his body weight to his opposite foot, to get a better vantage point for the butterfly.

For a tall, strong man he was surprisingly quiet on the crunching leaves and twigs of the woodland path. Now he'd moved even closer to her, encircling her with his scent, clean, musky and undeniably male. It reminded her of being held in his arms, his sure strength banishing her nightmare.

Her corset felt tight. Spring in Cornwall was hotter than she had anticipated. This morning she felt as if she were burning up.

She crept closer to the butterfly. Sir Dominic moved with her, their bodies in tune.

Her damp fingers nearly slipped on the net handle. It was more than the heat. She knew that. She forced herself to focus on the fairy creature before her, her eyes on the fluttering wings.

She angled the net. As she did so, the butterfly moved even higher.

'Do you want to catch it?' Dominic murmured in her ear.

'I do,' she whispered over her shoulder. 'Not to keep it. Just to see it close up. But it's too high.'

'Here.' He closed his hand around hers on the handle of the butterfly net.

She slid her fingers out from underneath his.

He moved in front of her to get a better position. She tried not to start as he brushed past, but his proximity took immediate effect on her body, sending her heart into a rapid tattoo.

With a stealthy grace that told of his hunting skill, he prowled silently over to the oak tree.

Then he leapt, the net flying through the air.

'Oh, you have it!' Maud could see the butterfly, unharmed, but inside the net.

He gave a slight bow. 'At your service.'

A few eager steps and she was beside him. Both bent to look at the specimen through the netting, so close, their heads almost touched.

'Is it a male or a female?' he asked. 'Can you tell?'

She nodded. 'It's a male. It's a bit bigger and a fine specimen, too.'

Her awareness of him vanished as she examined the butterfly, gently spreading the netting so it had plenty of room. 'I've never managed to catch a White Admiral.'

'Well, you didn't this time.' He chuckled. 'Not that it matters. But tell me, why is it called an Admiral?'

'I *would* have caught him if you hadn't been lurking in the undergrowth, scaring him off. He probably thought you were going to accuse him of trespassing, as you did me, once upon a time.' She laughed. He did not feel like her employer, here in the woods, catching butterflies. 'No one knows why they're named Admirals. It may have something to do with the navy and the flags on their ships. But you can see how fine he is, a real nobleman. Large, with a broad wingspan.'

'Indeed.'

'There are some collectors, I have read, who believe that the name was originally "admirable", not "admiral".'

'Is that so?'

She looked up to find him gazing at her, a strange expression on his face.

'I'm talking too much,' she said, flustered. 'You must excuse me. I tend to make everything a lesson. It is a schoolroom habit.'

'Not at all, Miss Wilmot. Thus far, I have enjoyed your lessons.'

As he passed her back the butterfly net, their fingers

touched. For a moment, everything stilled. She forgot the butterfly in the net, forgot everything, except Sir Dominic Jago and the way he was looking at her.

She raised her face to his. His eyes had turned dark, filled with a strange intensity as he studied her face, as if *she* were the butterfly and not the creature in the net. His gaze slipped over her—her hair, her forehead, her cheeks, her nose—to settle on her lips.

She had parted them—to speak—but no sound came.

There was only the hush of their breathing, as long moments passed.

A blackbird in the oak tree above them broke into song, as loud as any chaperon.

Maud jumped. With a start, she dropped the butterfly net.

He caught it neatly.

'Oh!' she cried. 'I've never dropped my net before.'

'It's all right,' he said. 'I've got it.'

He held out the net, with the butterfly undamaged inside it.

'It needs plenty of air,' she said.

'Of course.' He gave it more room as she observed it, her head bowed.

'Have you seen enough?' he said after a moment, in a voice that sounded more husky than before.

'Thank you. Now we must—'

'Set it free.' He finished her sentence.

With a gentle flick of Dominic's wrist, he sent the White Admiral flying away.

'You've caught your first butterfly,' she said.

'Have I?'

Silence fell between them, strong as a cord.

'A White Admiral was a fine choice,' she said at last.

He gave her his half-smile.

'I believe it is the coppers that have taken my fancy,' he murmured. 'Are there variations on the copper we saw this morning?'

'I believe so,' she said. She hardly knew what she was saying with him looking at her so intently. 'There are fritillaries. They are multicoloured. Striped. They are cousins of the coppers, I suppose, not the same family, exactly. And there are large coppers. They are bigger. Of course.'

She knew she rambled.

'Ah,' he drawled. 'I would like to see one again up close. Are they hard to catch?'

'They can be.'

He still didn't move.

Nor did she.

Yet there was movement between them, flourishing into life. She could not see it or hear it, but she could feel it.

Stop, she warned herself. *Stop.*

She had to ignore the swirling sensation, so strong, sparking between them. She had to fight all the sensations that were growing in her mind, in her body.

In her heart.

It began to pound as he continued to study her as if she were the rarest butterfly in the world.

'I believe it might be worth the effort to investigate.' He glanced again at her hair, then back to her eyes, down to her mouth. 'Copper has always been highly valued here in Cornwall.'

It was as if he touched her.

As if he kissed her.

She wanted him to.

The realisation flamed in her body before it reached her mind, heating her skin, tilting her head up to his. She could not look away from him. The sound of the woods, the birds, the wind in the trees—all vanished as he summoned her.

She took another step forward before she fell back. Came to her senses, an unsteady hand clutched against her bodice as she tried to recall what they had been talking of, before her heart had begun to thump that dangerous beat, still resonating through her entire being.

Butterflies.

Butterflies.

'The small coppers are not particularly rare, nor sought after,' she said at last.

His gaze remained on her mouth. Like fingers. Like his own lips.

Would they be gentle? Hard against hers?

More unruly thoughts swirled up into her head.

'I've told you already, Miss Wilmot,' he said. 'I am a man who trusts my own judgement.'

Still he held her, with his eyes.

What did her own eyes say? Oh, she must not let her feelings for him show! With all her will, she cast her gaze downwards to stare at the woodland floor.

The leaves crackled around them as he stepped back. 'I will leave you here. I assume you know your way back? Thank you for the lesson, Miss Wilmot.'

Without another word, Sir Dominic strode away.

Chapter Thirteen

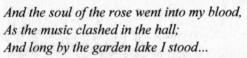

And the soul of the rose went into my blood,
As the music clashed in the hall;
And long by the garden lake I stood...
        —*Alfred, Lord Tennyson:* Maud *(1855)*

Dominic made his way to the stables to where Taran was stalled. He had been riding more than usual of late. It had been more than a week now since he had accompanied Miss Wilmot through the sunlit woods, yet what had transpired between them had stayed with him.

How had he overlooked such beauty? That was the question that now plagued him, for Miss Wilmot was beautiful. Ever since their walk, whenever he looked at her it was as if a lamp had been lit in an exquisite but dormant vessel. He was a moth who could not help but flutter near. It was not an ordinary beauty. Hers was the kind in which a painter would delight, an artist trained to look beyond the obvious, like the self-evident beauty of Averill Trevose.

He was not a man to fool himself. He trusted his own

judgement. The walk in the forest had sparked something between them, something rare and fine.

No, not sparked, precisely. But it had fed the flickering flame.

He found the new governess attractive. He hadn't, at first, and he could not possibly indicate in any way, of course, that he found her so now. Not only because of the hypocrisy involved in having told her that he was weary of governesses with romantic ideas, but because he could not, as her employer, imply any kind of interest, let alone make any advance upon her that could be considered untoward. His sense of honour would not allow it. He despised men who behaved in such a manner and, God knew, he had encountered more than a few of them.

Many men of his background treated female servants as property, as of lesser value. He did not share the view of a working woman, or a working man, being less valuable than one of the upper classes. Quite the contrary. He despised such class divisions. Many Cornishmen did. He wanted it to be part of the past. It was why he liked the railway business, taking Cornwall into a new future.

'If I'd been a different kind of man, I would never have let that moment in the woods pass by, would I, Taran?'

He smiled at himself, confiding in his horse as he led the stallion out of the stall and put on the saddle. What that moment would have turned into, he could only surmise.

His body flared into life as he remembered. He would never have allowed himself, of course, to act upon such impulses. He was a man who could control himself. He had never allowed himself any hint of impropriety with any of his staff and he never would. Since that woodland walk, he had ensured that his behaviour towards Miss Wilmot, as a woman in his employ, was entirely appropriate.

Yet he knew that the moment they had shared had been extraordinary. It seemed as if she was part of him—that the landscape had enfolded them both. He had never known such a moment before, even with Sarah.

He mounted the stallion and headed for the open fields, let the air blast against him as they cantered along. It was not only the physical sensations he had experienced in the woods, but also the sensitivity and understanding she had shown listening to him. It had made him aware that a true partnership was not something he had previously experienced. Not in that way. It had made him realise what was possible between a man and a woman.

Yet he had been unable to forgo the nightly pleasure of listening to Miss Wilmot's storytelling. Each evening he continued to climb the stairs to the nursery, lean against the doorframe and enjoy the evolving tale. Or was it simply her melodious voice and the fluttering of her hands as she told the tale, as delicate as any butterfly, that drew him back, night after night?

How could he ever have thought her plain? She was not plain—she was simply trying to disguise herself. For hers was a rare beauty, the kind of beauty that grew on a man, the kind of beauty that would mature with age, not fade like a spring flower. No, Miss Wilmot's beauty had the edge of the autumnal to it, the lasting, the fruitful, the coppery turn of fallen leaves, red, gold and brown on the ground. He would never tire of looking at such a face. He would want to see it at every age. Even as she grew old her eyes would not lose their beauty, he could not imagine them ever fading. Her enchantment was of a kind that could not be limited by any age.

He pushed back his hair from his forehead. Perhaps she *was* Scheherazade. She had protested that Scheherazade was not an enchantress, but a storyteller, yet her tales seemed to have cast some kind of enchantment upon him. Another half-laugh of incredulity escaped him. He was a practical man. He was never fanciful. His own sense of the possible and the improbable had altered irrevocably.

With his heel, he spurred Taran on.

He could do nothing about the situation. Not in the circumstances. He could only sit in silence each evening and listen to her tell a fairy tale. Their relationship must continue as one that befitted master–governess. It was, after all, he who had set the terms of her employment. What he had demanded of her, he would demand of himself.

Nor could he deny that his relationship with Sarah still scarred him. His reasons for never wanting to marry again, his sense of guilt—these still preyed on his mind and his heart. His inability to move past Sarah's death and how he had treated her—his conversations with Miss Wilmot had helped to ease that burden, but even so, he still had doubts about his ability to be a good husband.

He urged Taran faster into a gallop.

He would outride these feelings, these thoughts.

When he got back to Pendragon Hall, he returned Taran to the stables and made for his bedroom. Stripping off his coat and shirt, he threw cold water on to his skin, before putting on fresh clothing and returning to his study. Normally, work was his escape from any other matters on his mind, but he had to admit that since Miss Wilmot's arrival he had found it hard to concentrate.

He went to the window, hauled back the curtain. He had to focus, but Miss Wilmot was proving a serious distraction. The other governesses who had come before hadn't taken up so much of his attention, even though they had wanted to. Yet he found himself thinking about Miss Wilmot. To his own appalled amusement, he often stood, as he was now, by the study window, watching for her.

A knock came at the door.

Instantly he swung around. 'Yes.'

The footman entered the study.

Dominic raised an eyebrow.

'That delivery's come for you, Sir Dominic.'

Dominic smiled. He hadn't expected it to arrive so soon. 'Bring it in.'

The nursery door opened.

Maud tried not to show how affected she was by Sir Dominic merely entering the nursery. She did not look up, but she knew her voice faltered as the door creaked wider, followed by the sound of his tread upon the floorboards. Her head lowered, her mind went blank and she could not remember where she was up to in the story of Princess Swallowtail.

Rosabel, tucked up in bed, had been listening so intently she barely moved when her papa came in. Not so Maud. The minute Dominic entered the nursery—or any room, for that matter—she was instantly aware of him.

'What happened next, Miss Wilmot?' Rosabel asked.

Maud felt a flush building in her cheeks as her mind

remained stubbornly blank. Why, such a lapse in story-telling had never happened to her before.

Then she looked up and started.

In the nursery doorway, Sir Dominic stood holding a huge wooden box. The top had been opened.

'Papa!' Rosabel exclaimed. 'What have you got?'

'A present for you, Rosabel.'

Instantly, the little girl was out of bed. 'What is it?'

He carried the large box with ease across the room and placed it on the table by the window. There was only just room for it, crowded as it was with glass bottle insect homes and Rosabel's drawings of the caterpillars and butterflies inside them—for every day, under Maud's instruction, she sketched the insects' changes and labelled them. Rosabel enjoyed drawing so much she barely realised how much she was learning, to Maud's satisfaction.

'Miss Wilmot can tell you what it is,' Sir Dominic said now.

'I can?' She got to her feet.

He ran his hand through his hair. He wore no jacket, only a navy waistcoat with a crisp white shirt underneath. 'Indeed.'

She approached the table.

Rosabel, clutching her doll, leaned forward expectantly, her eyes wide.

Maud peered inside the wooden box. 'Why, it looks like a butterfly vivarium! However did you manage to get it here, Sir Dominic?'

His half-smile curved.

'I have a railway at my disposal, Miss Wilmot,' he replied. 'It arrived today. From London.'

She tried to ignore the unsettling effect of his sheer

physicality as the muscles flexed beneath his white shirt as he lifted out the rectangular wood-and-glass box that had been nestled, wrapped in straw, inside the wooden packing box. 'I hope it is satisfactory,' he said. 'The frame is made of rosewood. It is based upon a particular design of insect case by Mr Ward. I believe that was the name you mentioned.'

Maud gazed at it in awe. The vivarium was a large one. The back of it was made of wood, but both the sides and front were constructed of thick, clear glass. The front lifted like a door, for ease of access, and there was metal mesh at the top, so that there could be plenty of air. She'd never seen one so fine.

'It's marvellous,' she breathed. 'This will make it so much easier for us to observe the insects. Look, Rosabel.'

She put her arm around the little girl and drew her closer.

'*Vivarium* is a Latin word,' she explained. 'It means "a place of life".'

'*Vivo, vivas, vivat!*' chirped Rosabel, with a sideways glance at her father.

He grinned and ruffled her hair. '*Vivamus, vivatis, vivant.* Well done, O Latin scholar. Miss Wilmot has taught you well.'

Maud looked away in pleasure. 'We live and learn.' She pointed to the floor of the vivarium. 'Here, we can plant some ferns and other foliage into some earth, so that there is always fresh food and somewhere for the caterpillars to make their cocoons. We can even make a little lake, so they have water. And look how big it is! It's a very grand insect home. There's plenty of space for caterpillars and butterflies to grow, but they will be perfectly safe.'

She felt Sir Dominic's gaze upon her.

'Can we make a little lake for the butterflies now?' Rosabel asked eagerly.

Maud laughed. 'There will be plenty of time in the morning. Now, back to bed, Rosabel. You can dream of butterflies for now. It's getting late. We will begin work on the vivarium tomorrow.'

With a last look at the vivarium, Rosabel climbed back into bed. 'Is there still time for the rest of the butterfly story?'

'Of course,' said Maud.

If only she could remember where she was up to and then manage to tell it with Sir Dominic in the room, she thought to herself.

Across the other side of the bed he had settled in his usual chair. He stretched his long legs in front of him and tucked his thumbs into the small pockets of his waistcoat, in the relaxed manner she had come to accept as part of the nightly ritual.

While she'd managed to stay away from him at other hours of the day, there was no way she could avoid him in the nursery when he came to say goodnight.

He gave her his half-smile. 'Do go on with your story, Miss Wilmot. I didn't intend to interrupt by bringing in the vivarium. What happens next?'

For a moment she fancied that his deep voice seemed to hold a different question, a more intimate, personal question, but of course she had imagined it. Wishful thinking. No, perilous thinking.

She smoothed her skirt over her petticoats.

'Princess Swallowtail had found a friend,' she said at last.

'A friend?' His eyebrows quirked.

'Yes,' she said, 'a friend.' The slightest emphasis on that last word.

'Was it another butterfly?' asked Rosabel.

'It certainly was,' said Maud. 'It was a butterfly she had not expected to be friendly towards her. It was a very grand butterfly. To begin with, she was quite shy of him, but that soon changed.'

'Oh, what kind of butterfly was it, Miss Wilmot?'

'It was the White Admiral,' she said.

Dominic's smile broadened. She almost smiled back, but stopped herself just in time.

'What did it look like?' Rosabel asked. 'I don't think I've ever seen a...a White Ad—Admirable butterfly. Have I, Miss Wilmot?'

Maud couldn't help but glance at Dominic over Rosabel's pillowed head. A smile flashed between them. 'No, no...you haven't seen a White Admiral, Rosabel. But he is quite dashing in his black-and-white dinner suit with his orange waistcoat underneath. Most handsome,' said Maud, then flushed. What *was* she saying? She hurried on. 'It is the one I told you about, Rosabel, that I caught recently.'

A cough came from Sir Dominic's direction.

'I mean that your papa caught,' she corrected herself, again fighting a return smile. She would not look up again. She would keep her gaze fixed on Rosabel. The ease that had developed between them must not be her undoing. She had to remain as severe as possible.

'It is a black-and-white butterfly with very clear markings,' she went on. 'It is mainly found in wooded regions, in forests and clearings. It can be spotted when out for a walk, or perhaps out riding.'

'Like you do, Papa!' Rosabel exclaimed. 'You go riding in the woods. Do you often meet the Admiral in his dinner jacket and waistcoat?'

'I believe I may have made his acquaintance once or twice,' Dominic murmured.

'When it is a caterpillar, it feeds on honeysuckle,' Maud went on. 'It finds it most delicious.'

He raised an eyebrow. 'How did the White Admiral meet Princess Swallowtail, if I may ask?'

'It was a very strange thing,' said Maud. 'As you know, Rosabel, there are two rival courts among the butterfly fairies. There are those that support King Swallowtail and those who are on the side of the Red Emperor.'

Rosabel drew in her breath.

'One day,' Maud went on, 'Princess Swallowtail had been on a lovely flight when she came home and landed a little way out of the vegetable patch. Two of the Speckled Woods, soldiers of the Red Emperor, caught Princess Swallowtail and took her captive!'

With a shriek Rosabel clutched her papa's hand.

'They trapped Princess Swallowtail in a spider's web!' Maud continued. 'Its threads were so sticky. She flapped her wings, but she could not get free. Poor Princess Swallowtail. She tried and tried, but the harder she tried to escape, the more trapped she became. Then, to her surprise, the White Admiral landed in front of her. He was a much larger and stronger butterfly than Princess Swallowtail. To begin with, she was frightened of him. But then she thought: maybe, just maybe he would untangle her from the nasty, sticky spider's web and set her free! "Will you help me?" Princess Swallowtail asked the White Admiral, ever so politely. "I will help you to help yourself," he told her. "You must learn the ways of the wind." With that he flew away, leaving Princess Swallowtail quite perplexed. But she knew the White Admiral was a wise butterfly, so she settled in to learn the four ways of the wind. The north wind came first. It was so powerful it nearly blew Princess Swallowtail into the trees, spider's web and all, but she did not get free. The wind from the east made her shivering and cold. The wind from the south was warmer, for it blew from the faraway deserts of Africa. But it was the west wind that was just right. It carried the scent of the sea. And the next time the west wind blew she ran with it and caught the wind, and flew free.'

'Hooray!' cried Rosabel. 'Did you like that story, Papa?'

'Certainly,' he said. 'It's always wise to wait and see which way the wind blows.'

Maud picked up the globe that was now always nearby and showed it to Rosabel. 'Here we are in Cornwall. And here is north, east, south and west. See if you can find the deserts of Africa, far, far to the south.'

As they studied the globe, she felt Dominic's gaze remain upon her.

'Goodnight, Sir Dominic,' she said, finally. She always made sure she went straight to her room and didn't linger, but it had become more difficult of late. 'Goodnight, Rosabel.'

Idly he reached out and spun the globe with a long finger. It was another habit of his that had become part of the nightly ritual.

Then, unexpectedly, he stopped it, mid-turn. 'Miss Wilmot. I almost forgot. It slipped my mind in the excitement of the vivarium. I have something for you, too.'

'For me?' she asked, amazed.

He nodded as he reached into the pocket of his waist-coat. With a flourish, he pulled out a beautiful black-and-gold fountain pen.

Their fingers touched as he handed it to her. She had to school herself not to snatch her hand away. The warmth of his fingers seemed to burn her like fire. She focused on the pen. It, too, was imbued with his body heat.

'So that you can write down your stories,' he said.

'This is far too fine a pen for my tales,' Maud protested. It was one of the more expensive kinds, with a reservoir of ink inside it. She would not have to constantly dip the nib in a pot.

'You do yourself an injustice.' He moved back to the table and found a blank piece of paper from among the pile of Rosabel's drawings. 'Here. Test it, if you will, Miss Wilmot. Sign your autograph. Rosabel and I shall keep it for posterity.'

Maud's fingers clenched around the pen.

Her heart thudded as she crossed the room and leaned over the table.

He slid the paper towards her.

She could not refuse to sign her name. It would appear strange.

With a heavy, reluctant hand, she formed the letters of two words: Martha Wilmot. At least her surname was as she usually wrote it, with the W half-flying across the page.

Dominic glanced down at the paper, his half-smile on his lips.

Then his face changed. He frowned at the rapidly drying ink.

Hastily Maud stepped away. 'Thank you, Sir Dominic. For the pen.'

He did not look up, merely inclined his head. 'Thank you, Miss Wilmot. Goodnight.'

Maud hurried from the nursery, the fountain pen clutched between her fingers. Inside her own room, she shut the door and leaned against it, her breath coming quickly.

If only she did not need to live a lie to remain at Pendragon Hall. She had never foreseen such difficulties. The more time she spent with him, the harder it became. Sir Dominic Jago was a man who lived by and deserved integrity.

Maud unclenched her fingers and stared at the fountain pen in her hand.

Chapter Fourteen

A shadow flits before me;
—*Alfred, Lord Tennyson:* Maud *(1855)*

Through the mullioned window Dominic caught sight of a movement on the gravel drive outside. Crossing to the glass, he rubbed the pane, steamed by the fire, and stared out into the near darkness. Yes, there it was again. A movement as someone left the Hall.

She carried no lamp, but he saw the flick of her shawl catch the moonlight and knew instantly who it was.

Miss Wilmot.

It was later than usual, much later. She had not come to sit by the fire and read. He glanced towards the chair where she often sat. He'd become used to her being there.

He went back to his desk, looked again at the piece of paper she'd written on earlier and smiled.

He'd wanted to give her something, to show his appreciation of her work.

There was Miss Martha Wilmot's signature, written in the black ink of the fountain pen he had just given her to write her stories. He couldn't disguise to himself that the gift of a pen had been more than appreciation. He found himself thinking about her, about her needs and desires. What might make her happy. The irony did not escape him now that he was the one who could be described as having romantic notions about a governess, rather than the reverse.

Since that moment in the woods, he had known himself to be beguiled by her. Or perhaps it had happened before, when he first heard her tell a fairy tale.

It was her stillness and her reserve, too, that made her even more attractive to him. Rather than the usual clamour of women trying to get his attention, she never aimed to catch his eye or to make witticisms to try to amuse him. She never wore clothing that could be deemed sensual or striking. Her grey dresses, which he had begun to become accustomed to seeing about the Hall, were no fashion pieces and almost severe in their simplicity. Knowing she did nothing to entice him was part of her unconscious charm, yet it was her sweetness of character, and an apparent inner strength, that truly attracted him. She was full of moral integrity. It could not be hidden. It could not be disguised. The stories she told Rosabel were full of wisdom beyond her years.

The Butterfly Fables. They were not only enchanting, they were educational. She was a storyteller with a true gift. It was fashionable, she'd told him, for fairy tales to be published in magazines as moral fables. Hers were good enough for a magazine, or even a book of their own. He truly believed it. He hadn't exaggerated on that score. Far from it.

Miss Wilmot's stories were clever because, although she had an idealistic nature and an ethical bent, she was not heavy-handed in her moral instruction. Her approach was as light and airy as a pair of butterfly wings. The world she created in The Butterfly Fables was full of advice, lightly given, in the search for happiness and goodness.

But there was danger in the imaginary world she created, too.

Dominic frowned. The sense of threat and menace in the tales was, he suspected, emanating from more than a flair for drama. He had seen her fingers clench as she spoke of binding cobweb or fleeing from predators. She knew of what she spoke. She had experienced true terror, true menace.

The thought of it made his fingers tighten in echo. He cared. He cared *for her*. He could no longer deny it to himself.

He opened a drawer and tucked the signed piece of paper inside. As it slid closed, he noticed a black box. It had been half-hidden between the papers. Puzzled, he yanked back the drawer, extricated the box and snapped it open.

A wave of memory came over him as he stared, incredulous, at what lay inside.

He wasn't sure how long he stared at it before he came to a decision.

With one last draught of brandy, he stopped in the hall, seized his coat and headed out into the night to find her.

Maud slipped further into the garden, away from the house, lamp and net in hand.

She needed nature around her tonight, no matter how late the hour. The clock had chimed midnight, but she couldn't sleep. Not yet.

The wind was high and the leaves made a welcoming sigh as she crossed the lawn to the entrance of the woods.

She would not go too far. She was not brave enough for that, not yet. But ever since the walk in the woods with Sir Dominic, she had felt it welcome her.

Sanctuary.

She was safe at Pendragon Hall.

She slid her hand into her pocket and touched the smooth, cold metal of the pen, and smiled.

The past few hours had vanished into another place, another time, another world. Thanks to Sir Dominic.

She had never imagined that writing down her stories would be so absorbing. One Butterfly Fable after another had poured out of her, each instalment more exciting than the last. She had always enjoyed telling the tales to children, especially to Rosabel, but she had never imagined that writing them, being able to follow the story at speed, would be so enjoyable. It had been a revelation. She had used up page after page, her hand flying across the writing paper. The pen had flowed as fast as her words, spurring her on, until at last it had stopped. She'd shaken it, but only a few blots of ink came out. The pen would need to be refilled.

She'd leaned back and stretched, amazed to see how many hours had passed. She had entirely forgotten to eat the meal on her tray.

She ought to have gone to bed, she supposed, but she could not. Her mind was still buzzing with unwritten tales. Instead of her nightgown, she seized her lambswool shawl and flung it around her shoulders, picked up her lamp and net and crept down the stairs. From under the door she could see that a lamp was still burning in Sir Dominic's study. He, too, was still up, then.

Now she took a lungful of air. It was a relief not to be wearing her corset, for she'd thrown it off earlier, before she'd begun to write. She had been determined that nothing would hold her in. Her hair was in the loose braid that she usually wore at nighttime, though she hadn't undressed and put on her nightgown. Instead, she'd thrown a shirtwaist dress over her petticoat, without her corset. Perhaps that was why it had been so easy to write. She had been able to breathe. She had felt free.

Yet it wasn't only the thrill of writing that was keeping her awake now, so awake she wondered if she would ever sleep.

She put the lamp in position to allow the moths to come, though she didn't have much urge to cast her net. As she watched them begin to swirl around the lamp, she could not stop thinking about Sir Dominic. There was something in him, something rare. He was not like all the other masters of the house she had encountered in her employment. He was admired and spoken well of by all those who worked for him, which was unusual below stairs, and he worked harder than anyone she knew.

But it was more than that. There was a part of her that connected with a part of him, something deep.

Nor could she dismiss the memory of the way he had held her the night that he had awoken her from that dreadful dream. She had not had another nightmare since. It was as if his arms continued to hold her in her sleep, protecting her from harm, from the horror that had tormented her for too long.

Momentarily she moved away from the lamp. An unseen bough scratched her face. It brought her to a standstill in the dark. Brought her to her senses.

No matter how grateful she was for that magical moment of connection in the woods, she would not allow her thoughts to stray in his direction. She would fight the feelings that were growing inside her. She would squash them out of existence.

An owl hooted, soft and soothing above her. The wind caressed her with the scent of moss and primroses. Maud stood still in the nighttime forest, gazing up at the restless leaves, black tossing shapes against a glittering sky.

It seemed as if time had lost all meaning, such was the depth of her new-found emotions. They tossed her like the leaves above, but were as breathtaking as a starfilled sky.

There was no future for them.

She would have to let these feelings wither and fade. But could such consuming, all-encompassing emotion simply fade away?

And how was she going to cope with these feelings, seeing him every day, and every night in the nursery? After all that had happened to her, she thought that her heart would never concede to such feelings. But she could no longer deny them.

Maud froze.

Was that…steps? Her ears strained to sift through the sighing wind, the unstill leaves, to discern what was probably just a figment of her overheated imagination.

A crunch of snapping twigs. Another. Closer now. It was undeniable.

Someone else was in the woods.

But she was not afraid. She knew who it was. And she waited, steadying herself against a sturdy oak.

The moon lit his features, turning his jaw to exquisitely carved marble, his dark hair to shadow. His coat was unbuttoned, as if he had thrown it on with haste, and his cravat had been loosened around his neck as if he had needed to free himself from its confines. It was a habit of his, she'd noted. It emphasised the strength and grace of his neck.

She moved towards him.

He moved towards her.

They stopped, only inches apart. So close, she could hear his breathing.

They stood, unmoving. Yet all about them, in the dark rustling forest, was that force of colour and life, of invisible, bright wings.

'I didn't mean to startle you,' he said at last.

'You—you don't startle me. I sensed it was you. I… have learnt your footsteps.'

'I'm surprised you have ventured so far into the woods at this hour, in this weather,' he said.

'I feel safe here,' she said. 'I'm not frightened. Not any more.'

Silence fell again between them, broken only by another call of an owl.

'Miss Wilmot,' he said quietly after a moment. 'There is much I know about you. But there is a great deal I do not know.'

Her breath hitched. She could not move.

'It's curious,' he mused, 'because, through your stories, there is a part of you I know—intimately.'

'What part of me is that?' It was a mere whisper.

Even in the darkness, she could sense the intensity of his gaze. 'Your morals,' he said. 'Your true character. You try to be so stern, yet your stories tell me other things about you. Your hopes and dreams.'

She bit her lip.

'I know how you love children,' he went on, 'and butterflies. But there is a great deal I do not know of your background, of your experiences in life. Apart from your character references, of course. From your previous employment.'

She could hardly breathe now. She'd become a statue, unable to move her limbs.

He moved closer. 'I do not intend to interrogate you, Miss Wilmot. You need have no fear.'

Fear? What *was* it she was feeling? No, the chaos inside her would not be analysed. It was all she could do to breathe.

'I do not want to pry,' he said. 'I am not by nature a curious man. But I must admit, you intrigue me. I want to know who you are.' He moved even closer. 'Dine with me tomorrow night.'

'What?'

'It is not such an outrageous request. It is not uncommon for governesses to dine with the family.'

'But your rules about governesses…'

'Ah. But you are no ordinary governess, are you?' He glanced at the lamp, surrounded by beating wings, then back at her. 'You pretend to be a moth, Miss Wilmot, but I think you might be a butterfly.'

Maud couldn't move as their gazes held in the dim light.

Moments passed, soft and slow in the night air, before he spoke again. His voice was husky. 'I do not want to alarm you in any way. But if you would permit, I would like us to get to know each other even better.'

'Why?' she asked.

'I think you know why,' he said quietly. 'There is an affinity between us.'

She felt the full force of that affinity flare as he studied her.

'I believe you feel it, too,' he said at last. 'Do you?'

She inclined her head. Just once. She couldn't deny it, not now. Not with that attraction fluttering to life between them. Not with what she had discovered, about the powerful truth of her feelings.

'We are master and governess,' she protested.

He ran a hand through his hair. 'Indeed, it is ironic that we find ourselves in this position. I know what I told you when you arrived. That's why I am inviting you to dine with me. As an equal. I am not trying to take advantage of my position, nor yours.'

'But surely even dining together would be improper?'

His smile gleamed in the moonlight. '*More* improper than meeting by night in a forest? But if you do not wish it…' He paused. 'Please feel free to refuse my invitation. I am aware that as master of the house you may feel compelled to accede to my desires.'

'You are not compelling me.' She swallowed hard. 'I would like to have dinner with you. Thank you for the invitation.'

She sensed, rather than heard, his exhalation.

'My thanks go to you, for accepting it.' He bowed. 'I will leave you to your moth-hunting.'

He turned and walked away.

No, she did not want him to leave! She wanted to call out to him.

But to say what?

Instead, she leaned against the oak tree and listened to his tread on the leaves.

Then his deep voice came floating back to her through the darkness like a promise. 'Until tomorrow night, then—Miss Wilmot.'

Chapter Fifteen

The brief night goes
In babble and revel and wine.
— Alfred, Lord Tennyson: Maud *(1855)*

'*Dine with me.*'

Maud went into her bedroom, closed the door and leaned against it. Momentarily she closed her eyes end let the feeling flow over her. All day she had thought about Sir Dominic's invitation. She had scarcely seen him since the night before, when he had issued the invitation. He had been at the railway all day, as he so often was.

She had been so busy trying to unravel her tangled emotions that, until he had appeared in the woods, she had never dreamed the feelings she fought so hard against might be something more, something that might also be shared by him.

He was the master of the house. She was the governess.

'*But you are no ordinary governess.*'

His voice came back to her.

Her pulse quickened. She put her hand to her throat. She could feel it there, fluttering.

Earlier that evening, she had told Rosabel the latest instalment of The Butterfly Fables. She had not expected to see Sir Dominic, but she had come in to find him seated in his now-usual place at the other side of Rosabel's bed.

'Dinner is at eight,' he'd said to her in an undertone, after she had tucked Rosabel under the covers. 'If you are still willing to accept my invitation.'

Her stomach had fluttered then, too, in anticipation. It was probably just hunger, she had remonstrated with herself, for she was used to eating much earlier than eight o'clock. She'd nodded quickly in reply, without Rosabel noticing.

With a slight incline of his head, Sir Dominic had disappeared from the nursery.

Now she hurried over to the wardrobe and flung open its wooden doors. Inside hung a distinctly meagre array of clothing. The grey and brown dresses, her drab grey dressing gown, and the green dress that she brought with her, never imagining that she might wear it in the grand dining room of Pendragon Hall.

She took the dress from the wardrobe and laid it on the bed. The fabric shimmered in the sunset glow from the window. It was so green it was as if it were alive itself. This satin was thick and had impressions of leaves from certain angles or lights. She slipped it from the hanger and held it up against her in front of the mirror.

She sighed. How she wished it was in the latest style. Perhaps she might put in some panels, one day. She had no shawl to wear over the dress, except for the serviceable cream knitted one. It would have to do. It was a soft lambswool and, even if it didn't go with the dress exactly, it would keep her warm.

She moved to the dressing table. It displayed a scattering of her few possessions, a vase full of bluebells and her hairbrush. Now, though, the fountain pen lay in pride of place on the polished surface.

She reached out her finger and glided it over the pen. It was almost too beautiful to use, but it meant so much that he had given it to her. He believed in the power of her stories. He believed in her.

She picked it up and revelled in its smooth weight. The point was sharp, but not too sharp, and it wrote so effortlessly, the ink flowing thick and smooth. She'd known it the first time she'd set it to paper, as she'd signed her name under her employer's keen gaze.

No, Martha's name.

The sharp nib of the pen nicked her finger. Quickly she laid it carefully back on the dressing table. In place of the indigo ink she'd used up last night, a drop of red beaded upon the pen's tip. She was at Pendragon Hall under false pretences. But she would set aside all her concerns tonight.

About everything.

'You pretend to be a moth...but I think you may be a butterfly.'

Had he really said that to her?

She stared at herself in the glass.

He meant it. Every instinct told her he was telling the truth.

Her entire body seemed to tingle. It had been numb for so long. She had answered yes to his invitation, before she had asked herself whether it was wise.

She peered closer at her face in the mirror, at her pink

cheeks. They had admitted an attraction to each other, she thought to herself, vexed, but she was behaving as if she were being courted. She rubbed at her cheeks, but that only made them pinker.

She'd fought against her romantic notions.

It had become infatuation.

She had fought against infatuation.

It had become so much more.

Now that she knew she had developed such a flurry of feelings for him, was it sensible to dine with him?

It was not. She knew it. Such powerful feelings were exactly the kind sensible governesses ought to avoid, especially for a man such as Dominic Jago.

Yet she felt it, deep within her; the current growing stronger and stronger, pulling her towards him. It could not be denied. She would cherish this moment of feeling so alive. Since her last position as governess, she had been only half-existing. She would not deny the flourishing force within her now, or pretend it wasn't there.

Maud took a deep breath.

She frowned as she surveyed what lay in front of her on the dressing table. She had no jewels. None to wear around her neck, or on her wrists or fingers. Jewels were not for governesses. Yet she still wanted to add something more to her attire.

An idea came to her. Casting aside the dress, she seized her wrap and hurried out into the garden before it became too dark. The woods were not far. She was sure she would find what she was looking for.

Maud stood outside the great wooden doors that led to the dining room of Pendragon Hall. It seemed strange never to have entered a room when she had lived in the house for months, but the occasion had never arisen. She had her meals upstairs or with Rosabel, or occasionally, if she was asked especially, she ate in the servants' hall below stairs, but she was always careful never to overstep her welcome or lower herself in the staff's estimation. They would be shocked if she became too 'familiar'. She knew the unwritten rules.

She was breaking the rules now.

She smoothed the bodice of her green dress. The décolletage dipped lower than her usual grey dress.

Suddenly she felt uneasy. Was she being too impulsive? Having dinner with the master of the house was unheard of for a servant or a governess. She still couldn't believe that he had invited her in such a manner, as if he truly wanted to get to know her.

Taking another deep breath, she put her hand on the round doorknob. The brass was cool and smooth. The door swung open as if a butler had been waiting on the other side. She gasped. It was not the butler holding the door most courteously open for her, his white gloves ushering her in. Instead Dominic stood in front of her.

'I dismissed the servants for tonight,' he said quietly. 'I have arranged for a private supper, if that is acceptable to you.'

She nodded her consent. It had worried her. She wasn't sure if she'd have been able to be at ease with all eyes upon her.

But he'd thought of that.

'I expect we've already caused a great deal discussion below stairs,' she said. Netta and the other servants had been giving her curious glances for weeks. They all knew she spent some of her evenings reading in the library, with Sir Dominic present, but no one had asked any questions.

'I expect so, too,' he replied. 'But that is not our concern. Is it?'

She shook her head.

He bowed slightly and she stepped into the room, her legs not entirely steady. She lifted her head to examine the room. She could not meet the gaze of her host quite yet. He evidently felt no such inhibition. As she took in the elegance, the unexpected formality and the quite intimidating size of the room, a part of her burned with the touch of his gaze upon her.

It was panelled in part with dark wood, like the library, with granite walls and mullioned windows. At one end of the room there was a fire lit—there was often a chill in the air, even in springtime, in Cornwall.

Tiny goose pimples crept over her arms. He was still looking at her, silent and intense.

She drew a breath and turned to face him.

She focused on his clothing. Yes, that was the safer option. He, too, was formally attired, wearing his tailed dinner jacket with the crisp white shirt and the black tie, dressed as formally as when he had gone to dinner at Trevose Hall, with Averill Trevose. The notion suffused her like April sunshine. Her goose pimples disappeared. He had dressed that way for *her*.

It made her glad that she had worn her green dress, even if it didn't have hoops. She touched the oak leaves in her hair. She had bound them into her usual chignon.

'I see you have made use of your knowledge of botany.' He smiled. 'You look like a wood nymph, Miss Wilmot.'

She touched them again lightly. Perhaps it was ridiculous, to have put leaves in her hair, but she didn't have anything else.

His smile vanished as a darker expression came into his eyes. 'The effect is charming, if I may say so.'

'Thank you,' she said, after a moment. 'I hope you do not mind. They belong to you, after all.'

'The woods are at your disposal,' he said quietly. 'Day and night.'

Again, that current wavered between them.

'Allow me.' He moved aside and indicated the long dining table. The tablecloth was snowy white. The candles in their silver holders glowed.

Two places had been set at one end of the table. That at the head of the table was set before a large carved chair, almost a throne. At its left was another place, evidently awaiting her.

Maud burst out laughing.

Dominic raised an eyebrow. 'What is it?'

'The table,' she said. 'It's so long. It must seat more than twenty people. I'm sorry. It just looked rather funny to have only two people sitting at that long table. And that chair.' She pointed to the head of the table. 'I believe you've misplaced your crown.'

To her relief, he chuckled. She'd been worried for a moment he might have taken offence.

He rubbed his head. 'The crown gives me a headache.'

The smile that flashed between them seemed a living, growing thing.

Her glance skittered away. It was too much, too real, this ease, this sense of shared pleasure, between them. Surely she was deluding herself.

'One thing we do not lack here at Pendragon Hall is

space,' he continued in a more normal tone, as if sensing her discomfort.

'Perhaps the table will be full again one day,' Maud said.

'That would make me the father of twenty children, Miss Wilmot. I think that is a few too many, even if they have an excellent governess.'

He crossed to the end of the table. The fire, lit near that portion of the table, outlined him in flickering light.

'Allow me, if you please.' He drew out the chair for her. She had to move entirely too close to him as she slipped into her seat. All senses dimmed to the awareness of his tall form behind her, his gaze upon her, his sheer physical proximity. She sat down as if in a dream and then spent a tense ten seconds adjusting her shawl to rest at her elbows rather than upon her shoulders. Anything to wrench her attention away from utter absorption in him.

'May I offer you some wine?' He indicated a crystal wine jug with a silver top. 'There is white wine of the German variety for our first course and a rather fine claret to accompany the lamb.'

'Oh!' Maud said, flustered.

'Are you as unused to drinking wine as you are to drinking brandy?'

'I am unused to being served,' she admitted.

His half-smile curved. 'I am quite capable of serving you, Miss Wilmot. I can pour wine, among other things.'

'Yes, of course.' She lifted her wine glass. 'I will have some wine. Thank you.'

He took the glass, his fingers lightly brushing hers, filled it and replaced it on the table.

'What kind of table did you have in your home growing up, Miss Wilmot?' he enquired, after he had filled his own glass and taken a seat. They had begun to eat the Cornish crabmeat terrine.

'Not one this size,' she said. 'It was round and made of oak, with legs that twisted like barley sugar.'

'Is your sister a storyteller like you?'

'No, but she's a governess, as I've mentioned before. She always wanted to be one.'

'Did you?'

The directness of his question startled her.

She shook her head. 'No. But butterfly-chasing does not earn a living. And I cannot be a burden upon my sister. That would be unfair.'

Maud checked herself. 'Do you know the story of *Beauty and the Beast*?' she asked, to change the subject away from Martha.

'Indeed. I have not read the tale to Rosabel, but I am familiar with it, I believe. It is the tale of a young woman who lives in a large house with a beastly gentleman. Was the young lady a governess?'

Maud burst out laughing. 'I don't think so. And you are not to suppose that I imply *you* are a beastly gentleman. But do you know who wrote the story? Or who translated it into English, at any rate?'

As he lifted his wine glass, he shook his head.

'The author was a governess,' Maud told him. 'Or should I say, the translator. Her name was Madame Leprince de Beaumont and she wrote and published educational guides for young ladies. They were called *Moral Tales*. She did not make up the story, I understand. It is an old French tale. But she was the one who made it well known in England.'

'Is that so?'

Maud hesitated. She had become so used to keeping secrets, it was hard to reveal her dreams.

'Madame de Beaumont is a hero of mine,' she said, after a moment. 'I would like to do something similar. I don't expect I'll ever have the opportunity, but if I could I would like to publish tales for children that could be shared among governesses.'

'That is your ambition?' he asked.

She nodded. 'It would be so helpful, you see. If governesses could share materials, it would make it easier for us. In my previous post…' She hesitated. 'I mean, I often had to stay up at night preparing lessons. If we had ready-made resources, they would be very useful indeed.'

'I must say I had never thought of that. It is an admirable idea, Miss Wilmot.'

'I have teaching methods that I think other people might benefit from.' Now she had started to tell him, she couldn't stop. She had never confided her ideas to anyone, not even her sister. 'Other governesses might use my methods, if I could find a way to communicate them. They are ways of teaching that you have seen with Rosabel. I believe all children, even girls, should be outdoors as much as possible in the fresh air. But that doesn't mean that they would not be learning at the same time.'

'I'm learning a great deal just listening to you,' he said.

She flushed. 'I'm talking too much again.'

'Not at all. I invited you to dinner to get to know you, Miss Wilmot. I'm glad to hear about your ambitions.' He laid down his glass. 'I'm pleased you feel you can confide in me.'

After they had served themselves from the large silver

dishes that had been left on the side, he brought up the subject again. 'If you do decide to pursue your dream, perhaps you can bring a proposal to me.'

'To you?'

'As a business venture,' he explained, as he poured her a new glass of wine, a claret to accompany the lamb.

'You would consider backing *me* in my business venture?' she asked.

'Why not?' he asked, amused. 'I presume the publications you mentioned would be sold for money.'

'Yes, I suppose they would.'

'It would take some calculations, but I dare say it would be an excellent investment,' he said. 'Selling stories would probably not in the end work out to be much different from selling train tickets.' He smiled. 'And if you wish I could offer you a good rate to carry your publications from Cornwall to London.'

She laughed aloud. 'You make it sound so easy.'

'Life is easy, once you get started. It is thinking about things that is always difficult and holds us back. Action propels itself.'

'Like a train,' she said.

'Exactly. Like a train.' He looked her in the eye. 'Once it is started, it's difficult to stop.'

Maud took a hasty glass gulp of the red wine.

'Be careful with that,' he said, 'if you're not used to it.'

'I am quite all right.' She thought for a moment. 'You've been kind enough to listen to my ambitions. What of yours, Sir Dominic? For the railway?'

'Ah. Are you sure you want to hear? I know that railway talk is not usually considered appropriate for the dinner table.'

He'd told her that his first wife, Sarah, had been uninterested in the railway.

'You could never bore me,' she said quietly.

The silence that she had begun to appreciate between them hovered over the table.

He took a mouthful of wine. 'Very well. Let me tell you my plans. In the summer, the train becomes very busy, with holidaymakers going to the seaside. Have you ever bathed in the sea, Miss Wilmot?'

She shook her head. The curls she had left out on either side of her head brushed against her cheeks. Normally, she pulled her hair back so severely, but now the light strands danced against her skin. It felt most frivolous.

'Sea-bathing is something to look forward to, if you wish to try it,' he said. 'I would be most pleased to convey you and Rosabel to the seaside.'

The thought of bathing in the sea was even more frivolous than her evening's hairstyle. She had seen, in a magazine, an advertisement for a most daring bathing costume that came only to the knees, with pantaloons underneath it.

'Do you swim?' she asked.

'Indeed. I have done so since childhood. And you?'

She shook her head.

'Then it will be my pleasure,' he said, 'to teach you something.'

Maud took a hasty sip of wine.

'Sea-bathing is a most healthful pastime, I believe,' she said.

The corner of his mouth quirked. 'It is also most enjoyable, Miss Wilmot. And the Cornish coast is spectacular.'

Maud touched her cheeks. She was sure they had flushed. She could not allow herself to dwell on the thought of sea-bathing with Dominic Jago.

'Do your trains run along to the coast?' she asked, making a slight change of subject.

'Not yet,' he replied. 'Currently there are two separate lines. My goal is to make them meet. One day, we will have a straight run to the coast. But that will take considerable investment.' He glanced down the long table. 'Would you like to see the most valuable item we transport from Cornwall to London on the train? It's right here, on the table.'

She glanced down the long snowy tablecloth, mystified.

He showed his half-smile. 'It is in plain sight. Right in front of you.'

'I can't work it out,' she confessed, after staring at all the silver pots and dishes for a time.

'Have you eaten a saffron bun since you have been here?' he queried. 'They are bright yellow in colour.'

She nodded. 'Why, yes. They're delicious.'

'They are also called revel buns,' he told her. 'They have long been used for feast days in Cornwall.'

He leaned forward and lifted a small silver pot from near the salt dish and pepper caster.

Lifting the lid, he slid it over to her. 'Do you know what this is?'

She shook her head.

'It's saffron,' he replied. He lifted out one of the fine, orange-red strands. 'It is the stigma of the crocus flower. It is grown here, in Cornwall. It's a rare spice—the most expensive on the market.'

'I had no idea,' she said. 'Rosabel and I have enjoyed

saffron buns on our picnics out of doors, but I admit, I enjoyed them without enquiring any further.'

The stigma glowed in his hand. 'Saffron can be added to food, or to wine. It's said to increase—pleasure. It's long been used in marriage customs here in Cornwall, for good luck.'

'Oh.' Maud felt herself flush.

He dropped the saffron stigma back into the pot and slid it away.

'There is Cornish cream, too, of course,' he said casually. 'We also take that to London, packed in ice. I believe they are quite partial to it at the palace.'

'The Queen?'

'Possibly.' He grinned. 'You can eat like a queen tonight, too, Miss Wilmot, if you care for some cream with your pudding. I believe we have been left a fine syllabub.'

'I'm not sure I can eat any more,' she confessed.

He looked at her directly. 'Will you join me in the study for another nightcap of brandy?'

Maud nodded. She wanted the evening to last as long as possible. 'I would like that.'

Dominic stood and tossed down his linen napkin. The firelight, now behind him, left his face in shadow. 'Very well. I have something I wish to show you.'

Chapter Sixteen

The souls we loved, that they might tell us
What and where they be.
    —*Alfred, Lord Tennyson:* Maud *(1855)*

Maud sat by the fire in Sir Dominic's study.

The masculine room seemed so familiar to her now. The smoke from the fire, the leather scent of the chairs, the train timetable on the chimney piece and Sir Dominic himself. They had spent other quiet evenings in it, without needing to talk, her reading by the fire, him at the desk, running his fingers through his hair as he worked.

But tonight was different.

He had shrugged off his tailed dinner jacket, leaving only his white shirt with its black jet buttons and the loosened bow tie. He had built up the fire again, kneeling beside the grate himself rather than calling a servant in.

He had done it before, but tonight Maud had not been able to tear her eyes away from the scene. A simple task, deftly completed, the shift of his shoulder blades beneath the fine shirt, the tightening of trousers over his thighs.

Now Maud no longer needed her lambswool shawl. She laid it aside over the edge of the leather chair.

'Thank you,' she said, as he lifted the brandy in an unspoken question. The hot scent of the spirit rose up as Dominic passed it to her. Her eyes lingered upon the fingers extending the glass to her, strong and lightly tanned from his daily rides, yet sensitive.

'Are you regretting declining the syllabub?'

'Not at all.' She laughed. 'But I am curious about the effects of saffron.'

Had she really said that? The wine must have loosened her tongue, or was it just the effect of his presence? She could get drunk on him. No, no, she must rein her unruly thoughts back. Who knew when they, too, might come tripping out?

'Are you indeed?' he murmured.

She looked at him over the edge of her glass.

That invisible connection flared between them again, hotter than the flames of the fire.

'You said you had something to show me,' she said at last, when she could bear it no longer. The intensity was almost overwhelming.

He seemed to hesitate, in a manner unusual for him. 'Ah. Yes.'

He laid down his own brandy glass, untouched. The topaz liquid glowed.

The fire crackled.

He moved over to the desk, loosening his bow tie in what seemed to be a practised gesture. She remembered how the tie had been loose the night he had come and woken her from her nightmare. How long ago that seemed. Yet it had been the beginning of that powerful link between them, that sense of security and safety she had unexpectedly found in his arms.

Now she found herself watching his hands as he rolled back the upper section of the desk, after taking a brass key from a drawer underneath. It made a sound like falling dominoes, tumbling against each other as he rolled it back.

'It's in here,' he said, 'what I have to show you.'

He reached inside the desk. For another long moment he seemed to hesitate. Then he took something out—what it was she could not see—rolled the desktop down again quickly and locked it once more.

Tossing the key aside, he came back to Maud by the fire and sat opposite her.

He drew his leather chair closer to her. Their knees, hers clad in the dark green satin with its imprint of leaves and his in the black trousers of his evening attire, were now only inches apart.

In his hands he held a black felt box about the size of a watch case.

'I found this yesterday,' he said. He paused for a moment. Again, she sensed he hesitated. 'I came across it while sorting some papers. I wanted you to see it.'

'What is it?' she asked. An indefinable jumble of emotions jumbled inside her as she laid down her brandy glass.

'Open it and see.'

His fingers touched hers as she took the box from him. It couldn't be construed as accidental, that contact. It was deliberate, though it lasted only a heartbeat. She had to school herself not to spring away like a startled hare—or let her hand linger in that warmth for ever.

It wasn't covered in felted material, she realised as

she stroked her finger over the surface. It was velvet, thick and black. It was the sort of case used to protect expensive jewellery. She had never held such a thing in her hand.

He noticed her hesitation. 'Is something wrong?'

'It's just I've never held a jewel box before,' she explained. 'Let alone opened one. I've only ever seen them in shop windows.'

'Let me help you.' He leaned in, ran his index finger around the edge of the velvet box and found the tiny gold catch that held it closed. It opened with a click.

Maud gasped. 'It's a Swallowtail.'

He chuckled. 'I thought as much. I hoped you might be able to identify it.'

'I can't believe it,' Maud exclaimed. Nestled in white silk was a delicate hair comb, surmounted by a beautiful butterfly enamelled in creamy yellow and black, with a blue frill at the bottom. At the base, where the wings met, was a touch of red, shaped almost like a heart.

Maud peered closer. 'It's not precisely a Swallowtail, but it's close. Did it belong to Rosabel's mother?'

Dominic shook his head. 'No, it didn't belong to Sarah. It belonged to my mother and to her mother before, I believe.'

He leaned back in his chair. 'When you first started telling the story of Princess Swallowtail and described the butterfly, it enchanted me.'

Maud put her hand to her bodice. 'It did?'

He nodded. 'Indeed. I must confess that I have been most beguiled by your stories and now I realise that it was because it was as if something from my own childhood came to life in the telling of your tale. My mother often wore this butterfly ornament in her hair. I remember seeing it and thinking how beautiful it was when I was young. It seemed to dance and move and fly as she walked along. It captured her character in a way.'

He gave a half-chuckle.

'Now I am being the fanciful one.' He crooked a smile. 'When I came across it yesterday it captured my attention. It reminded me of the happiness I had experienced growing up here as a child. You have brought that kind of happiness here again.'

'Me? I have done so little for Rosabel so far. I have only been here three months.' Or at least *nearly* three months. A little frown wrinkled her brow. Would Sir Dominic allow her to continue now, given this...feeling between them? 'I have only done my duty.'

'You have done a great deal,' he corrected her. 'Rosabel is a different child. Pendragon Hall is a different place.'

Dominic leaned in to lift the butterfly from the box. 'I want you to have it.'

It was as well the leather chair held her up. Her legs certainly wouldn't have.

'You can't give it to me,' she whispered.

'Why not?' he replied lightly. 'I want to show my appreciation for all you have done for Rosabel, but it is more than that. Consider it a token of friendship from the White Admiral.'

She had to smile. Still, she protested. 'Surely it isn't appropriate.'

'What could be more appropriate? As soon as I saw it, it seemed to be made for you.' His mouth curved into a smile. 'Do you not like it?'

'Of course. It is truly exquisite. But you gave me a fountain pen only yesterday.'

'Ah, yes, the fountain pen.' His smile twisted. 'This is not a gift of that nature, Miss Wilmot.'

She held out the box to him. 'I can't accept it. It's too much.'

He held up his hands, flat palms facing her. 'Are you averse to receiving such a gift?'

'I don't know,' she said frankly. 'I have never received such a gift before.'

She stared down at the butterfly. It was exactly the kind of ornament she would have dreamed of owning, if she ever allowed herself such idle dreams. The hair comb was the finest one she had ever seen. In London, in shop windows, she had seen combs made of silver and gold, or coral, or ivory. They were worn to balls, or fine dinners. She had even seen one in the figure of a jewelled bluebird on a fine wire, but she had never seen a butterfly. She'd certainly never held such a jewel in her hand.

'It isn't appropriate,' she repeated, uncertainly.

'I want you to have it,' Dominic said. 'Please. Do not deny me the pleasure of seeing you wear it. Will you at least try it in your hair?'

The sincerity in his eyes was unmistakable.

She couldn't resist. She gave a quick nod.

'Here.' He took the box and laid it on the table.

He reached out his hand and raised her to stand next to him, in front of the mirror that hung over the mantelpiece.

She could smell the woodsmoke on him from the fire he'd built in the grate, mixed with that freshness that clung to him from his rides, and now the scent of brandy.

'May I remove your crown of leaves?' he murmured. 'Not that I do not admire it.'

In assent she lowered her head.

His touch was gentle, yet there was a firmness to it. He lifted the leaves from her hair, one by one, and laid them on the chimney piece. The leaves had been green and fresh when she had placed them in her hair earlier that evening. Now the edges were curling.

Without speaking he turned and lifted the jewelled butterfly from its box. She watched him in the mirror.

He turned back. His dark eyes were now opaque.

She bent her head further towards him.

She felt the touch of his hand on her neck, just below her chignon. Then it glided up, pausing as he deliberated, before he slid the comb into her hair, near the top. A tiny shiver ran through her as it went in. He halted, momentarily, then pushed it a little further. Then he took his hand away.

'Look,' he said.

She raised her head, angling it from one side, then the other. She gasped aloud.

The green dress with its imprint of leaves had always been a favourite of hers. She knew it made her look different, better than she did in her normal grey attire.

But the butterfly hair comb…

It sat high in her hair, glistening as if it were alive, as if it were real. It brought out the dark red depths of her hair, contrasting with the colour of her eyes. Surely her cheeks were not so pink, her lips so red, her eyes so luminous?

She had never looked like this before.

She caught his reflected gaze as it rested upon the comb in her hair, then travelled down, over her face, to rest on her lips.

She saw her own lips open, like a flower to the sun.

He didn't move.

They were close, closer than they had been the night before in the woods, when she had realised the full force of her feelings for him.

She'd stopped then, stood apart from him.

But tonight, she would not.

Maud turned and lifted her mouth to his.

She felt his body pause, jerk, as he went to pull away.

But their lips had already touched.

Now she turned her body completely, lifting her arms to twine around his neck.

With a groan he pulled her to him, his mouth hard on hers.

She opened her lips, throwing back her head to drink him in. The taste of him, the brandy on his tongue and hers, the heat of his body beneath the white shirt, pressed against her satin dress.

He reached for her hair, curling strands of it around his fingers as he continued to search her mouth with his, in a wild, passionate discovery. She searched, too, for the truth of him, in that kiss, in that connection, that had flared between them for so long now.

Then, with a groan, he pulled away.

He ran a hand through his hair. 'I didn't intend that to happen.'

She drew in a shuddering breath. She could taste him still. Her whole being cried out for more. But would he give it?

'It wasn't your fault.' Her voice did not seem her own. It seemed to come from far away.

She hadn't known it was inside her, that passion. It was *still* there now, crying out for his touch, his taste. She had thought it had been taken away, that it had been destroyed, by what had happened to her.

It had not. Not with him.

He moved away to the window and stared out into the darkness. She studied his back, the set of his shoulders, the angle of his head. What was he feeling? What was he thinking? That she had thrown herself at him, wantonly, with utter inappropriateness for the governess of his child? That he would like to kiss her again?

When he turned back, he shook his head. Her stomach lurched.

'This wasn't what I intended when I asked you to dinner. Nor when I gave you the hair comb. I must ask you to believe that.'

She touched the comb in her hair with unsteady fingers.

'You have captivated me,' he said, low. 'I have never had such feelings, even for Rosabel's mother. This is so entirely unexpected.'

'It is for me, too,' Maud managed to reply.

'Then you…'

'Yes,' she said. 'Yes.'

He reached out and cupped her face in his hand. His fingers were warm and strong.

He groaned. 'This isn't possible.'

'Because I'm a governess?'

'Because I didn't know such sensations existed.' He brushed a finger over her lips. 'I want to explore what this is. I want to explore you. Can you believe that? Do you believe that?'

'Yes, Sir Dominic.'

He gave her the half-smile that dented his cheek. But there was a light in his eyes, an expression she could not read. 'You cannot continue to call me that. Not any more. Call me Dominic. Unless you want to call me by my other name.'

'Your other name?'

'In some nurseries I am known as "The White Admiral",' he said.

She laughed aloud.

'Dominic.' She tasted the name on her lips. 'I prefer that, I think. Dominic.'

'And by what name ought I to call you?'

She turned still, then drew back, out of his grasp.

'What do you mean?' Her voice was a fearful wisp.

'I cannot call you Princess Swallowtail,' he said as he, too, stepped back. 'Unless that is your wish, of course.'

She tried to laugh again, but this time it came out high and hollow.

Dominic moved closer. She looked so beautiful, just then, with the jewelled butterfly perched in her coppery hair. It suited her to perfection, even more than he had imagined. He felt as if he were near a winged creature that he had to ensure he did not startle, or it would fly away.

Now she was staring at him.

'Well?' he asked softly.

She backed away.

Fear had come into her eyes, as if she were trapped. As if he might cause her harm, catch her in a net and seal her in glass.

'I'm sorry,' she gasped. 'I can't accept this!'

She tugged the butterfly comb from her hair, so strongly that the chignon collapsed. Her hair tumbled about her shoulders.

She held it out, trembling.

'Please. Take it! It isn't right that you've given it to me. I—I don't deserve it.'

'Keep it.' He raised his palms flat. 'I want you to have it. It's yours.'

'No. I—I can't!'

She released it from her grip.

The butterfly hair comb almost flew to the floor, but he caught it, just in time, as speedily as he had caught the butterfly in the woods.

But in doing so, he had taken his eyes from Miss Wilmot.

He heard the door slam.

When he looked up, she had vanished from the room.

He stared down at the hair comb.

His brandy glass was nearby. With his other hand he picked it up. Drained it.

Finding the butterfly hair comb had seemed to be some kind of strange sign.

He didn't want to catch her in a net. He wanted her to come to him, to alight upon his outstretched hand. He truly was becoming fanciful now.

He stared at the ceiling, its ancient beams, the pale plaster.

That kiss.

He hadn't planned on it. He would never have stepped over the bounds of propriety, lured her into his study for such a purpose. Yet when she had turned to him, reached for him, he'd been unable to fight the urge to take her in his arms. He had barely managed to hold back from seeking more when she'd kissed him, her full lips warm and soft.

Dominic unclenched his fist.

He dropped the jewelled butterfly from his hand.

Chapter Seventeen

O young lord-lover,
what sighs are those?
                    —Alfred, Lord Tennyson: Maud (1855)

'Miss Wilmot! Miss Wilmot! You almost let the butterflies out of the vivarium!'

'Oh!' Maud exclaimed.

With a slam she closed the glass door.

'They would have escaped,' Rosabel said, reproachfully. Her ringlets bobbed. 'And they have only just hatched!'

'Oh, dear.' Maud bent down and peered through the glass into the vivarium. The ferns they had collected had grown bigger, more delicate and beautiful, and most of the white chrysalises were open now. The newly emerged butterflies were still fluttering among the plants; the small and large coppers, the blues, the fritillaries with their multicolours.

'Are you feeling all right, Miss Wilmot?' Netta asked, from where she was seated by the window, mending one of Rosabel's white ruffled pinafores.

'Yes. Yes, of course,' Maud replied, flustered. 'I'm perfectly all right. Thank you. I'm just a little tired.'

Netta gave her a friendly, knowing look that told Maud it was all over the servants' hall, as Maud had expected, that she had had dinner alone with Lord Jago in the grand dining room.

Maud flushed and put her hands to her cheeks.

Did they know that Sir Dominic Jago had kissed the governess?

Or, more accurately, that the governess had kissed Sir Dominic?

She put her hand to her lips. She had been able to think of little else, other than the sensation of Dominic's mouth on hers. That searching, seeking pressure, as if he wanted to know everything about her. She had met his kiss with that same urgent, seeking desire.

All night, it had not abated.

Certainly, she was not doing justice to her employment as governess this morning. It wasn't fair to Rosabel that her teacher was so distracted.

She needed to be alone.

She needed to think.

'Netta, I want to go to the woods and collect some more ferns for the vivarium,' she said, after a moment. 'Would you mind looking after Rosabel for a little while?'

'Not at all, Miss Wilmot,' Netta replied promptly.

'May I come with you, Miss Wilmot?' Rosabel asked.

'You come along to the kitchen with me,' Netta said to Rosabel, with a quick pat of her ringlets, before Maud could reply. 'I think Cook is baking this morning. She'll need your help with the saffron buns.'

Immediately Rosabel jumped down from her chair. 'Are they going to have currants in them?'

'I believe so, Miss Rosabel. And she is making lemon tarts, I think.'

'Perhaps we can go for a picnic, Rosabel, when I return,' Maud said.

Rosabel jumped up and down. 'A picnic? Can Polly and Papa come, too?'

Maud bit her lip. 'If he wishes.'

'Can we make some plum tarts for the picnic?' Rosabel asked Netta.

'It might have to be lemon tarts, not plum tarts, miss. The greengages and damsons aren't ripe yet in the orchard. Got to wait for the summertime for those.'

'We're going to the seaside in the summer,' Rosabel confided to Netta, as she took the nursemaid's outstretched hand. 'Papa is building a train line and Miss Wilmot is going to take me bathing in the sea.'

'Is that right, Miss Rosabel?'

Netta gave Maud a wink as she went out the nursery door. 'You take your time, Miss Wilmot. You've had a busy few days.'

As Rosabel left the nursery, hand in hand with Netta, Maud let out a sigh of relief.

She had barely been able to concentrate all morning. It went entirely against the grain to neglect her duties as a governess, but she hadn't slept a wink the night before. She'd tossed and turned, unable to sleep, until dawn had come. With her lambswool shawl wrapped over her nightgown, she'd watched the sun rise, golden and full, over the treetops of the green woods beyond. Then she had washed and dressed, aware all the while of every part of her body still yearning for the kiss they had shared. She had never imagined her entire body would flare into life, as if she were emerging from a chrysalis herself. That part of her that had been bruised and numb for so long had been awoken.

She stared at the butterflies, fluttering in the vivarium.

She hurried to her bedroom and seized her bonnet and butterfly net.

She would walk in Pendragon Woods until she knew what to do.

Surely, in that sanctuary, an answer would come.

Dominic stood at his study window. He felt like a sentry at a gate post, waiting for Miss Wilmot to come out of the woods.

All morning he had watched for a sighting of her. The sun was bright, but there were clouds in the sky. She often took Rosabel out in the morning, he knew, but he hadn't wanted to lie in wait for them on the lawn, nor had he thought it appropriate to go up to the nursery.

But this morning, Miss Wilmot and Rosabel hadn't gone butterfly-chasing or fern-hunting together. It had been much later that Miss Wilmot had appeared and hastened alone to the woods, and disappeared.

Dominic fought down his urge to follow her yet again. He loathed the idea of her feeling pressured by him, but God knew, all he'd wanted was to go after her and take her in his arms again.

He'd paced up and down the floor of the study, keeping the window in sight, awaiting her return. But he'd not seen her, only the copper-coloured butterflies that now he connected with her. He'd seen plenty of them, dancing across the lawn, as if tempting him to follow.

He released a self-mocking laugh. He had been pursued by governesses and now all he wanted was to go in pursuit of one himself.

He would not, could not. Every fibre of his body wanted to hold her again, but every fibre of his mind instructed him to wait.

To let her come to him, if she did.

It was the only way.

He swore under his breath. Waiting never had been his strong suit. He would rather build a train line than wait for a train.

He'd vowed to himself that there would be no impropriety between them. He was keenly aware of the power imbalance between him, the master of the house, and the governess. He'd intended to make it clear to her that he wanted them to begin a relationship, one where they could be on equal ground. That was why he'd invited her to dine.

He'd been unprepared for what it had led to.

His energy coiled inside him as he paced faster.

Now she might think he meant to entrap her by his invitation. That he was a hypocrite who declared he was weary of governesses with romantic ideas, but then made advances upon her. That he was a master of the house who used his position against a governess in his employ. That he was a man entirely without honour.

He rubbed his jaw. He was still unshaven. He'd barely slept. That kiss was enough to keep a man awake for nights on end. He had known intimacy with his first wife—of course he had—but that kiss with Miss Wilmot had been the most revealing encounter of his life.

He knew now that the emotions he'd had as a younger man falling in love with Rosabel's mother were a mere shadow of the real experience. He'd heard, of course, and witnessed men who fell in love and cast all propriety to the four winds. But he had never expected it to happen to him—and not with a governess.

Then Miss Wilmot had arrived, with her chin high and her practical manner which he now knew disguised her romantic nature. Her fairy tales were full of longing, full of dreams and desires for a different kind of reality. She was not made to be a governess. She was a true artist, a storyteller of the greatest enchantment. He smiled wryly.

He'd warned her off. Told her not to develop any romantic notions about him. He knew now that his aversion to any idea of remarriage had been to do with his own regrets. Then he, the confirmed widower, had been hit by the proverbial lightning bolt of which he'd always been so dubious. Could a man fall in love in such a way? It had never happened to him, even with Sarah, God rest her. That had been a mere youthful romance, whereas this was so much more.

He was ready to move on.

To discover what that kiss could become.

In the woods, it had felt as if they touched, so vibrant was the attraction between them. But when they had kissed last night, it was as if they had communicated themselves, each to the other, through the touch of their lips. It was a sense of having met her, reached her and of her having reached him in a way no woman ever had before.

It was a revelation.

She had been badly hurt. She had not told him the facts, nor had he pressured her to do so. The expression in those deep green pools of her eyes had been enough.

He clenched his fists in his pockets. The idea that something—someone—had hurt her, or caused her pain, was intolerable.

He moved to his desk. Drummed his fingers. Perhaps work would take his mind off her, while he waited.

He pulled open a drawer and winced.

There was the black box that held the butterfly hair jewel.

He slammed it shut, opened another and winced again. In it he had kept all the correspondence regarding employment of a new governess.

Pulling out the file, he proceeded to leaf through the papers. A pile began to amass upon the green leather desk. By God, he really ought not to let his correspondence build up so. Perhaps he should employ a clerk. As he went, he dropped letters in the wicker wastepaper basket from governesses who had been unsuccessful in their applications and governesses who had been and gone. Yes, indeed, how he wished he'd chosen Miss Wilmot first—for so many reasons.

There had been a break in the communication early on. He had put out the call for applicants and had received numerous letters from governesses, most sent to him directly. In one or two cases, the governesses had been represented by agencies, intermediaries who had provided introductions and letters of reference, but Miss Martha Wilmot had provided her own handwritten letter of introduction. It was after he had made those disastrous decisions to employ other governesses that he had turned back to his pool of applicants and chosen Miss Wilmot and renewed their contact.

He picked up the letter to read it again and frowned.

He ran his fingers through his hair. He realised now

what it was about the letter that had arrived from her sister that had bothered him so much. It had been out of proportion. But it had nudged a memory in his brain, one he could not at first grasp. He was not entirely sure he had grasped it now.

He laid down the piece of paper on the leather desk-top and leaned back in his chair.

Then he wrenched open another drawer and rummaged inside until he came to it, the piece of paper that Miss Wilmot had signed with her new fountain pen.

Dominic swore.

He'd watched her curve those letters, sign that name.

There could be no mistake.

He stared at the slip of paper, unseeing.

Handwriting can alter, he told himself. Why, the pen he had given her probably ran across the paper with quite a different motion than whatever she had used to write with all those months ago. Which was perhaps why he had even bothered to note the odd discrepancy in her handwriting.

For a moment, he wanted to tear it into pieces. To crush it in his fist and throw it into the fire, to not look any closer.

It crumpled in his hand. It became a ball. He looked at the fire, the coals now mere embers, and took aim.

Then, before he knew what he was at, his hand was lowered and engaged in un-crinkling the paper to compare it to the letter.

All handwriting had a slant to it. This handwriting on the letter leaned a little to the right. It was rounded, copperplate, but rather cramped.

One thing was certain.

It was not written by the hand of his current governess.

His fist clenched as he again took up the handwriting sample that he had asked from her. He had witnessed her reluctance to form the letters of her first name. Now he knew why. It was patently clear.

She was not Miss Martha Wilmot.

He stared down at the papers spread over the desktop. He studied her signature again, held it to the lamplight to examine it more closely, as if it were a counterfeit banknote.

Miss Wilmot was not the original applicant for the post of governess to Rosabel. That woman's handwriting was completely different. Her signature was small and decorous. That of the governess upstairs, however, was curved, generous, even slightly flamboyant, with a touch of the artistic. The W looked practised: it almost seemed like wings. The handwriting fitted the woman he had come to know. She was an artistic being, a story-teller. And he knew it was her own hand. He'd watched her curve those letters himself, with the new pen she had obviously liked so much. Her innocent gratitude had been touching.

The chair scraped as he pushed it back, dropped the papers down on the desk.

Anger flamed in his gut. She'd lied to him. Deceived him. He strode to the window, but she did not appear.

He swore beneath his breath. Who in damnation was she? Why had she come to him? How had she managed to use the other Miss Martha Wilmot's name without the first Miss Wilmot appearing on his doorstep?

He exhaled in a half-laugh, half-choke.

She was a complete mystery.

She was a complete impostor.

Miss Martha Wilmot.

But that was not her name at all.

He went back and sat at his desk, studied again the papers that lay there, with those two sets of differing handwriting. He wanted to see something different, but no. There could be no mistake.

The two papers lay there—proving beyond a shadow of a doubt that the woman he had held in his arms the night before was not who she pretended to be.

It hit him like a horse-kick in his stomach. He considered himself a good judge of character and he didn't like the feeling that he had been duped.

It made no sense. She did not seem to be the kind of woman who would choose to be deceptive. He had tasted truth on her lips.

She was of good character. He *knew* it to be so. It had made no sense that she had come to Pendragon Hall, based on a lie. Her warm, beautiful nature, beneath the calm and proper exterior. Her bravery and willingness to stand up for what was right, beneath the nervousness.

A knock came at the door.

'Enter.'

'Good morning, Dominic.'

'Averill.' He bowed. 'I wasn't expecting you.'

She swept into the room, looking enchanting in a blue dress and an elegantly trimmed bonnet. It looked as though it had come straight from Paris, and, knowing Averill, it probably had.

'It's such a lovely day,' she said. 'Won't you come for a walk with me?'

'I'm surprised you have the time,' he said, managing to be civil, even though the last thing he wanted, just then, was to entertain a visitor. 'I thought you have guests at Trevose Hall.'

Averill toyed with the ribbons of her bonnet. 'They have other pursuits this morning. In fact, some of them are out walking—in your woods, I believe, Dominic. You know you've always said neighbours could access them and they do border my lands, of course. It's another thing we share.'

Dominic hesitated. The woods. In his mind he could see Miss Wilmot there, among the trees. Her sanctuary, she had called it.

Averill tucked her gloved hand into his arm. 'Don't dream of saying no, Dominic. You work far too hard. Fresh air will do you good.'

'Have you taken up nature walks now, Averill?' he asked drily.

'I have a fancy for one today,' she said. 'I have a feeling we might chance upon something of interest to you.'

'Is that so?' He smiled briefly at her. She'd presumed too much from their friendship, but she'd gone to the trouble of arranging possible investors from London.

'Very well,' he said. 'A walk would be most pleasant.'

Perhaps it would be the best way to spend the time, as he waited for Miss Wilmot. The situation could not go on. As soon as she returned, he would have to tell her what he knew.

She had to tell him.
The bluebells were still out in force and their fragrance was heady as Maud followed the path through the woods. Butterflies played above the blooms, but for the first time in her life Maud did not stop to look at them, even though she had come out with her butterfly net.

She had to tell him the truth.

The opportunity had been there, the night before. She knew it. But she had pulled back.

She could not allow herself to be held in his arms, to be entwined in his embrace, without being honest with him. There was now a chill in the air. She wished she had brought her shawl.

As she walked the now-familiar path, it became clearer and clearer.

She had to tell Dominic.

Dominic.

The name stopped her in her tracks.

When had he become Dominic, not Sir Dominic, in her mind?

He had told her to use his first name.

She creased her forehead. When he'd asked to use her name, it had almost seemed as if he already knew that she was not Martha. But that was impossible. She pushed the idea away.

There could be no delay. She had to reveal her real identity, that she had disobeyed the instructions he had given her at the start.

But that was not all.

It came in an overwhelming rush.

In her months at Pendragon Hall, in her time spent with him, near him, close to him, she had developed much, much more than romantic notions.

It was more than infatuation.

She knew it then, with every part of her being. She had fallen in love with Sir Dominic Jago the moment she saw him in a swirl of steam on the railway station platform.

She no longer cared if he was master and she was governess. She did not care if he was a railway magnate or a railway worker. She loved him. She loved Sir Dominic Jago.

It was a force of nature, surging through her. Her heart was now pounding so loudly in her chest it threatened to leap out.

He had brought her to life again.

A cuckoo called overhead. Spring was ending; summer would soon come.

How could she tell him anything without revealing what had happened to her in her previous post?

She couldn't bear to think about it, let alone speak the awful words.

How could she trust anyone, with that terrible tale?

'I want you to trust me,' he'd said to her.

The safety and security she had experienced in his arms, the connection of his touch, the taste of his mouth on hers…

Surely that could be trusted.

She froze.

Footsteps came on the path behind her.

It was not Dominic. She knew his tread. These footsteps were heavier on the leaves and she could hear deep breathing.

She picked up her skirts and started to run.

A branch caught at her hair as she thrust her way through the bushes.

Something caught at her leg. She stumbled, almost fell.

The footsteps came, heavy near her, and the sound of a laugh.

She could not outrun him.

Maud raised the butterfly net and spun around.

Chapter Eighteen

Mix not memory with doubt;
—*Alfred, Lord Tennyson:* Maud *(1855)*

'Well, well.' Lord Melville bowed. 'If it isn't Miss Wilmot. When Averill told me about the charming governess who told fairy tales with such imagination, I guessed it must be you.'

He stood in front of her, blocking the path back to Pendragon Hall and safety. Perfectly attired, he was dressed in a black top hat and black riding coat, with a pair of white jodhpurs and boots. His cravat was red. His light-coloured hair was smooth, his eyes a pale blue. In his gloved hand he held a horsewhip.

A wave of nausea swept her, dizzying, utterly debilitating. She was planted in the woodland path, like a tree buffeted by breeze. She couldn't move her legs.

She stared up at him. It was the weight of his body, the way she had been crushed beneath him, that she remembered most of all. That weight was what came back to suffocate her in the night terrors she experienced, those that Dominic had finally pulled her out from under, as if releasing her from beneath a stone.

But now that weight threatened to crush her again. His stare, his physical presence, was all it took. She couldn't move. It was as if she had become Princess Swallowtail, trapped in the strands of the spider's web. She wanted to run away, yet that dreadful feeling, numbing her limbs, silencing her voice, held her in terrible captivity.

'How delightful to see you again.' Holding the whip in one hand now, with the other he caressed its tip. 'Still chasing butterflies, I see.'

Maud gripped the butterfly net tighter.

'You're just the same,' Lord Melville said. 'But I must say I prefer the recollection of how you looked when I last saw you.'

Again, Maud tried to speak, tried to move. Still, she stayed frozen. Her legs would not obey her.

'You left my employ so hastily,' he drawled. 'It quite caught me by surprise. We'd only just begun to get to know each other. There are so many lessons you needed to learn. A governess's place isn't only in the schoolroom. Sometimes she needs to be governed elsewhere.'

Bile rose in Maud's throat. 'You're disgusting.'

He smiled without it reaching his eyes.

'Get away from me,' she whispered. Her voice seemed choked in her throat.

'Now, now. Is that any way to greet an old friend?'

'We're not friends.'

'But we became very close before you left. How sorry I was when you departed like a thief in the night.'

'I am no thief. You spread rumours about me that weren't true.' The accusation still stung. 'You said I had stolen from you.'

He shrugged. 'But you did steal something from me, my dear. You stole my pleasure.'

Maud shuddered.

'I had anticipated us spending many more nights together. Once I'd found the way to your bedroom, I had planned to visit you there nightly. I told you so. You must recall.'

Maud clenched her fingers together around the net handle. Oh, yes, she remembered. The attic bedroom had been small enough to begin with. With Lord Melville in the room it had become stifling. Her lungs constricted as the recollection came. She felt ready to choke.

'You're...you're a monster.'

He tutted. 'Now, now. That's not pleasant talk, is it? Hardly befitting a governess.'

He moved another step closer, his boots crushing the leaves. 'I don't want you telling tales about me. Especially since you have such a talent for stories.'

Maud leapt back and raised the butterfly net, like a weapon. 'Stay away!'

He laughed. 'What are you going to do with that net, my dear? Catch me?'

Fast footsteps and a voice came from behind her. 'What in damnation is going on here?'

Dominic slid to a stop as he took in the scene on the woodland path in front of him. Miss Wilmot was backed against a tree stump, her butterfly net raised.

A tall, sleek man dressed in hunting attire stood nearby. He gave a low bow. 'No need for alarm, old chap.'

'No?' Dominic asked shortly. 'I'll be the judge of that.'

In two strides he was beside Miss Wilmot. 'Are you all right?'

She lowered the butterfly net, but that was all. Her eyes were huge in her face. When he moved a step closer, she shrank away from him.

Dominic fell back, his hands clenched. What were they doing? Had he interrupted some kind of assignation? The instant the idea came into his mind he dismissed it. There was too much tension in the air; he could sense it.

Averill swept up beside him. She had been beside him on the woodland path, chatting of inconsequential and amusing matters. Now she glided forward. 'Allow me to make introductions. You know Lord Melville, don't you, Dominic? He is one of my guests at Trevose Hall. He is interested in the Cornish railway.'

Lord Melville bowed. 'Sir Dominic. We haven't met before, but we are members of the same club in London, I believe.'

'Indeed,' said Dominic, adding nothing more. The last thing he wanted just then was to engage in introductions. He'd seen Melville several times at the club, always at the gaming table. Melville was not a man whom he admired, nor one he would have wanted to meet, let alone consider as an investor in his railway company, but he had no choice other than to acknowledge him, now Averill had brought the man to Cornwall as a guest.

'I was just becoming reacquainted with Miss Wilmot.'

Dominic stared from Miss Wilmot to Lord Melville.

'You know each other?' he asked, mystified.

'We've most certainly met before,' Melville replied. 'We are very well acquainted.'

Dominic narrowed his eyes. There was something deeply repellent about the man, in spite of his courteous manner. 'How so?'

Melville smiled. 'Miss Wilmot was in my employ for some time as a governess, among other things.'

Dominic turned to Miss Wilmot. 'Is that true?'

Wordless and white-faced, she gave a nod.

'I don't remember Lord Melville's name from your character references,' he said to her, unable to keep the edge from his voice.

'Ah.' Lord Melville shook his head. 'I'm sorry to say that doesn't surprise me, Jago.'

Dominic looked to Miss Wilmot, but the leaf-green eyes were cast down.

'She's been lying to you all along!' Averill broke in, triumphantly.

The butterfly net slipped from Maud's fingers. She stared down at it as it lay on the ground.

She couldn't raise her head. She couldn't face him.

His voice came, low and penetrating. 'What is your name?'

'I never wanted to lie to you,' she whispered, still staring at the empty net. It was all she could manage to say. Her whole body was still numb, frozen. Her voice came out a dry croak.

Trembling, she looked up.

The expression on his face. She'd expected it to be as hard as the granite stone of Pendragon Hall. Instead, she saw the flash of comprehension in his eyes. 'You knew.'

He nodded. 'I discovered it today. Your handwriting did not match the first letter of application. Tell me. Are you Miss Wilmot?'

'Yes,' she whispered. 'No.'

'You'll never get a straight answer from her, Dominic!' With a swirl of her skirt, Averill Trevose moved between them. 'That's what I'm trying to tell you!'

'My name is Maud.' She could barely utter her own name. 'My name is Maud Wilmot.'

He exhaled. 'Ah.'

'Martha is my sister's name,' she faltered. 'She is, was, a governess, too. She's married now.'

Dominic stepped around Averill. 'I'm beginning to understand. When I sent Martha Wilmot a fare to come here to Cornwall…'

'I used the ticket.'

'You used your sister's name to gain employment.'

She couldn't bear to look at him. The shame of it. The betrayal. She bowed her head again, as if an axe was about to fall. 'Yes.'

'I've never heard of a governess being so deceitful.' Averill's lips pursed. 'She's not fit to be around children. I knew there was something about her, all along. I warned you, Dominic!'

'That is fraud,' Lord Melville commented. 'A potentially criminal offence.'

'I didn't think of that. Not at the time. And you mustn't blame Martha,' Maud added quickly, looking up at Dominic, almost pleading. 'It was all my idea.'

Dominic's dark eyebrows were still drawn together. 'Do you mean you used your sister's references to ensure you gained the post here at Pendragon Hall?'

She couldn't deny it, but it sounded so much more dreadful now.

A muscle moved in his jaw. 'I employed you as Rosabel's governess based upon the excellence of your character, extolled by your references. You must realise what a predicament that puts me in, now I discover that they were not your own.'

'I needed employment. My only skill is as a governess. I was desperate.' She choked as she tried to explain, but she knew her excuses sounded weak.

Leaves rustled as he moved closer. 'You could have come to me. Trusted me. Surely you realised that. You had more than one chance to do so.'

How she wished she had taken the opportunity!

'And what, pray, of your moral example?' Averill put in, with a toss of her ringlets. 'A governess must be above reproach. Especially looking after our *dear* Rosabel.'

Lord Melville cleared his throat. 'Being above reproach cannot be said of this governess, I'm afraid. I'm not surprised to hear she has no character references of her own, not after her dismissal from her previous employment with my family. No, indeed.'

Maud's heart sank. She pressed her back against the tree trunk for support as tears stung her eyelids.

She mustn't cry.

She hadn't before.

She wouldn't now.

With all the power in her, she blinked them back.

Lord Melville moved forward. Instinctively Maud slid further away from him. She wanted to run, to flee, to hide. The nightmarish sense of suffocation threatened to overwhelm her again.

'Allow me to explain, Jago,' he said smoothly. 'Miss Wilmot accompanied the boys when they came to stay at my home. She often invited me to listen to her tales in the evenings. I had no idea what she was scheming. Soon enough she became all too…' he paused '…familiar.'

Maud shuddered. Lord Melville was twisting it all

around, but she still couldn't bring herself to speak of what had really happened. The very thought of it made her feel ill.

'That's a lie.' It was all she could say, but her voice came out merely in an anguished whisper.

'Now, now. You're not in a position to accuse your betters of lying,' Lord Melville chided, with a glance of warning. 'I believe we all know how fond this young woman is of telling stories. Too fond. And she's here under false pretences—we all know now. One of the reasons I had to insist she was dismissed without references from my employ is that… No. I won't go on. It isn't appropriate to discuss such things in front of ladies.'

Melville gave Averill one of his polite smiles that made Maud feel sick.

'I think I've heard enough,' Dominic cut in.

He turned to Maud. His expression was inscrutable, his emotions reined, just as when she had first met him. 'I should like to hear Miss Wilmot's side of the story.'

Chapter Nineteen

Get thee hence, nor come again.
—*Alfred, Lord Tennyson:* Maud *(1855)*

'Dominic!' Averill exclaimed. 'Don't tell me you're going to listen to any more of a governess's fairy tales!'

'There are two sides to every story, Averill,' Dominic replied curtly. 'Miss Wilmot has a right to tell hers.' He glanced at Maud. 'But perhaps we should return to the house first.'

'Ooh!' Before Maud could move, Averill set her hoops whirling as she stepped between them. 'I knew there was something about you, something sly, from the minute I met you.'

Maud stared at her. Her throat choked. Then all the words she had kept inside for so long surged out of her. They could not be stopped. Not any longer.

'How can you be so cruel to a member of your own sex?' she asked, shaking. 'I am a governess, but I am also a woman, just like you. I do not deserve you to be so unkind to me, simply because I have found myself in more straitened circumstances than yours.'

Averill's cheeks reddened. 'How dare you speak to me like this!'

Maud raised her chin. She had nothing to lose. Not any more. 'I didn't ask to have fallen on hard times. It was tragedy that propelled my sister and I into poverty. I took up employment as a governess, not merely because I needed the wages, but because I believe in education. If women are not educated, they are forced to rely upon the mercy of others. Without an education, women have no chance in life. You ought to thank governesses, not revile them.'

Averill gave a little laugh, turning from Dominic to Lord Melville in an attitude of amazement.

'Governesses ought not mingle with their employers as if they are their social equals,' Averill declared.

'Perhaps,' Maud replied. 'But I have always done my job with pride, no matter what you think of it, and nothing you can say can diminish my belief in my work.'

Taking a deep breath, she put one foot in front of the other until she was in front of Lord Melville. Every step seemed like a mile.

'And you, Lord Melville.' Her voice had disappeared, becoming a whisper. She forced herself to raise it, even as she trembled. 'You treat your staff as if they are nursery toys, not people. You disgust me. You are the worst of all kinds of men. What you did to me, what you do to all the female servants in your employ, is utterly immoral. You have said that a governess must be upstanding and of good moral character. What of your character? What example do you offer your nephews?'

'That's libellous.' He didn't meet her eyes.

'Is it?' she demanded. 'You and I both know what occurred when I was in your employment. You are the one who has libelled me.'

She clutched at her bodice, her breath coming in heaves. She felt as if she might be sick as the memories came flooding back. She couldn't go on.

Then her breath came in a huge gust. 'But that is your story. It is not mine.'

She lifted her chin. 'No matter what happened to me, no matter what you did to me, you cannot take away my story. And it is this. That I can still see the beauty in the world. That I can hope for happiness. You cannot destroy that for me. You can only destroy it for yourself.'

Maud turned to Dominic. Everything she had ever wanted to tell him, she tried to communicate now, through her eyes. For a moment, it was as if they were the only ones in the woods, just as it had been when they had seen the White Admiral.

But no more words would come. Her throat was too choked, with tears, with pain. There was no way she could ever tell him of her feelings now. That the love she felt for him was so much more than infatuation. Only the night before, she'd reached out and kissed him. But everything between her and Dominic had been tainted now.

No one will believe your story.

Her breath kept coming in painful gasps, as she bent, trying to control her nausea. There was no way she could explain or defend herself, without having to reveal the full, unspeakable horror of what had happened.

A twig snapped as Dominic moved. His hands were clenched.

'I'm sorry,' she whispered, at last. It was all she could

say, with Lord Melville looming so near. 'For everything.'

She lifted her eyes, but their connection had snapped,
broken, like a twig underfoot.

Now Dominic was staring at Lord Melville, with an
expression Maud could not make out.

Without another word, Maud turned and stumbled
away as fast as she could.

Dominic took a stride forward on the path. Miss
Wilmot had almost disappeared, a moth-grey flicker
among the trees.

'How extraordinary,' Melville drawled. 'I told you
that governess was a storyteller.'

Dominic tensed. Blood pumped through his veins. He
wanted to go immediately after Maud, but he couldn't
let it pass. Not the way he spoke about her. The man had
to be put in his place.

He shoved his fists deep into his pockets as he swung
back towards Melville. 'You caused Miss Wilmot harm.
Then blamed her for it.'

'Steady on, Jago.' Melville's tone remained smoothly
cordial, as if they were at their club. 'Surely you want to
know if your servants lie to you. She admitted it herself.
You don't know anything about her.'

Dominic shoved his fists deeper into his pockets. 'I
know everything I need to know about her. I know her
from her stories.'

His voice was calm now and it reflected a sudden
certainty, deep-seated and sure. He'd told Miss Wilmot
that he was a man who trusted his own judgement and
he knew it now, for certain. He trusted her, too.

Melville's lip curled. 'I'm surprised you believe a governess's tattle.'

Dominic couldn't restrain himself any longer. He reached out and grabbed the horsewhip from Lord Melville's hand. 'I suggest you leave my land, Melville.'

The other man took a step back. 'You can't be serious.'

'Deadly serious.' Dominic tightened his grip on the horsewhip. 'And if I hear that you ever repeat those repugnant lies about Miss Wilmot again, I'll be coming after you, with this.'

Melville shook his head. 'You'll regret making an enemy of me, Jago. I know you need money for your Cornish railway.'

'Do your worst. I wouldn't go into business with you even if the railway never runs again,' Dominic told him in disgust.

Melville shrugged. 'I'll be forced to let everyone know your trains are a bad investment, then. They won't run for long without my money.'

'You would sully the reputation of anything you touch,' Dominic retorted. 'I wouldn't take your money if it was the last penny in England.'

His blood was still pumping as he swung back on to the path. Miss Wilmot had vanished now.

'Dominic!'

Taking a deep breath, he turned to look at Averill, saw shock and sympathy in her eyes.

She put a gloved hand on his arm. 'I'm sorry. Please believe me. I didn't realise the full story.'

He couldn't stop to talk to Averill. Not now. She'd caused enough trouble. 'I have to find her.'

Averill nodded.

Dominic threw aside the horsewhip and strode away.

* * *

Maud ran through the woods. She heaved in one breath, trying to draw in strength and peace from the forest. Then another.

Her legs felt like quivering aspic, but still she ran. Moments ago, in front of Lord Melville, they seemed to lack even the strength to hold her up, let alone carry her further through the woods.

No one will believe your story.

Dominic had heard all those terrible allegations being made about her. That she was a liar. A man-chaser. A thief.

The shame of it.

How could he believe her now? Well, of course he wouldn't. She'd lied to him, after all. She had admitted it to him. Now he would be the same as all the other men she had encountered, all the other masters of the house. He would take the side of Lord Melville.

There was no question of Lord Melville's reputation being besmirched, only hers. He'd accused her of theft. Of being of low moral character. That she was not a fit person to be around children.

She stopped and took another aching breath as the thoughts pounded in her brain. Her ribs hurt from running as if a knife had pierced them, just below the heart. She put her hands to her forehead as if she could drive the thoughts out. But still they came.

Dominic would judge her guilty. He would not want her to care for Rosabel, not any more. All the moments they had shared together would count for nothing now.

All there was between them had been erased at one blow. She could not help the sob that burst from her throat at that moment, choking her, suffocating her like a fist about her heart. She clapped a hand to her mouth, stifling the sobs. She leaned against the oak tree, letting it bear her up when nothing in her own frame would. Finally, the shuddering sobs stilled. She managed to stand upright, telling herself firmly, bleakly: it was nothing but a dream, one that had just turned into a nightmare. But it would have made no difference, in the end.

No matter what her name, she was just a governess. *No one will believe your story.*

Maud stumbled on. These were the woods where she had shared those fairy-tale moments with Sir Dominic. But that was all it had been—a fairy tale.

Perhaps he was laughing about her now with Lord Melville. Perhaps he had been treating her the same way that Lord Melville had treated her. As a plaything. As a nursery toy to pass the time. If he had been toying with her, his ploys were worse than Lord Melville's advances. He had lulled her into a false sense of security. He'd shown an interest in her true self, or at least that was what she had thought. But it might not have been so at all. Perhaps it had all been a pretence.

It couldn't be! a voice in her head cried out. What they had shared together, surely it couldn't be counterfeited.

No! Maud shook her head. She would not fall prey to such doubts about Dominic. He was not the same kind of man as Lord Melville. She knew that of him, deep in her mind, her heart, her soul. But she was lucky that it had not gone too far.

She loved him, but he could never love her. He never would, not now, not after what he had been told about her, and she could never tell him the truth.

She picked up speed. Her shuddering weakness was past. She raced through the woods, the wildflowers dragging at her skirts. She hurried across the lawn towards Pendragon Hall and stopped.

She had imagined living there for ever, she realised, her fingers clenched. Oh, how could she have been so foolish? She had started to imagine so much. Now those dreams and hopes were shattered. She had not found sanctuary. She had not found a home.

With a cry, she turned away from the house and ran down the long drive.

Chapter Twenty

And the roaring of the wheels.
　　　　　—*Alfred, Lord Tennyson:* Maud *(1855)*

Dominic strode through the woods. He could not recall ever being so angry. The rage surging through his body was like a triple shot of the brandy that he had drunk with Miss Wilmot the night he had first held her in his arms. It was like fire, sending his fists clenching and his body pulsing.

How he had managed to hold back from seizing Lord Melville by the scruff of his cravat and shaking him like the dog he was, Dominic would never know. He had wanted to kill the man. By God, the thought that he had laid his pudgy hands on Miss Wilmot, forced himself upon her. Dominic swore aloud and aimed a vicious kick at a clod of dirt. He only wished it was that clod Melville. He had never wanted to punish someone as much as he had wanted Lord Melville punished. And he had wanted to do that punishing himself.

His paces lengthened, quickened. His rage wasn't directly solely against Lord Melville. It burned against any man who would take advantage of a woman in his employ. Miss Wilmot was not the first governess who had experienced such hideous treatment. Dominic knew better than that. No, she was not alone. Lord Melville considered himself entitled, in a kind of outdated *droit de seigneur*, to be able to help himself to his servants. It was not something that Dominic could imagine ever thinking was acceptable behaviour. It was about as far a cry from gentlemanly conduct as he could think.

Only the fact that he would be reducing himself to Lord Melville's level by using violence against him had stopped Dominic from using that horsewhip, taking him and forcibly throwing him off his land. He had been angered, too, by the role that Averill Trevose had played in the whole saga, even if she'd seemed appalled by what she had done. She had allowed, in fact encouraged, Lord Melville to catch Miss Wilmot by surprise.

How Miss Wilmot managed to be so kind and loving to Rosabel, such a beautiful person in spirit and character after all that had happened to her, Dominic could hardly perceive. She was an extraordinary woman. She had not become bitter or full of hatred. Instead she had continued to do her work, educating children and telling her enchanting stories. All the while she had been suffering a secret pain from a horror that had destroyed her world. Yet she had overcome it. He didn't like that she had lied to him about her identity. He wished that she had trusted him enough to tell him her story. Perhaps she would have told him, in time. Yet now he had heard what had happened, he understood that she had told him in so many ways. Her nervousness, her nightmares—all was explained. He knew now: she was someone special who needed to be treated with the utmost care. She needed to be treated with all the gentleness of a butterfly.

He wanted to be with her, always. He knew that now.

He would tell her; as soon as he got back to the Hall.

He swore beneath his breath at the recollection of how she had cowered away from Melville. His slightest move sent her jumping, as if she were a creature still full of fear. It had been hard to witness. Miss Wilmot was no thief. Nor was she a man-chaser. She would never have thrown herself at Lord Melville in the way he had implied. Dominic knew her soul. He also knew he had to get rid of all the anger that he felt before he went back and said to her what he needed to say.

To Maud.

'Maud.'

He said it aloud. The name suited her. Again, he felt that pang that she had not been honest with him. When the truth had been laid out before him by Melville, mixed among the lies, he'd had to piece it together. He'd been angry at first, to hear of her deception. But the anger towards her had died away so fast. The desperation on her face had gutted him to the core. Now he could see why she thought it had been necessary. She'd been desperate. Hunted.

He reached the lawn, looked across to the house.

The truth could not wait any longer.

Maud raced to the end of the gravel drive, hardly looking where she was going. As she passed through the tall iron gates, she ran a hand across her eyes. She couldn't bear to look back at Pendragon Hall.

She stopped, gasping, and placed a hand on the gates to steady herself. She leaned over, the nausea overwhelming. Almost crouching, she bent her body, but nothing came.

Still bent, she took a step, then another, before more pain sent her keeling over by the side of the road.

The sound of horses' hooves and wheels came to a stop beside her.

'My goodness! Are you all right?' came a sweet voice.

Maud looked up, still clutching her stomach.

From the carriage window a kindly old face in a ruched bonnet was staring down at her with concern. 'Why, my dear! I don't believe it. Do you remember me? We were travelling companions, months ago, on the West Cornish Railway.'

'Oh! Yes, I do remember.' Maud tried to smile, but her mouth would not make the shape.

'You were so kind to me,' the old lady said, with a beaming smile. 'You made sure I kept my seat by the window even though I was in the wrong place. I've always remembered it.'

It was when she had first met Dominic, Maud remembered with a pang.

'I was glad to be of help,' she somehow managed to reply.

The old lady peered at her. Beneath her bonnet and grey curls, her blue eyes were surprisingly sharp, but her voice was gentle. 'Are you quite all right, my dear?'

Maud shuddered.

'Are you going to the station? I'm on the way there myself, to catch the train to London.'

The train.

Dominic's train.

Maud wiped her hand across her eyes.

She had a chance now, to flee, before she had to face

him. She would not wait to be dismissed, for that was surely what he must do. He could not keep her on as governess, knowing she had lied about who she was.

After Lord Melville's cruelty, she had never dreamed of experiencing the feelings that she had shared with Dominic. She had never known the pleasure that she had experienced with him, of being safe in his arms. The way he had held her after her nightmare. The touch of his hand, in the woods. His lips, hard and searching upon hers. To think that she had nearly succumbed to those dizzying, overwhelming sensations and had wanted more and more of him. Where would it have all ended but ruin?

'Please,' Maud choked out. 'I need to catch the train.'

Dominic flung open the nursery door. 'I'm looking for Miss Wilmot. Where is she?'

The nursemaid, Netta, bobbed a curtsy. 'I don't know, Sir Dominic. I thought she'd be back by now. She said she needed to go and get some ferns in the woods, but she hasn't come back to fetch Miss Rosabel.'

'Miss Wilmot nearly let all the butterflies out of the vivarium this morning, Papa,' Rosabel told him. 'Where is Miss Wilmot? Polly and I have been waiting for her.'

'She is usually so reliable, Sir Dominic,' Netta said. 'We've all become so fond of her.'

'Miss Wilmot told me such a lovely story last night, Papa.' Rosabel's face lit up. 'It was all about Princess Swallowtail and the White Admiral again. And today, she said that we might be able to take a picnic out into the woods and eat our luncheon among the butterflies.' Her small face was alight with excitement. 'Would you like to come, too? Would you like to spend the day among the butterflies, Papa?'

Dominic arranged his face into what he hoped was a calm expression.

'Very much,' he said, 'but we will need to find your governess first.'

He swung to Netta.

'I'm concerned for Miss Wilmot,' he said. He kept his tone neutral. He didn't want to indicate that anything in particular was amiss. He would not have gossips guessing at what had happened in the woods. 'So, you haven't seen her?'

'No, Sir Dominic.'

'I need to find her. Will you go into her bedroom, please, and see if she is there? I'm concerned that she might be unwell.'

'Of course, Sir Dominic.'

Netta hurried out of the nursery through the connecting door that led into Miss Wilmot's bedroom.

Rosabel slipped her hand into her papa's.

Dominic stared at the butterfly vivarium. He couldn't presume upon Miss Wilmot's privacy to go into her bedroom himself. He didn't want to cause her any more anxiety and distress. After what had happened in the woods that morning, he knew that her nervousness was not part of her character. She was not an anxious woman. She was a brave one. The nervousness he had witnessed had been caused by what had happened to her at Lord Melville's hands.

Dominic stared around the room. The only sign of life were the butterflies, fluttering in the vivarium. He glanced at them in the glass case. The bright colours of their wings seemed to dim in front of his eyes, the butterflies turning to grey.

Netta came running back into the nursery. 'She's not there, Sir Dominic.'

Rosabel's lip trembled. 'Where is Miss Wilmot?'

Dominic looked at Netta. One look at his face and the nursemaid blanched.

'Take Rosabel downstairs,' he said.

Immediately, Netta obeyed his instructions.

'Come along, Rosabel. I'm sure Miss Wilmot will be back soon.' She took the little girl's hand and led her away.

All his instincts were on alert. He ought to have caught up to her by now. He had to see for himself that there was no clue to her whereabouts. Without another word, he pushed through the connecting door and into Maud's bedroom.

Miss Wilmot's absence was palpable. The fragrance that always seemed to emanate from her clothing and hair still hung in the air. Yet the room was empty. He'd been so sure they would find her there.

Where had she gone?

The wardrobe door was ajar. There hung her grey and brown dresses, the meagre array of clothing she possessed. The green dress, with its imprint of leaves, swayed slightly on its peg.

He slammed the wardrobe door shut.

Gritting his teeth, he moved to the dressing table.

A bundle of manuscript lay there, tied with a ribbon. The fountain pen he had given her lay beside it.

He picked up the sheaf of papers.

The Butterfly Fables:
For Rosabel,
with love always,
from her governess,
Miss Maud Wilmot

Dominic exhaled.

She'd dedicated them to his daughter. He hadn't known she had done that.

But then, she had given them both all she had to give.

He gripped the fountain pen in his fist and practically ran out of the governess's bedroom and into the corridor and down the stairs.

'Have you seen Miss Wilmot?' he snapped at the butler. He never usually spoke in such a tone.

'Excuse me, Sir Dominic, but I saw her down near the gates,' a footman piped up.

Dominic relaxed his tense shoulders. She was on foot. She couldn't go far.

'Get Taran,' said Dominic.

Maud clambered on to the train, half-blind with tears. She couldn't stop them falling, no matter how hard she tried.

The old lady had pressed some money into her hand. 'You don't have to tell me anything, my dear. But please let me help you.'

Maud's eyes filled with tears again.

'Thank you.'

'Not at all. One good turn deserves another.'

It had almost broken Maud's heart to buy a one-way ticket back to London.

'You're the governess up at Pendragon, aren't you,

miss?' the ticket master at the station had asked her. 'You don't need to pay the full fare.'

'I want to pay full price. And I'll need a second-class ticket, please.' She didn't want to be further indebted to the old lady, even though she had suggested they share a first-class compartment.

Yet when she had looked down at the ticket in her hand, she saw that the ticket master had nonetheless given her a first-class ticket.

He winked as he passed it to her.

'This isn't what I paid for.' She slid it back towards him.

'It's the ticket Sir Dominic would want you to have,' the ticket master replied. 'He'd want us to look after you, he would.'

Maud choked. 'He would?'

The ticket master nodded. 'You've been doing a fine job up there with Miss Rosabel these past few months, from what we hear.'

'Thank you,' Maud had answered faintly.

Now, the ticket clenched in her glove, she made her way to the first-class carriage where the old lady was in the corner seat. She gave her a sympathetic pat on the hand as Maud took her own seat.

The memories came rushing back of when she had travelled in the opposite direction, on her way to Cornwall. Oh, how she wished she could turn back time! How she wished it had all been different. She held back a shudder. Seeing Lord Melville had brought it all back, the terror and fear that she had experienced. How she wished she had not been forced into such a dreadful position to have had to lie to Dominic in the first place. But he was a man, an independent businessman, not a dependent governess. He would never have been able to understand the kind of desperation that drove her to make such an error, to make such a choice. Perhaps, looking back, she *had* had a choice. Perhaps she could have chosen a more honourable path than disguising her identity. But she had not been able to think of another way to find employment and she had not wanted to make Martha's life more difficult by staying with her in London and being an extra mouth to feed. Now she was going to have to go back and do just that while she worked out what to do.

Rain began to fall, hard, loud drops on the roof of the train. Her vision blurred as she stared out the window. Her Cornish idyll. It was ending, just as it had begun.

She twisted her fingers together. She had not been able to say goodbye to Rosabel. Perhaps it was just as well. She couldn't bear the thought of saying goodbye to the little girl whom she had come to love. It would break her heart. It was better for her to simply leave. Rosabel would forget her, in time.

A puff of steam obscured the platform, then swirled away.

She had first seen Sir Dominic Jago through such a cloud of steam.

Tall, dark-haired, long-legged, he had worn his long dark grey coat, with a scarlet cravat tied carelessly around his neck. He often wore his cravats and ties loose; she knew that now. His hands had been gloveless, she recalled, and she had seen the flash of a gold signet ring on his right hand, the same flash of gold that glowed when he pushed back his hair from his brow, in the habitual gesture she had come to know. That was how she would always picture him, in her mind.

From now on, that was all he would be.

A memory.

A picture.

'Goodbye,' she whispered.

The rain pelted down. His hat was off and his hair trickled rivulets down his neck. And it was nothing more than he deserved.

It had come on suddenly, one of those early summer showers that could turn Cornwall from blue to grey in a matter of minutes.

With his heel he urged Taran onwards. He never used a whip; he used his legs and his hands to get the best from the stallion. Now, as if they were one, he flew at speed down the long drive through the gates and on to the open road.

There was no sign of her.

Dominic swore beneath his breath.

Had she cut across a field, gone cross country?

He turned Taran and went the other way along the road, searching through the driving rain.

Again, no one was in sight.

Then it struck him.

The train.

He knew the timetable, knew every arrival and departure. The train would be pulling out of the station in a matter of minutes.

He urged the stallion onwards again, as if, through the sheer force of his will, horsepower could match steam power.

The trees, the landscape flew past him in a wet blur. The rain made it harder for him to see in front of him, but still he rode on, fast and hard, trusting to the horse's senses above his own, until at last he reached the station. He slid off the stallion and ran to the railway platform.

It was empty except for the ticket master.

'Sir Dominic!' He bowed.

Dominic grabbed the man's arm. 'The train?' It was all he could get out.

The ticket master nodded with pride. 'On time as usual, Sir Dominic. You can always rely on the West Cornish Railway.'

Dominic swallowed his reply.

'The governess from up at the Hall was on the train today,' said the ticket master, eyeing Dominic's damp clothing. 'I remembered what you said about her deserving special treatment. I made sure that she got a first-class ticket even though she only paid for a second-class fare. I escorted her to her seat myself, sir.'

'How far did her ticket go?'

'All the way to London.'

'She told you nothing else?'

'No, sir.'

Dominic bowed his head.

'I hope I haven't done anything wrong, Sir Dominic,' the ticket master said, glancing at Dominic's hand upon his sleeve. 'Giving her that first-class fare.'

Dominic cleared his throat.

'Not at all,' he said, releasing the fellow and giving him a half-hearted pat on the shoulder. 'Miss Wilmot deserves a first-class fare, wherever she goes.'

He had to turn away.

Dominic stared at the railway tracks.

Damn his damned punctual trains.

The governess had flown.

Chapter Twenty-One

Pass, thou deathlike type of pain;
—*Alfred, Lord Tennyson: Maud (1855)*

Maud couldn't breathe.

She was suffocating, pressed beneath a heavy weight that she could not fight. She tried to break free, to kick, to scream.

With a cry, she woke up, shuddering in fright.

The nightmare. She hadn't experienced it for so long now, those horrors. Not since Dominic had come to her and pulled her out of the terrifying dream.

'It's all right.' His low voice had been full of a strange tenderness. 'You're awake now. You're safe. I've got you.' His strong arms raised her up, out of the nightmarish depths.

She had leaned into those arms. Her whole body had known instinctively that she was safe, protected from the horrors of the dream.

Her heart still pounding in her chest, she opened her eyes and looked around the darkened room. In the gloom the shapes of the furniture were dark and mysterious.

It wasn't her bedroom at Pendragon Hall.

Sir Dominic Jago wasn't holding her in his arms.

He never would again.

Instead, Maud lay half-on, half-off the horsehair sofa in Martha's sitting room. Gaslight from the lamp post outdoors streamed into the room at the edges of the curtains and she could hear the shouts and voices outside as men left the public house on the corner. It must be past closing time.

She had only managed a few hours' sleep. The sofa folded out at one end to form a *chaise longue*, but the resulting 'bed' was still narrow and slippery. She had become accustomed to her large, comfortable bed at Pendragon Hall, with its down-filled pillows and mattress. She knew she wouldn't be able to sleep again tonight, but it wasn't only because of the sofa. It would be impossible for the sense of terror to abate enough for her to rest.

And—more devastating, by far—the heartbreak that had become her living reality. Day and night.

She would never see Sir Dominic Jago again.

She'd arrived at Martha's to find her sister was now quite visibly pregnant. At least Maud would be able to help with the baby, if she stayed that long, but by then room would be even more tight.

'Never mind,' Martha had said firmly. 'You can stay as long as you like.' But Martha had cast an anxious glance at her husband, Albert, as she'd made the invitation, and Maud knew that it was too much to ask to stay for long.

'I only want to stay for a few days,' she'd said, quickly, even as her heart sank. 'I am sure I can get another post as governess. Or perhaps I'll try a school, or an orphanage.'

In truth, she wasn't sure of finding employment at all.

Perhaps she would need to go abroad to find a post. To France, or somewhere in Europe. Or perhaps she would go further afield still, to another country such as Australia, where no one knew the name Maud Wilmot.

She buried her face in her hands. Dominic had heard all those terrible allegations about her.

The way he had looked at her in the woods…

Her nails dug into her forehead. She simply couldn't bear it.

If only she had told him the truth from the start. But once she had taken the post as governess and had begun to care for Rosabel, she had found such peace at Pendragon Hall. She hadn't wanted to risk her new-found sense of safety.

It hadn't only been timid Rosabel who had benefitted from their happy days in the grounds. Maud, too, had been healed by the wild beauty of the place, the woods, the gardens—the butterflies.

Sanctuary.

A vivarium.

Dominic had seemed to know that she needed to be coaxed into spreading her wings, just like Rosabel.

How she would miss the little girl. It had broken her heart not to say goodbye. She would have to hope that the little book of stories would give Rosabel some solace.

Stories would give Maud no solace now. Not any more.

But it wasn't only Rosabel who had kept her wanting to stay at Pendragon Hall. She knew that now.

On the train journey to London, as the wheels had whirred and the steam blew, over and over in her mind she kept reliving the time she had shared with Dominic. Their first meeting, when he had made her furious and determined not to show any attraction to him, even though, she realised now, she had been attracted to him from the start. The way he'd held her in his arms, the walks in the woods, the dinner and brandy, the time they had spent together...

And his kiss.

She touched her lips with her finger. His kiss had been imprinted on her, deep into her soul.

Now it all seemed like a dream.

Like a fairy tale.

She never wanted to tell another fairy tale again. She didn't believe in them any more. They were lies, fantasies. She'd told the stories of Princess Swallowtail, always believing, in her heart, that she, too, would have a happy ending.

But there would be no happy ending for her. She would be destitute, unless she could find some way to earn a living and quickly. And even if, by some miracle, she secured a job? What sort of living would it be—a half-life, emotions stifled, living in fear of a master's domineering interest.

A half-life, without him.

Maud got up from the horsehair sofa and crossed to the window. She clutched the bodice of her nightgown. In a few hours, the milk cart would come, clattering down the street.

Soon, she would have to face the day and the dismal future that lay ahead.

Without Dominic.

'Are you sure you wouldn't like a sandwich with your cup of tea, Maud?'

Maud shook her head. 'I am not hungry. But don't

concern yourself with me. You are the one who needs nurturing. Let me pour you another cup, Martha.'

Her sister lifted up her teacup. 'It was kind of you to prepare breakfast for me. But don't think I didn't notice that you didn't eat any.'

Maud smiled. 'You need your rest. And I was already awake. I was happy to do so.'

She didn't tell Martha, of course, that she had spent a second night on the horsehair sofa barely sleeping at all.

There was a rap at the front door.

'I'll get it.' Martha bustled out of the sitting room and into the hall. 'It's probably the postman.'

Maud glanced towards the sitting room window. She could just make out a dark hansom cab drawn up outside, a rather smart carriage, from the little she could discern through the lace curtains.

She heard the front door open. Then came Martha's voice, sounding more high-pitched than usual.

Then another voice.

Maud froze, her teacup in her hand.

His voice.

His very faint Cornish accent, warming the clipped enunciation of a gentleman.

Martha reopened the sitting room door. She stood there for a moment, blocking the entrance. Her pretty forehead was drawn into a frown. 'Maud. There's a visitor for you. It's—'

'I know who it is,' Maud faltered.

The teacup clattered on to the saucer as she laid it down with shaking fingers.

Sir Dominic Jago entered the sitting room.

His gaze sought hers. She could not tear her eyes

away. He stood there in the doorway, completely oblivious to her sister, and simply looked at her with his dark eyes.

The small room suddenly seemed even smaller. Her breath came short and fast. She was suddenly aware of how tall he was, as he stood in the doorframe, or perhaps the high ceilings and vast rooms of Pendragon Hall had altered her sense of proportion. Yet he did not seem at all discomfited by his surroundings, for, after an eternity, he seemed to recall himself and turned to smile at Martha.

'I hope you do not mind me calling unannounced,' he said. Beneath the courteous tone, his voice was husky, even a little deeper than she remembered. 'I'm sorry to intrude.'

'Not at all,' Martha replied, though clearly flustered, as she smoothed her apron gently over her stomach. 'Might I offer you a cup of tea, Sir Dominic?'

He lifted the carpetbag he held in his hand. 'I do not wish to intrude on your hospitality. I came to bring your sister's belongings.'

He turned to Maud, who was still seated as if frozen in place, by the tea table. She had never imagined he would come himself.

'I received your letter of resignation,' he said. 'I would like to have a few words with you, if you will permit it. Please believe me—I have no wish to discomfit you, Miss Wilmot. None at all.'

Maud inclined her head. She could do no more.

Her sister looked from one to the other, her eyes resting searchingly upon Maud's face.

Then she nodded. Martha lifted up the tea tray. 'I'll just clear the tea things.'

Dominic bowed and moved aside as Martha bustled out into the hall.

The door closed.

Dominic turned and looked directly at Maud.

Her eyes drank him in. He looked the same, the sculpted jaw, the dark, brooding eyes. But there were shadows beneath them now, as if he, too, hadn't slept. Yet that sense of suppressed purpose, of energy around him, remained palpable.

He, too, took her in, his gaze running over her. Yet his face revealed no expression that she could make out; his emotions reined in.

'I never expected to see you again,' she whispered.

'Did you not think I would come? I did not expect to find you gone. I thought you would wait for me at Pendragon Hall.'

'I'm sorry.' She twisted her fingers, over and over. 'I tried to explain in my letter. I couldn't stay.'

He studied her for a moment, taking her all in. Maud wished for a fleeting moment that she'd taken more care with her hair this morning. What would he see before him? A drab woman in a grey dress, her hair scraped back into an unbecoming bun and her eyes ringed with shadows, no doubt. She'd seen them in the looking glass that morning.

'I am sorry, too,' he said softly. 'That scene in the woods, Lord Melville's despicable behaviour, even the distress Miss Trevose caused you—I regret all of that, Miss Wilmot. Most deeply.'

She stared down at her lap and clasped her fingers together to stop them twisting. He ran his long fingers around the edge of his top hat.

He laid it down.

'I do not want to distress you any further.' From the inside pocket of his long coat he took an envelope. Beneath the coat he wore a striped waistcoat and a dark brown silk cravat. It was tied tightly about his neck today. 'You have been through enough. I know that now. But I wanted to see for myself that you were safe. And I wanted to give you these, too.'

He laid two white envelopes on the table, where the tea tray had been.

She unclasped her hands and picked one up, lifted the flap.

She gasped. It was full of pound notes. 'What is this?'

A muscle moved in his jaw. 'Your wages. Did you think I wouldn't pay you?'

Maud tried to keep her hand steady as she held out the envelope. 'I can't accept it.'

'Why not?' he demanded.

'They were not earned…honestly.'

He raised his eyebrow. 'How so?'

'You believed I was Martha,' she whispered, 'when I am not.'

His teeth gritted. 'You more than deserve your wages as governess, Miss Wilmot. Take it. You earned it. It's not charity.'

Maud clenched her fist around the envelope, then laid it back on the table. At least now she could offer Martha some payment for her room and board—if the sofa could be considered a room. It would be false pride not to take the money, even if she didn't want to take it. 'Thank you.'

He nodded curtly.

He touched the other envelope. 'This is your character reference. In your letter, you said you wanted to leave Pendragon Hall and my employment. I wrote it this morning, on the train.'

She took it, glanced briefly through the contents. The reference was glowing.

Her mouth fell open. 'I can't believe you would do this for me, after what happened.'

'Your opinion of me is low, it seems.' He shook his head. 'Could you not have waited for me to return to the Hall? At least you might have said goodbye to Rosabel. She is most distressed. You must have known your leaving would break her heart.'

Maud's eyes filled with tears.

'I'm sorry,' she whispered. 'It broke my heart to leave her, too. I never wanted to hurt Rosabel. I never wanted to hurt anyone. But I had no choice. I couldn't gain employment any other way. I'm sorry I didn't tell you, that you had to find out from Lord Melville.'

'Your character was never in question, Miss Wilmot.'

The tears spilled over now. Gushed down her cheeks.

'But in the woods. What Lord Melville said about me…' Maud couldn't go on. Her throat hurt, the words like stones.

'I sent Lord Melville packing.'

'What?'

'Did you think I don't recognise lies?' he said harshly. 'Yours certainly never rang true. And when I matched your handwriting to the letter from your sister, I knew for certain. It wasn't yours.'

'So you always suspected.'

For a moment his half-smile glimmered. 'You are a good storyteller, Miss Wilmot, but a poor liar.'

'Why didn't you tell me of your suspicions?' she asked.

'I could ask the same of you.' He exhaled. 'We both didn't trust each other. And yet in a way we both did.'

The trembling spread over her body. 'What do you mean by that?'

'There was truth between us,' he said, low. 'You know it.'

Maud looked down at her shaking hands.

He turned away, gazing through the net curtains into the street. After a moment he swung back. 'I didn't want to rush you or confront you. I knew there was something you weren't telling me, something that troubled you. I asked you to dinner, to give you time to get to know me, to learn to trust me. I wanted you to have that chance. It wasn't easy, but I was prepared to wait. You taught me that, the way you wait for butterflies. So still. So patient. I wanted you to come to me.'

'But in the woods…' she faltered. 'You were angry with me. I am sure of it. I saw it on your face.'

He closed his eyes briefly. When he opened them, his expression was unreadable. Chagrin, regret, a flicker of anger still?

'I'd just discovered my suspicions were true. I hadn't wanted to believe that you had been lying to me, all along.'

'I thought you were going to ask me to leave.'

'That was a fair assumption, I suppose, after the way you had been treated before.' He breathed in. 'But as soon as I understood what you had been through… I wanted to tell you that I understood. But you had already gone.'

'I was a coward,' she whispered. 'I knew I was damned

in your eyes and that it was inevitable that I should leave. I could not face any more humiliation and pain.'

'You are not a coward, Miss Wilmot. You expressed yourself admirably to Melville and Averill that day.' A little smile flickered, but then fled. 'But we all have our breaking points. You had reached yours, although I am still not certain why. You ran away. From Pendragon Hall. From me. From Rosabel. There was only one thing that would soothe her.'

At her look of query, he replied, 'The Butterfly Fables.'

Tears smarted her eyes.

From his pocket he took the folded piece of paper. He held it out to her. 'This is from Rosabel.'

She opened the folded page. A cry escaped her lips.

'I suppose you recognise them.' Dominic pointed to the drawing, where Rosabel had drawn Princess Swallowtail and the White Admiral. She had painstakingly printed a rather shaky message beneath.

Dear Miss Wilmot
Come back soon.
From Rosabel

Maud made a choking sound. 'Thank you for bringing this to me. I will treasure it always.'

She laid it on the table.

A silence. Although her head was bowed, she felt the force of his gaze upon her.

She looked up to see him looking down at her with a little frown, his mouth twisted.

He picked up his top hat. 'I'll be catching the train

back to Cornwall later today, now that I have delivered these to you.'

Her heart felt as though it was tearing in two, like paper.

Dominic stepped closer.

'Come with me.'

Maud gasped. She could not have heard him correctly. It was impossible. 'What did you say?'

'Come with me,' Dominic repeated. 'Come back to Pendragon Hall.'

'You can't mean that!'

'But I do.' Dominic exhaled. 'Rosabel misses you. I—I miss you.'

She stared at him, incredulous. 'But you wrote me a character reference.'

He shrugged. 'If you want to find new employment, I cannot stop you. But my having written you a character reference does not preclude your return to Cornwall. If you so wish.'

Her heart began to pound. She shook her head.

He moved closer. 'Not all masters of the house are the same. I am not such a man as Lord Melville.'

'I know it…' she faltered. Her heart had told her so, from the very beginning.

'I realised afterwards how distressed you must have been, seeing him.' He tightened his mouth. 'I greatly regret that Lord Melville came upon you by surprise, in my woods. I hoped you had found safety at Pendragon Hall.'

'I did.' Safety. Solace. And so much more.

'Then will you come back?' His voice was low now, his gaze piercing.

'As governess?'

He passed a hand over his brow. Then he appeared to come to a decision.

'If that is what you want,' he said at last.

All she wanted was to say yes. To travel back to Cornwall with him, on the train. To return to Pendragon Hall, to chase butterflies with Rosabel in the woods again.

It was impossible. She couldn't return to Pendragon Hall as a governess, knowing of her love for him. Her days there had been the happiest time of her life, but too much had changed. Seeing Lord Melville again had shaken her too deeply. She would never be able to cast off the shadow of the past.

Her throat tightened. The words wouldn't come. Everything she had wanted to say, all the feelings she had kept hidden. But they were locked inside. She had been forced to keep everything inside her for so long now.

Her chest constricted. She could not settle for anything other than love. But any hope of that was gone for ever.

Her gaze blurred as she turned away and stared at the snowy-white curtains.

'I can't come with you,' she whispered. 'I'm sorry.'

From behind she heard his sharp intake of breath.

She bowed her head.

'Then this is goodbye,' he said at last. The words were husky, low, near unrecognisable.

She could still not turn back to look at him. Her heart would be in her eyes. He would read everything. All her foolish, helpless love for him. She was just another governess with romantic notions after all and he would see it. She simply could not bear it.

She stood, unmoving. The mantel clock ticked.

Her pulse pounded loud and fast in her ears.

'Maud.'

He had never spoken her first name before. Not her real name.

The word rang and echoed in the room, in her heart.

But she could not turn around.

There was a long silence, then a movement behind her.

The sitting room door closed.

Then she heard the sound of his footsteps in the hall—those footsteps that had become so familiar, that tread she knew so well—receding.

Every sound seemed louder than it ever had before.

The click of the front door opening, the sound of the wood reverberating against the doorframe as it closed. The echo of his boots on the pavement outside.

Suddenly galvanised, she flew to the window and flung aside the lace curtain. A flash of brown, his coat swirling as he got into the hansom cab that would take him to the station, away from her for ever.

The hansom cab drew away. She heard the wheels turning and the horses' hooves ringing, steel on stone, down the street.

She remained, like a statue, staring out, the curtain in her hand.

She had no idea how long she stood there, staring into the empty street. Time had ceased. It had no meaning, any more.

She would never see Sir Dominic Jago again.

She let go of the lace curtain, let it fall.

Finally, she stumbled away from the window.

On the tea table were the envelopes he had brought. Her wages. Her letter of character reference. The drawing from Rosabel.

And something else.

Maud's brow creased.

She took another step.

It could not be.

On the table lay a black velvet box that she would not again mistake for felt.

Still she stared. With shaking fingers she fumbled at the tiny brass catch. The first time, it had been difficult to open. This time, it was easier. It clicked and she raised the lid.

The butterfly hair comb. It gleamed, as if it were alive.

He had left it for her. She smoothed a finger over the enamel wings.

She bent her head. Peered closer.

The night he had shown it to her she had not studied it so closely. The small antennae at the top weren't made of enamel. She touched them lightly. Now she could see, as she studied it more closely, that the tiny stones were made of rubies, small yet exquisite. And the body of the butterfly was finished in gold. It was not merely a hair comb. It was a hair jewel.

She lifted it gently from the case, as gently as if it were a living thing. Beneath her fingers it seemed to vibrate with life. Moving over to the small wooden-framed mirror that Martha kept by the sitting room door, she raised her arms and put the jewel into her hair. The mirror was not as large as the one at Pendragon Hall, but the effect was the same. The butterfly seemed to be almost flying, its wings glistening.

The sitting room door opened. Martha put her head around the corner. Maud saw her sister's reflection in the mirror, how her mouth fell open as she saw the jewel in Maud's hair. 'Maud. Is that...?'

'Princess Swallowtail. Yes.'

'From your fairy tales.'

Maud choked back a sob. 'Life isn't a fairy tale, Martha.'

'But, Maud,' Martha protested, 'you always said that there was more truth to life in fairy tales than in anything else.'

Maud looked back at her own face in the mirror. Life had entered it. The shadows beneath her brows merely emphasised the purpose in her eyes now. Her mouth was slightly parted, as if hungry for air, for life itself.

She could still love. Feel it. Give it. That power had not been taken from her and never would.

But she had to be more than just the princess in a fairy tale. She had to be both hero and heroine, as daring and adventurous as Princess Swallowtail, as she had once been herself, as a little girl. She had to fight for herself. Maud spun to face her sister. 'I must go to the train station. Now.'

Chapter Twenty-Two

The last wheel echoes away.
— *Alfred, Lord Tennyson:* Maud *(1855)*

'Stop! What do you think you are doing?'

Maud raced along the railway platform.

'Miss!' the voice bellowed from behind her. 'Miss, come back! You didn't buy a ticket!'

Ignoring the porter, she ran on. She hadn't taken the time to put on her bonnet. Wisps of her hair escaped, whipping in front of her.

'Stop, I say! What do you think you are doing? You can't get on that train!'

Still she ran on. A cloud of steam obscured the platform in front of her. She charged forward, let the steam cover her as she ran, dodging passengers and trolleys as she evaded the porter. He was getting closer; she could hear his puffing breath.

She had to find him.

She had to see Dominic, before it was too late.

When she came to the first-class carriage of the West

Cornish train, she slowed to peer up at the windows, gasping.

A hand touched her sleeve.

She spun around.

The porter's eyes bulged. 'I saw you, miss! Went right by the ticket master, brazen as brass!'

'I have to catch the train. I mean, I have to catch someone who is on it,' she panted, craning for a better view. It was about to leave. She knew it. She'd felt every precious second slip by as, in an agony of anxiety, she had rushed from Martha's to the train station. She'd managed to find a hansom cab, using some of the pound notes from the envelope Dominic had given her. Thank goodness she had accepted it. Even so...

The porter stood in her way. She tried to dodge around him.

'I must catch that train to Cornwall!'

'You won't be going anywhere, miss, except to the constable!'

'What seems to be the matter here?'

A cloud of steam swirled and parted to reveal Dominic.

He stepped forward. His voice was low, but the authority in it was unmistakable. 'Do you know who I am?'

The porter bobbed his head. 'Of course, Sir Dominic.' He pointed at Maud. 'This young woman's trying to get on one of your trains without a ticket!'

Dominic looked to her.

Even in the steam cloud, their powerful connection flared. Soundless as the movement of a butterfly wing, it pulsed between them.

They both stood motionless as they stared at each other.

'You can leave this matter to me.' Dominic addressed the porter.

'But she—' the porter began to protest.

'The train's soon to depart,' Dominic broke in. 'I will take responsibility for this young lady. You can go about your business. I thank you for your diligence.'

Reluctantly the porter stepped back. 'Very good, Sir Dominic.'

With one last look of annoyance at Maud, a look that now contained curiosity, the porter marched away.

Maud let out a sigh of relief.

Dominic moved closer, the steam swirling around him. 'I didn't expect to see you here.'

'I—I had to see you. I wasn't planning to catch the train. It's just that there's something I need to say.'

He glanced around the platform at the people milling about, carrying the bags and luggage.

'Come inside the carriage for a moment,' he said.

He stood aside, so that she could board the first-class carriage, and held out his hand to assist her. His fingers were warm as he held hers. Like her, he wore no gloves. She remembered how the touch of his hand had felt at their very first meeting on a train. She hadn't known who he was then. She hadn't known all that would happen between them and all that would tear them apart.

Nerves, restless as butterflies, swirled in her stomach. She couldn't let him leave without taking a chance. She knew that now. She'd said it was cowardly to have fled Pendragon Hall. It was. She would be a coward no longer.

With something between a leap and a stride, evidently well practised, he was up beside her, inside the carriage.

'Excuse me!' A woman with a large portmanteau

huffed past. 'These corridors are not designed for standing in. The train is about to move!'

'Here.' With a flick of his wrist Dominic opened the door to one of the first-class compartments. As Maud stepped inside, she inhaled the now-familiar scent of the leather seats. The carriage was mercifully empty.

He turned to face her. She was so close, she only had to reach out to touch him. 'What did you come to say?' he asked, as calmly as if they had all the time in the world.

For a moment, words failed her.

It was too painful, too raw. She could never tell him.

Running after him had been a mistake. A governess, running headlong and reckless after her handsome employer. Oh, how could she?

The whistle blew, piercingly loud. Her gaze darted to the window. The steam had, if anything, increased. The porters were closing the doors. The train was about to leave the station.

The whistle shrieked again.

Then it came to her, how she could tell him.

She lifted her head. 'I want to tell you a story.'

An eyebrow lifted. 'A story.'

'Yes. It's one of The Butterfly Fables. It is about Princess Swallowtail. But it is not a pretty tale and certainly not one for little girls.'

He exhaled. 'Go on.'

'Once upon a time,' Maud said rapidly, 'Princess Swallowtail was caught by the Red Emperor. He was a big, ugly butterfly. Quite nasty and domineering. The Red Emperor held her captive and Princess Swallowtail fought to be free, but she couldn't escape.'

Dominic stepped closer. His gaze found hers.

She looked into his eyes, finding the courage she needed to go on. 'The Red Emperor was very cruel, you see. Princess Swallowtail was employed in his court and she had to obey him. He was too big and powerful for her to fight off, even though she tried. She tried with all her might. But he…he tore her wings.'

His face was frozen. His eyes held a question.

'Irreparably,' she whispered, agonised.

Dominic turned away and stared out of the carriage window.

Maud stared at his broad back. The set of it had become so familiar to her. She would have been able to recognise him anywhere, simply from the way he held his shoulders. And his dark hair, the same colour as Rosabel's, brushing the high collar of his coat.

It had taken every ounce of her courage to tell him the truth.

She crumpled on to one of the leather seats. Her legs were trembling too much to hold her any more. She felt the train begin to move beneath her, as if her shuddering had transferred to the engine itself.

His back and shoulders blocked most of the view from the train window. She could just make out porters clearing the platform of onlookers, while inside the carriage time seemed to have stopped.

At last he swung around.

Maud clambered to her feet. She smoothed her skirt.

'I will have to get off at the first stop,' she murmured, gripping the seat as the carriage began to sway.

'How did the story end?'

She had not been looking at him, but staring dismally at the roiling steam outside. It was like the mists of an endless nightmare, one from which she would never break free. Now she ventured to meet his eyes. It was out. Now came the final rejection, the scorn. She would face it, not run away. She was not a coward. Not any more.

She met his eyes. Dark eyes, gazing down at her with something that, if she had wanted to delude herself, she might have read as tender concern.

'I don't know...' Maud faltered.

'I do,' Dominic said.

'Let me finish the story.' Dominic pushed back his hair from his forehead. 'If I may?'

He allowed himself a small smile. 'You may as well take a seat, Miss Wilmot. Our first halt does not occur for some time and I will not have it said that I force my passengers to stand for the duration of their journey, even if they have not paid the fare.'

She very nearly collapsed back into her seat. It was only with great effort that Dominic reined back the urge to tuck a supporting arm around her. No, both arms, dammit, and lay her head against his chest.

Instead he sat down on the seat opposite and studied her from across the carriage. Her hair was loose, curling wildly around her face from the run she'd made along the railway platform. His lips curved at the image, but he managed to force them back into more reassuring lines. She had looked so beautiful and wild, a creature of air and motion, flying through the steam. She wore no bonnet or cape, only one of those grey dresses he had come to appreciate more than any fine silks or satins.

Not that she did not deserve fine satin. She could have anything she wanted, as far as he was concerned. He wanted her to have it all, always.

Her face was white, so white he saw a smattering of

faint freckles across her nose. They hadn't been there when she first arrived at Pendragon Hall; he was sure of it. She had caught the sun out of doors with Rosabel, chasing butterflies. Her bonnet had often fallen back from her head, hung only by its ribbons. And her eyes… her eyes were those deep green pools that he wanted to dive into for the rest of his life.

He stood up and, with a key extracted from his waist-coat, locked the carriage door.

'I do not want our story interrupted,' he explained, at her wide-eyed look. 'Now, if I may finish your tale?'

'What are you saying?' she asked wildly.

He leaned a little closer, but he didn't touch her. Not yet.

When he had found her at her sister's, he'd wanted to say so much more to her. He'd wanted to gather her into his arms and take her home, back to Cornwall, back to Rosabel, back to the woods and the butterflies. But she'd shrunk away from him. At Pendragon Hall, he had seen the blossoming beautiful beguiling side of her, but it had been shut down again, once Lord Melville had hunted her in the woods. She'd appeared even less trust-ing than before.

It had compelled him to change his course, seeing her like that. He'd intended to declare himself, but he'd re-alised he could not. He'd decided, at that moment, that if all she wanted was to return as governess, he would not ask for more. He would offer her the home she needed so badly and hope she was able to accept it—even if he could not offer her his heart.

He winced. Given his experience with Sarah, he was wary of being able to give a woman what she needed. He'd needed to be absolutely sure she wanted him.

'You don't understand what I'm trying to tell you about—Lord Melville.' She shuddered. 'He began to make advances. I avoided him all I could, but it proved impossible. He had…keys to every room.'

Dominic clenched his fists even harder, so hard the muscles cramped, hard as rock. His pain was nothing to hers; he knew that. Her green eyes were an ocean of tears. He could hardly bear to witness the torment in them.

'I used to see his face coming down towards mine, every time I closed my eyes to go to sleep,' she whispered.

The night terrors. He'd witnessed them and would not make her relive the horror yet again.

He leaned towards her abruptly, yet still not touching. 'You don't need to tell me any more. Unless you want to.'

She shook her head.

'I only wish I had used his own whip while I had the chance. It's time for my story.' He leaned his hands on his outstretched thighs and offered her a half-smile. 'Railways are more my skill than stories, Miss Wilmot, but I will try. I hope you will not judge my beginner's attempt too harshly. Once upon a time…' he said.

Her smile glimmered through her tears, like sunlight on water.

He smiled, too, then sobered as he focused on his tale. 'Let me tell you about the White Admiral,' he said quietly. 'I believe I know his character. The White Admiral admired Princess Swallowtail from the moment he met her.'

Another faint smile. 'He did?'

Dominic nodded. 'Indeed. The more he observed of

her, the more beguiled he became, until all he wanted to do was be near her.' He leaned closer. 'Always.'

She was silent, except for her breath, coming in tremors, lifting her bodice.

'It didn't matter to the White Admiral if Princess Swallowtail's wings were torn,' he said, at last. 'He saw her whole beauty. There was so much more to Swallowtail than her wings.'

She put her hands to her lips.

'But I am…ruined,' she whispered, anguished. 'That's what is said when such a thing happens to a woman. And then there are all the other things Lord Melville said about me, the lies he told. That I pursued him. That I am of low moral character. Everyone will believe him. No one believes a governess.'

'I believe you,' Dominic said. 'My dear Miss Wilmot.'

She released a muffled sob.

He enclosed her hands in his. 'Allow me to reach the end of my story, if you will.'

She gazed up at him, so vulnerable. So utterly dear to him.

'The White Admiral realised he loved Princess Swallowtail.'

He lifted a hand to her cheek, stroked it. Smoothed away the tears.

'As I look back, I realise I did not defend you as I ought to have in the woods, before Lord Melville and Miss Trevose.'

'I wanted to defend myself,' she protested. 'I needed to do so.'

'And you did, admirably. But perhaps I ought to have ordered them away instantly.'

'I thought that you might have believed them, for a

moment,' she admitted. 'Even that you might have sided with them against me. I am ashamed that I doubted you.'

He made a rueful expression. 'I am ashamed that I ever made assumptions about governesses, especially the kind who read fairy tales.'

She smiled. 'I made assumptions, too. About masters of the house.'

'Then we are both corrected.' He looked directly into her eyes, dropped every barrier and discarded every doubt. There should be nothing but honesty between them.

He bowed his head.

'Miss Wilmot, will you give me another chance?' He took a deep breath and looked up at her. No matter what had happened in the past, in his previous marriage, he wouldn't hold back. 'I will ask you again. Come back to Pendragon Hall.'

A little frown descended on her brow. The urge to kiss it away was nearly overpowering.

'To be the governess?' she managed to ask at last.

He shook his head. That wasn't an option. Not any more, not after her bravery in coming to him. He knew what she needed now; knew he could give it to her. It had to be all—or nothing. 'To be my wife.'

She gasped. 'You can't want to marry me!'

'Why would I not want to? You're the bravest, truest woman I have ever met. You have enchanted me with your stories. With your courage.'

'You said you never wanted to marry again,' she protested.

'I didn't know I did, until you arrived at Pendragon Hall.'

He smiled, then sobered.

'After what happened with Sarah, I didn't want to take the risk again. To marry. To try again. But I didn't expect you to come into my life.'

She held still. He ran his thumb over her cheekbone, then drew his fingers through her curls, smoothing their wild disarray. Finally, he placed his hands together on his lap, giving her space and freedom.

'Marry me,' said Dominic. He would say it again and again. As many times as she needed to hear it. Until she believed it was true.

Tentatively, she reached out a hand and touched his. She curled her white fingers over his larger, browner hand. She looked at him. 'I didn't run from Pendragon Hall only because of Lord Melville. I ran from you, too.' She hesitated. 'I'd discovered my feelings for you were not at all what they should be.'

'Ah.'

'I discovered I had…romantic notions,' she said, a little smile playing at her lips.

'I warned you against developing those, Miss Wilmot.'

'You did. Then they grew more unruly. They developed into what I thought was an infatuation. Then, worse still, it dawned upon me that it was even more than an infatuation.' She took a deep breath. 'You see, I discovered I love you.'

'That is very fortunate,' he replied. 'Since I had discovered some romantic notions of my own.'

He took her hands in his and pulled her gently towards him, across the rocking carriageway. 'I love you.'

He wrapped his arms about her and held her close, laid his cheek against her hair. She shifted against him, her form against his. Nevertheless, he drew back a little. Had he gone too far, too fast?

Heaven forbid. He looked down into her up-tilted eyes. Beautiful eyes, that took his breath away. They held no fear, nothing but trust—and something else.

Her lips parted. He lowered his head, so gently, to touch his lips to hers. Just in case. The touch of her lips was like a bolt of coal fire. It shot through him. It rocked him in the carriage seat. He gasped, but she did not hesitate. She opened to him as he told her with his lips, his tongue, his hands just how much he needed her. Adored her. Wanted her for ever.

'You warned me,' Maud reminded him breathlessly, when at last they broke apart.

His signet ring glinted as he pushed back his hair. 'I am most relieved that you didn't listen.'

'I didn't,' she confessed. 'But I didn't want to be yet another governess chasing the master of the house.'

'You did the opposite. I understand why now.'

'I'm not the chasing type,' she said, with a smile. 'Well, not entirely. I prefer to chase things a good deal smaller than me. Like butterflies, for example.'

His arms encircled her. 'Is that so? You never wanted to chase me?'

His half-smile teased her.

'Perhaps a little,' Maud confessed. 'You must know that you're quite the catch.'

Dominic's smile broadened. 'Consider me caught.'

Chapter Twenty-Three

From the lake to the meadow and on to the wood,
Our wood, that is dearer than all;
       —Alfred, Lord Tennyson: Maud *(1855)*

Rosabel jumped up and down, her ringlets bobbing. 'Is it time?'

Dominic laughed. 'It certainly is, Rosabel.'

Maud reached down and hugged the little girl. She'd been unable to stay in her chair for the whole of the wedding banquet. She had spent most of it perched on Dominic's lap instead, beside Maud.

She wouldn't have had it otherwise. Without Rosabel, she would never have come to Pendragon Hall.

She would never have found a sanctuary.

She would never have found Dominic.

Her husband.

At his nod, the footman stepped forward and clapped for silence.

Dominic stood. 'Ladies and gentlemen, if you would all like to follow us out to the lawn, we have a surprise for you.'

They had held the wedding banquet in the dining room. It rang with the sound of happy laughter. Guests had filled the long table, her sister, Martha, her husband and their new baby as well as Rosabel adding a sense of merriment and fun to the proceedings.

'We may have a chance to fill this table after all,' he murmured, as they made their way out of the dining room.

'Not twenty children!' She laughed.

He raised an eyebrow. 'It's not as if we would need to employ a governess. We have one already in the Hall.'

She laughed. 'I suppose we can only try.'

She flushed as he met her eyes.

She turned to take Rosabel's hand. The little girl looked as if she were about to burst with excitement. Her cheeks were pink and she was the picture of health as the three of them led the way out of doors.

On the lawn, everyone waited. It wasn't a big crowd; neither of them had wanted a large wedding. Some of the nearby families had been invited, but not Averill Trevose. Dominic had baulked at that, even though Averill had come to call on Maud and apologised for bringing Lord Melville to the woods.

'I'm not sure we can ever be friends,' Maud had said to Dominic, 'but we can be good neighbours.'

'You are too kind-hearted,' he'd said, lifting her hand to his lips.

Now the footmen came out of the Hall, each carrying one of the vivaria that had been set along the wedding table, fluttering with bright life. Dominic had ordered more of the glass cases from London, and Maud and Rosabel had been preparing them for months.

'These butterfly vivaria aren't big enough either,' he

murmured to her, as the butler and the footmen made their way to stand in front of the small crowd. 'I believe we must build a large one in the garden so that we can visit butterflies at any time of the day or night.'

'Do you ever stop building?' He had found new investors for the train line, too, and was planning to expand.

He shrugged.

'I would like that very much,' she said, 'but I would be sorry not to go to the woods.'

He looked at her with a curious expression. 'Is that so?'

He gave a nod to the butler. At his command, the footmen opened the vivarium glass doors.

It took a moment, as if the butterflies were unsure what to do. Then, one by one, they emerged, some large, some small, some patterned, some plain. Coppers. Whites. Browns. Blues. And Swallowtails. Bright wings, in all the colours of the rainbow.

For a few minutes they fluttered, like flowers in the sky. Up and out they flew, into the pale blue, before disappearing almost like a swarm, into the woods.

Martha dabbed at her eyes with a lace handkerchief. 'Oh, Maud. That was the most magical thing I have ever seen. Don't you think so?'

Maud blinked back her own tears. 'I think it might have been.'

Dominic smiled at her. Again, he had that curious look in his eyes.

She had been worried that after he'd ordered Lord Melville from his land, Dominic's plans for the development of the railway would be affected. Lord Melville had threatened to ruin Dominic and the railway, Dominic had told her. But either his threats hadn't been carried out or Melville did not possess the influence he had claimed. New investors had come forward. The railway would surge ahead.

'What is it?' she asked him, as they strolled back into the Hall after the butterflies had vanished into the sky. 'I do believe you're hiding something. I thought we promised to have no more secrets between us.'

He smiled. 'No more secrecy founded on mistrust and fear, certainly. But I never promised there would be no more surprises.'

'There are more?' He had already given her so much. They were to go on a honeymoon to the Continent, shortly, travelling by train, of course.

Maud's body tingled as Dominic leaned in and whispered in her ear, 'You will have to wait until tonight.'

'Something old,' said Maud. 'Something new. Something borrowed and something blue...'

Dominic grinned. 'I hardly dare to hope.'

She smoothed her hands over the lacy skirt of the white wedding dress that had transformed her into a fairy-tale bride when she slipped it on that morning. Even now she could not stop smoothing her hands over the hoops. They were as light as air compared to the layers of petticoats that used to weigh her down in the past. Now her whole body felt light and free. The dress itself was made of layers of lace and silk, one over the other, and drawn in at the waist to smooth over her corset, held together at the bodice with a row of tiny buttons shaped like butterfly wings. Her slippers were made of satin, too, with ribbon rosettes on them. She had been fitted for the gown by a dressmaker in London. Dominic and she had pored over a sheaf of designs in the shop and finally settled upon a mixture of two. But a picture on paper was quite a different beast to a fully fledged gown. She had hardly been able to believe that such a magical dress was hers when she drew it from its box upon delivery. The puffed sleeves, too, were so light and airy she felt as if she could float away.

Across the room, Dominic was still dressed in his wedding attire. His dark morning suit with its long black-tailed coat and the crisp white shirt he wore underneath reminded her of the tailed dinner jacket he had worn when he had first invited her to dine in the grand dining room of Pendragon Hall. She had teased him by showing him, in the pages of a magazine, a new fashion for gentlemen in Europe. The fashion was to wear a cravat, or a bow tie, shaped like a butterfly. Some even had embroidered wings. She had pretended seriousness about such a bow tie's suitability for his wedding attire until the sight of his horrified face had sent her into peals of laughter. She hadn't known that such ease and amusement was possible between a man and a woman. His half-smile could barely be termed such these days—it had grown to at least a characteristic three-quarters and she had hopes for a full four.

Now, with another laugh, she lifted her petticoat to reveal her blue stockings.

'My dear Lady Jago,' Dominic drawled, with his new three-quarter smile. 'For a while I was concerned that you had lost your passion for education.'

'Amid my passion for other things, do you mean?'

He lifted an eyebrow. 'What are your other passions?'

She raised the petticoat a little higher and stepped closer to him in a rustle of silk. 'Storytelling.'

He placed his hand on what could be seen of the blue stocking, just inside her thigh.

'And butterflies.' She lifted her skirt a little higher.

Again, he followed her lead, gliding his fingers further. A shiver like liquid honey rippled down her spine.

'Anything else?' he asked, as his fingers moved higher still.

Maud quivered. 'I am still discovering.'

'As I am you.' He ran a finger around her lips. 'You were most elusive.'

His lips went to her neck. 'I wanted to kiss you here.'

They moved upwards. 'And here.'

'And here.'

His hard mouth had found hers again now.

Then he pulled away, gliding his hands over her bodice.

'Allow me to enlighten you. If I may.' His hands released her. 'But not yet. You must wait a little longer.'

No! She craved his hands upon her thigh, her bodice, his mouth hard upon hers. A tiny part of her was still frightened, yes, but his hands negated all fear. She trusted him completely.

Her husband smiled down at her almost mischievously, reminding her of Rosabel as the dent played in his cheek. She saw it more often now. Then he took her hand in his.

'Come,' Dominic said.

Chapter Twenty-Four

Come into the garden, Maud,
For the black bat, night, has flown,
Come into the garden, Maud,
I am here at the gate alone.
—*Alfred, Lord Tennyson:* Maud *(1855)*

'Where are we going?' Maud asked in a whisper.

Dominic chuckled. 'You'll see.'

He took a hand as he led her through the woods.

Owls hooted in darkness. The trees in the dim light appeared quite black, twisted monstrous shapes, but Maud was not afraid, not with Dominic holding her hand so snugly. The moon was full and he carried a lamp, too, as they made their way along the woodland path. Moths danced beside them, attracted by its glow.

'We're almost there,' he told her. He stopped and raised her hand to his lips. He kissed her palm, then her inner wrist.

Maud shivered.

He drew her into his arms. 'Are you cold?'

'Not at all,' she murmured against his chest. 'Just a little impatient. It feels like I have waited for you for ever.'

It was a relief, to have those feelings. She had been so afraid that her desires would have been tainted, ruined in some way. But they had not been stolen from her.

Dominic tipped up her chin and claimed her lips. His mouth told her more clearly than words that he, too, was impatient. She wound her hands around his neck and told him in the same mode that she had been virtuously restrained long enough and that *now* was her wedding night.

'I don't want you to think I would treat you the way you were treated before,' he'd told her on the day he'd given her an engagement ring.

'I know you would never do that,' she had replied. Yet there had been some nerves she'd been unable to deny to herself.

But now the insidious fear Lord Melville had sown was quite swamped with desire for her husband. And he wanted her to wait, even now! Oh, it was enough to make a respectable governess develop all kinds of notions.

He drew back, disentangling her hands from about his neck. His fingers brushed the ring. It was made of diamonds with an emerald in the centre. He'd said it reminded him of her eyes, save it could never be so beautiful. She wore a golden wedding band now, too. When he'd slipped it on to her finger in the village church, she knew she had never imagined such happiness. She hadn't expected there to be more to follow.

'Tell me where we are going,' she pleaded again.

His smile gleamed in the moonlight. 'It's a further adventure for Princess Swallowtail and the White Admiral.'

She laughed.

'You're the one who is making up the stories now,' she teased him.

'Not far now.' He took her hand. 'Are you sure you don't want a honeymoon in a distant land? It was your dream to be an explorer, after all.'

'Cornwall proved to be adventure enough,' she told him. 'Does that count?'

'I believe it does.'

They walked on, in silence.

Then he stopped. 'We are almost at the place where we found the White Admiral. Do you remember?'

She nodded.

'I wanted to kiss you then,' he told her.

'You did?'

'Indeed. That's why I've brought you here tonight. To finish what we started.'

Her pulse fluttered.

He tightened his grip.

'I can see a light. There, just by the path,' she said, peering ahead.

He let go of her hand and indicated the path. 'Follow the fairy lanterns. They'll guide your way.'

She glanced up at him, trying to read his face, but it was in shadow.

She took a step, then another. More tiny lanterns appeared, some set by the path, others hanging from trees. Their flames flickered slightly in the breeze, sending ripples of dim light through the forest, shifting shadows, bringing the woods to life as if touched by magic. Moths fluttered. Maud continued, hearing the tread of beloved footsteps behind her, her shoes sure on the leafy lamplit path.

She had slipped off her satin slippers before she left the house and put on her walking shoes, but she still wore her blue stockings beneath her dress. She'd also thrown a shawl over her shoulders against the night air. Now it slid down. She let it fall over her elbows as she stepped onwards through the magic of the forest, not in the least cold.

'Maud.'

She paused at the low voice behind her, looked enquiringly over her shoulder.

'Allow me.' Dominic stepped a pace ahead and lifted a bough so that she could pass underneath.

'Oh!' Maud cried.

A glade in the forest opened up before her, twinkling with a hundred little lanterns. She gasped again as she recognised it. It was the dell in which they had caught the elusive Admiral.

But the glade looked quite different now and not just because of the lanterns in the night. Erected in the centre of the dell was a beautiful tented pavilion, made of white silk. Ribbons flowed from it.

'It's like a fairy tale,' she whispered.

'I wanted tonight to be a fairy tale for you,' he said. 'The beginning of your happily-ever-after.'

'It is a fairy tale. It's better than a fairy tale,' she said. She could not believe he had thought of something so beautiful for her, he, a practical man who built railways.

'You will have no nightmares, I trust, sleeping out of doors.'

'I don't think I will have nightmares ever again,' she said, honestly. 'Not with you sleeping beside me.'

'Then I must always sleep beside you. And you're safe here. I hope you know that.'

'I do.' It was a sanctuary within a sanctuary in Pendragon Woods. 'This place has not been ruined for me.'

She refused to allow it.

'You don't need any more time,' he confirmed.

'Only time with you.'

The silence that she valued as much as words hung between them.

'I want us to make new memories,' he said at last. 'Come inside.'

He lifted the silken door.

She ducked her head and entered.

The ground, too, had been covered in silk. Downy mattresses and pillows had been heaped to make a snowy bed.

Saffron was sprinkled over the covers. The tiny strands of orange-red stigma seemed to set the white counterpane alight. The whole bed seemed to glimmer with a strange fiery light, as if covered with fireflies.

'Look up,' he told her.

She looked up to see that the roof of the silk pavilion was made of netting. Through it, she could see stars winking down between stirring leaves. Moths of brown, white and grey, their wings silvered, danced over the sheer rooftop.

'I didn't bring my butterfly net!' she exclaimed with a soft laugh.

His grin flashed.

'That's most remiss of a governess,' he drawled. 'We shall have to explore other pastimes.'

'Shall we?'

'Indeed.' He took her in his arms.

'They're drawn to the light,' he murmured. 'Shall I put out the lamp?'

She shook her head. 'No.'

'You want to see the moths?'

She twined her hands around him. 'I want you to see me. I want to see you.'

He studied her face.

'Are you sure?'

She nodded.

'Then I shall release you from your cocoon.'

His smile gleamed in the low light and his lips descended upon hers. Then his fingers were upon the butterfly buttons. One by one, she felt them give way.

Maud shivered—not with fear.

With love.

And she was free.

Epilogue

Come hither, the dances are done.
—*Alfred, Lord Tennyson:* Maud *(1855)*

Rosabel leaned over the wooden cradle. 'Oh, the baby looks like my doll Polly!'

Dominic chuckled. 'This is a real-life baby, not a porcelain doll.'

'And even better than that, she's your new sister,' said Maud.

'She's so tiny,' said Rosabel in awe. She reached out and touched the miniature hand. As the tiny fingers latched around her thumb, Rosabel giggled. 'Look, she likes me!'

'And she'll grow,' said Dominic. 'Before long she will be as beautiful as her sister and her mother.'

From her place propped up in the four-poster bed, Maud gazed at Dominic. Her husband.

She still couldn't quite believe it. She had never imagined it was possible to be so happy. Her family were all together now at Pendragon Hall, their home: she, her husband, her daughter Rosabel—for that was how Maud thought of her—and now their new baby daughter.

After having looked after other people's children for so many years, she realised that it had been a dream she had never dared to dream: a family of her own.

She remembered how Dominic had asked her if she hoped for a family and children of her own. She had thought then that even her capacity to dream of a future for herself had been lost. But it had not. From the ruins, they had built a new future. Even with her gift for storytelling, she had never imagined such a happily-ever-after was possible. But now she had a family, a home: that undreamed-of dream.

A tear rolled down her cheek.

Dominic leaned over and with one finger wiped the tear away. 'What's the matter? Why are you crying?'

'They're tears of joy,' Maud said in wonderment. Such happy tears were something that she had heard of, but never really believed could exist. She had cried so many other kinds of tears in her life. Tears of exhaustion. Tears of shame. Tears of heartbreak. But these tears now were nothing like those.

'So, you're happy, then,' he asked, as he crooked a smile so full of love and intimacy that it made her heart race.

'How can you ask?' she whispered. 'Happy doesn't begin to describe it.'

In the cradle the baby gave a cry. Gently Dominic leaned over and picked her up and handed her to Maud.

Maud nestled the tiny soft bundle against her silk bed jacket and the crying ceased. She was wrapped in the finest flannel and a little cotton-and-lace gown, with a trimmed cap on her head to keep her warm.

Rosabel leaned against the bed. Dominic reached out to put an arm around her; drew her closer in.

'What's my new sister's name?' she asked.

'The right names are very important,' Dominic said, with a glance at Maud.

She bit her lip. It still pained her that they had met under such clouded circumstances.

'How about… Mergetrude?' Dominic went on, with a grin.

In relief, Maud laughed aloud. 'That's what I thought Polly was called. Do you remember, Rosabel?'

The dimple appeared in Rosabel's cheek. 'Then you said Polly's name might be Dorothea-Millicent-Margaret-Anne. You made it up.'

'I don't make things up any more,' Maud said, her eyes welling again.

Dominic leaned in and whispered in her ear, 'Not unless you want to.'

He straightened and smiled at Rosabel. 'We have decided to call her Vanessa.'

'It means "butterfly",' Maud added.

'Butterfly,' said Rosabel, with a sigh. 'Oh, look, Polly. I have a sister called Butterfly.'

'She's the newest butterfly in our collection,' Dominic said.

The baby opened her eyes as if she knew she were being discussed. They were a grey-blue colour now, but Maud suspected they would change in time. Perhaps they would be green, like hers. Dominic had said he would like that. Or perhaps a deep chocolate brown like Dominic's.

'She can open her eyes,' said Rosabel. 'My doll Polly can't do that.'

Dominic chuckled. 'No, indeed, and she'll be able to do many more things with you in the future. It won't be long before she's running through the woods with you, chasing butterflies.'

'She might like trains more than butterflies,' Maud put in, with a teasing smile.

Dominic's chuckle turned to a laugh, making the dimple appear in his cheek. It played there more often now. 'Indeed.'

He whispered again in her ear, 'I'm torn between the two myself.'

After Rosabel had gone and Vanessa was tucked back into the cradle, sleeping peacefully again, Dominic climbed on to the bed and took Maud in his arms.

'I have something for you,' he said.

'You've given me so very much already, Dominic.' She raised herself on her elbows against the pillow. 'What is it?'

He passed her a parcel, wrapped in brown paper. 'It came from London today. Open it.'

The paper slipped off easily to reveal a leather-bound volume, in dark green. On the spine and the cover, embossed in gold, were the words: *The Butterfly Fables: Moral Tales for Children by Lady Maud Jago.*

The title shimmered on the leather, green as leaves.

'My stories.' She had been writing more of them during her confinement, using the fountain pen Dominic had given her.

He smiled. 'I sent them to a printer in London. This is the first of many volumes for our children, I hope.'

'It's beautiful,' she whispered.

'You must never give up your stories,' he murmured. 'They brought us together.'

Maud grimaced. 'They nearly kept us apart.'

Dominic shook his head. 'I'd have caught you anyway. Somewhere. Somehow.'

Maud leaned into his arms.

Why, who'd have credited it? Fairy tales did come true, after all.

* * * * *

If you enjoyed this story, why not
check out these other great reads
by Eliza Redgold

Enticing Benedict Cole
Playing the Duke's Mistress
The Scandalous Suffragette

Maud's World

The Figure of the Governess

The governess was a familiar figure in Victorian England. Some of them, like Maud, were 'bluestockings'—a nickname for free-thinking women who fought for female education. Also, like Maud, many governesses were cultured women who had fallen on hard times.

In their employment they were expected to provide both academic and moral education, often for low pay and in insecure conditions. Many governesses existed between two worlds, not accepted by the servants or by the family, and some were at the mercy of their more unscrupulous employers.

The Governesses' Benevolent Institution, to which Maud turns, provided aid for needy and retired governesses in straitened circumstances. Today, this society still exists in the form of the Teaching Staff Trust.

Wise Women's Wonder Tales

Governesses were known to use fables and fairy tales for female education. Like Maud's *Butterfly Fables*, such tales were often full of wonder, wisdom and often warnings to women.

One such governess, Madame Leprince de Beaumont, published educational guides for young ladies. Her *Moral Tales* (1744 and 1776) became famous handbooks, and included an early English translation of *Beauty and the Beast*.

Louisa May Alcott, best known for *Little Women*, wrote *Flower Fables* (1860), to instruct and entertain Ellen Emerson, the daughter of Ralph Waldo Emerson, while author and illustrator Cicely Mary Barker ran a kindergarten with her sister—she modelled her famous *Flower Fairies* (1925) upon the children who attended it.

Beautiful British Butterflies

In Maud's era, many species of butterflies fluttered across British landscapes. Butterfly-catching was a popular hobby.

The Butterfly Vivarium or Insect Home: being an account of a new method of observing the curious metamorphoses of some of the most beautiful of our native insects, by Henry Noel Humphreys, published in London in 1858, became a bestseller.

Sadly, many British butterflies are now rarely sighted. The Swallowtail, Britain's biggest butterfly, is threatened with extinction due to the salination of Britain's lakes and marshes. The Small Tortoiseshell is also facing declining numbers.

Learn more about butterflies from The Association for Butterflies—you can even attend Butterfly College—support Butterfly Education and Awareness Day in the

USA, or aid their conservation in Britain by joining The Big Butterfly Count.

Visit elizaredgold.com to see beautiful images of a Victorian butterfly vivarium.

All Aboard! The West Cornish Railway

Dominic's background as a railway entrepreneur is set against the founding of the West Cornish Railway Company. In the 1840s and 1850s this railway company was formed by local businessmen and men of standing in the community, offering new economic hope to Cornwall.

Dominic's passion and energy for the railway captures the pride emerging in Cornwall at that time. Its heritage remained in the form of the Cornish Riviera Express— one of the railway wonders of the world.

For a romantic getaway you can still catch the Night Riviera sleeper to Cornwall. Or climb aboard the magical Christmas Train of Lights!

Sensual Saffron

Saffron has been grown in Cornwall for centuries and has long been used to flavour its local cuisine—not least its famous saffron buns.

The brightly coloured orange-red stigma of the crocus flower—saffron—turns food to gold when cooked and, because of the necessity to harvest the spice by hand, it is worth its weight in gold, too.

A natural aphrodisiac, saffron was often used in marriage customs. Rather than rose petals, the marriage bed was once sprinkled with strands of saffron to ensure happiness and good fortune.

The Stories of Scheherazade

Scheherazade's fairy tales are some of the most famous and fabulous fairy tales ever told. Known as *The Arabian Nights* or *One Thousand and One Nights*, her tales embroidered flying carpets, magical lamps and wish-granting genies.

Scheherazade told her stories to save her life and those of other women. As vengeance against his wife, who had betrayed him, a sultan vowed to take a new wife every night. One of these was Scheherazade, but she had a plan of her own.

On her wedding night, she told stories full of such adventure and intrigue that the Sultan could not resist asking her to continue to tell them. She told her tales for a thousand nights and by the end of them the Sultan had fallen in love with her and seen the errors of his ways.

Do read more about Scheherazade, or listen to the famous music by Rimsky-Korsakov, inspired by her tales.

Poetic Inspiration

Interwoven into my story is Tennyson's poem *Maud* (1855). Full of desire and conflict, it is the inspiration for Maud and Dominic's story—which for them ended happily ever after.

Visit elizaredgold.com for more.

Saffron Revel Buns

Saffron revel buns have long been made in Cornwall.
Believed to have desire-enhancing properties, they were
once part of marriage or anniversary feasts.

Like all good things, saffron buns take time.

This is a traditional version of these festive treats.

Enjoy!

Ingredients

A pinch or two of saffron strands
Half a cup of milk
A handful of raisins
400 grams of plain or all-purpose flour
A pinch of salt
Half a cup of butter
Half a cup of double cream—or Cornish clotted
cream, if you can get it
28 grams fresh yeast or dried yeast equivalent
1 teaspoon of caster sugar

Method

Grind the strands of saffron in a pestle and mortar into a fine red-gold powder. Mix with the milk to make a paste. Set aside overnight, for the saffron to dye the milk gold.

Place the raisins in a small bowl and cover with warm water. Set them aside to plump.

The next day, sift the flour and salt. Rub in the butter by hand.

Strain the saffron milk. Warm until it is lukewarm. Do not allow it to boil.

Place the warmed milk in a bowl and mix in the sugar. Sprinkle the yeast over top of the milk and let it stand for ten to fifteen minutes. The yeast will soften and begin to bubble.

When cool, gradually stir in the raisins, cream and beaten eggs.

Make a well in the centre of the dry ingredients and add the milk mixture little by little, until it forms a firm dough.

Turn it on to a lightly floured board and knead for five minutes. Make a ball and return the dough to a lightly greased bowl. Cover with a damp tea towel and stand in the refrigerator overnight, until doubled in size. Alternatively, you can place it in a warm place and it will double in size in approximately two hours.

Once it has risen, shape the dough into twelve to sixteen buns. Roll each piece into a ball, place on a baking tray and allow them to rise again in a warm place for about fifteen to twenty minutes. Again, let them double in size.

Glaze with warm butter or milk and sprinkle with caster sugar if desired.

Place in a preheated oven at 375°F—190°C—for about fifteen minutes, until they are firm and golden.

Acknowledgements

A big thank you to everyone at Harlequin Mills & Boon Historical in London, especially editor Nicola Caws— a complete star, who is always fantastic to work with.

Thanks also to the Harlequin Hussies—the online group of Historical authors, past and present, who are so fabulous, funny and full of wisdom.

Thanks to my erstwhile critique buddy, author and creative practice academic, Dr Carol Hoggart, who dived into an early draft of this work and helped get it into shape—and share some 'Writer's Tears' whisky while doing so.

Thanks to Dr Rose Williams, whose critical reading has become my favourite part of the process.

Thanks also to Pamela Weatherill and Pearl Proud—I hope you know how much your friendship and support mean to me.

To Anne Symes—whenever an encouraging email was needed, it arrived from you.

And to Joanne Macdonald—who left a bluestocking badge on my university office door at the 'write' moment.